CHICAGO
PRE-BOOMERS

Richard J. Jackson

Gotham Books

30 N Gould St.
Ste. 20820, Sheridan, WY 82801
https://gothambooksinc.com/

Phone: 1 (307) 464-7800

© 2024 *Richard J. Jackson*. All rights reserved.

No part of this book may be reproduced, stored in a retrieval system, or transmitted by any means without the written permission of the author.

Published by Gotham Books (March 22, 2024)

ISBN: 979-8-88775-849-7 (P)
ISBN: 979-8-88775-850-3 (E)

Because of the dynamic nature of the Internet, any web addresses or links contained in this book may have changed since publication and may no longer be valid.

The views expressed in this work are solely those of the author and do not necessarily reflect the views of the publisher, and the publisher hereby disclaims any responsibility for them.

CONTENTS

CHAPTER 1 Chicago Park System 1
CHAPTER 2 World War II 6
CHAPTER 3 U.S. Marines 10
CHAPTER 4 Troopship 15
CHAPTER 5 Guadalcanal 18
CHAPTER 6 Manila Military Hospital 20
CHAPTER 7 Walter Reed 24
CHAPTER 8 DC Trip 27
CHAPTER 9 A Butler Reunion 32
CHAPTER 10 Preparing for the Awards 36
CHAPTER 11 Ultimatum 40
CHAPTER 12 Silver Star 43
CHAPTER 13 Rex's Return 47
CHAPTER 14 Nick Brown 53
CHAPTER 15 Sidewalks & Libraries 56
CHAPTER 16 Young Shawn and Nick 63
CHAPTER 17 Post-World War II Chicago 68
CHAPTER 18 Prowling the City 73
CHAPTER 19 Wrigley field 77
CHAPTER 20 Grammar School 82
CHAPTER 21 Post-World War II Years 89
CHAPTER 22 Freshman Year 96
CHAPTER 23 Off-Season Training 103
CHAPTER 24 Shawn's Senior Season 106
CHAPTER 25 College Choices 110
CHAPTER 26 Pre-College Job 118
CHAPTER 28 Summer Romances 122

CHAPTER 29 Right Junior College 126
CHAPTER 30 Jerry Diminico 130
CHAPTER 31 Joan Conley 134
CHAPTER 32 Shawn's Love Life 138
CHAPTER 33 Social Jogging 143
CHAPTER 34 Chicago City College 148
CHAPTER 35 Chicago City College Drama 153
CHAPTER 36 Triple C's Graduation 158
CHAPTER 37 Courtney's Decline 163
CHAPTER 38 Nick Brown's Graduation 171
CHAPTER 39 Shawn's Marine Training 175
CHAPTER 40 Vietnam Tour I 180
CHAPTER 41 A Subdued Leave 184
CHAPTER 42 Shawn and Nick Apart 191
CHAPTER 43 A Second Vietnam Tour 195
CHAPTER 44 Shawn & Nick Reunite 200
CHAPTER 45 Buddies No More 205
CHAPTER 46 Silicon Valley, The Preliminaries 212
CHAPTER 47 BBW's Super Bowl Week 219
CHAPTER 48 BBW Goes For Broke 223
CHAPTER 49 Wedding Plans 228
CHAPTER 50 Butler-Wilson Nuptials 233
CHAPTER 51 Rita's Farewell Tour 238
CHAPTER 52 Weddings A Pair 244
CHAPTER 53 Newly Weds 249
CHAPTER 54 State Senator Butler 254
CHAPTER 55 A Bipartisan Idea 259
CHAPTER 56 Bipartisan Expansion 264

CHAPTER 57 Shawn's Campaign Plan 268
CHAPTER 58 The Campaign 275
CHAPTER 59 Butler-Brown Babies 280
CHAPTER 60 Shane 286
CHAPTER 61 Rex Fades 289
CHAPTER 62 Tragedy Strikes 294
CHAPTER 63 Twin Funerals 299
CHAPTER 64 Russo, the Nanny 303
CHAPTER 65 Life With Shane 308
CHAPTER 66 Shawn's Career Decision 312
CHAPTER 67 Pivotal Meeting 315
CHAPTER 68 Living With Betrayal 319
CHAPTER 69 Butler and the Environment 324
CHAPTER 70 Shane Grows Up 329
CHAPTER 71 Shane's Wedding 334
CHAPTER 72 Challenges 340
CHAPTER 73 Agent Orange 345
CHAPTER 74 Meeting His Maker 349
OBITUARY Shawn Michael Butler 354

To My Wife, Linda,
For Her Patience and Kindness

CHAPTER 1

Chicago Park System

An unremarkable seven pounder, Shawn was born on December 6, 1940 to Courtney and Rex Butler in Presbyterian-St. Luke's Hospital on Chicago's near west side. While Rex was filling out admission papers at the front desk, Shawn made his appearance, squalled for a few minutes, was cleaned up nicely, and got his first taste of external mother's milk.

Mrs. Butler had wanted a daughter, but that longing evaporated immediately upon looking at Shawn. He had a curious expression that touched her deeply, and she loved him more with each passing day.

Rex was an iron worker and usually worked high above the city. He had broad shoulders, a narrow waist, and a strong jaw. He might not have been the toughest guy on his twelve-man crew, but none dared to test him. When overtime was available, he took it, realizing that with the little one, there would be additional expenses.

Rex was interested in the baby, but he often felt like an outsider around his wife and young son. Had he confided in his co-workers, he would have discovered that many felt the same way towards their families. However, men did not talk much about such things in pre-WW II days. Rex in particular would not have considered discussing this matter with anybody. So also, there was not much literature available on the subject, and if there was, he probably would not have read it.

Men spent much of their free time at work talking about the festering world war and the role, if any, the United States would play. Rex neither led these discussions nor even participated actively, but his mind was made up. He had not discussed this with Courtney either, but she knew her husband as well as anyone and had already guessed the answer to an important question: If the United States entered the war, would he enlist? For now, Rex was biding his time and spent many of his non-working hours walking in the city parks.

Chicago's park system is one of the world's biggest and finest. The 1871 Chicago Fire cleared the landscape and permitted the planning of a 2,193 acre cluster of parks fed by water from artesian wells. Environmentally blessed, the parks spouted tasty water day and night from spigots which were turned on in May and off in October.

Other than water, the city's blessings from nature were predominantly commercial in the form of a splendid harbor, but not aesthetic, since much of the city was originally a swamp that needed filling. Most of the parks' beauty grew from plants, seeds, and bulbs imported from Europe and made to fit visions of three separate planning committees, the first from the north side and then the second and third from the south side and west side. Chicago has only a splinter bordering Lake Michigan on its east side. Shawn's park visits reaped the benefits of the efforts of three generations of urban planners with a deep respect for what growing things could do to raise the spirits of hard-working people and their families.

People think of Chicago as a great city, in large part because of its parks. From May to October, people of all ages use their picnic tables, benches, swimming pools, and playing fields. Nobody is too poor to use the parks and only a few are too wealthy. These parks served as a splendid retreat from cramped or unhappy homes and as an effective device for social leveling.

These oases signal welcome by being accessible from all sides. Its only locks were used by conscientious maintenance men for small, remote storage sheds and by the park director for the front door of the main building, which usually featured at least one basketball court, showers, ping pong tables, bats and balls for check-out, and well-maintained rest rooms. The park custodians treated the grounds as if they were their own; rarely were these men or the premises which they tended disrespected by park-goers.

If you visited the parks at different times of the day in this pre-television era, you would see all ages and classes: shopkeepers, executives, teachers, factory workers, homemakers, infants, retirees, and college students. For children, the park they frequented defined who they were as clearly as did the schools they attended.

On a warm July day in summer 1941, Shawn and his mother took the bus to Washington Square Park, known as Bughouse Square, which became a crude reference to the mental health of those who gave speeches there. The three-acre expanse had been donated to the city in 1842 and is Chicago's oldest existing small park. Popular among tourists, Bughouse Square is the most celebrated outdoor free-speech center in the United States, a site which has undergone several social evolutions, including a strongly communist orientation in the Depression to that of a gay rallying spot in the early Vietnam era.

On this day, Mrs. Butler wanted to hear a high school acquaintance speak in favor of non-engagement by America in the looming world conflict. She could feel the tension between pro-war and anti-war advocates while moving Shawn through the mob, when a fight started. In a city known for quick fists, it did not take much.

Mrs. Butler tried pushing her way through the mob, when she bumped into a husky young man with his back to her. He turned and was ready to swing at her reflexively when he caught himself. Embarrassed, he took her gently but firmly by the arm and guided mother and son to safety. From a distance, Courtney looked on, hoping that the swarming police would restore order so that she could hear her friend speak; instead, the police cleared the park.

Though this trip was a dud, Shawn's park outings usually exposed him to birds, dogs, children, and swings and were the highpoints of his days. Some children would sleep most of the time they were outside, but not Shawn, who studied the world around him intently. He was determined to commit to memory the characteristics of God's creatures and man's objects so that he could come to understand them.

On a beautiful fall day in 1941, Shawn was sitting in his stroller in the park near his home, listening to a robin sing behind him. Though unable to see the bird, he began stabbing at the picture of a bird on his blanket. His mother, ever watchful for signs of precocity, turned her son to face the chirping bird and patted Shawn's head gently.

To prolong this wonderful parenting moment, Mrs. Butler crumbled one of Shawn's crackers and dropped a few crumbs within fifteen feet of the bird, making a trail with the rest back to Shawn's stroller and then retreating to sit on a bench. The bird cautiously began eating the crumbs, getting ever closer to Shawn, who did not once take his eyes off the bird. Reaching the last of the crumbs, the bird paused and returned stares with Shawn.

When the bird flew off, Shawn raised his arms and laughed delightedly. For months, he would not relinquish the bird blanket and insisted on taking it on every trip to the park. When he saw a bird, he would turn to his mother and smile.

CHAPTER 2

World War II

In 1941, Shawn's body was growing steadily in tandem with the threat of war. On his first birthday, Saturday, December 6, he was toddling around his parent's squeaky clean second-floor apartment, two miles south of Wrigley Field. Occasionally, he would stop and listen to the screaming brakes and emergency sirens which punctuated his waking hours. Shawn knew that when his mother returned, she would take him to the nearby park.

Rex, who had worked four hours that morning, was listening to the radio and occasionally looked Shawn's way to make sure he was all right. Shawn knew that after his dad watched him, his mother often came home with food in a little cart. Though he had no idea what his dad was talking about, he heard Rex say that the purchase and preparation of food was "woman's work" and that a kitchen was a "woman's place." When Rex talked that way, he knew it made his mom angry.

After putting the food away upon her return, Courtney asked Rex if he would accompany them to the park, because "after all, it is his first birthday." Rex shook his head no and walked into the bathroom, closing the door on what would have turned into an argument. When he emerged, mother and son were gone.

Rex had become increasingly edgy in recent months. It was not Shawn who bothered him, since he was a quiet, healthy baby. It also was not Courtney, who was a good wife and a great mother. Somehow, though, he knew he was going to leave, one way or another, and felt guilty that it did not bother him more. Rex had a combative nature and no one to fight with except a defenseless child and a good woman. If he fought at work, he could lose a job he loved, wanted and needed. He felt hemmed in and his frustrations were growing.

From his armchair, Rex looked at mother and son when they came through the door and knew they had enjoyed themselves. As Courtney busied herself preparing supper, Shawn toddled across the tiny front room and stopped in front of his father. Impulsively, Rex reached out and lifted his son upon his lap, adjusting his teething ring and hugging him gently. Rex began to cry and Shawn made a game of catching his tears, while Courtney looked on in amazement. Later, this was a moment that both mother and father remembered more than any other, with Courtney wishing that things could always be this way and Rex wishing he could more often show how much he cared.

After supper, though, Rex became withdrawn and sullen as though the tender moment with Shawn had never occurred. The following morning, a Sunday, he arose early, ate breakfast at a small restaurant nearby, and took a walk. Upon returning to the apartment, he ate lunch, took a nap, and awoke to find Courtney riveted to the radio which continued to add details about the attack on Pearl Harbor. Rex knew that President Roosevelt had no alternative but to respond. He and Courtney exchanged a long look and never even discussed what he was about to do.

He went to work the next morning as though nothing had

happened. The men at work, though, talked of little else for weeks, until a local government office opened that was authorized to process military enlistments. As soon as they received notification of the office opening, nine of the twelve workers on his crew, including Rex and the foreman, left work early and submitted their enlistment papers. Rex was told to report for induction three days later, a Friday.

Shawn was eating supper noisily in his high chair when Rex entered the apartment. After Rex waved half-heartedly in Courtney's direction, he hung up his jacket and followed her into the kitchen.

He looked at her, then down at his shoes and said in a soft voice, "I leave on Friday. Tomorrow will be my last day of work. If you'll make a list, I'll do what you want on Thursday. If your mom will sit with Shawn, we can eat supper at Ernie's on Thursday night."

This was the longest he had spoken to her without stopping since they had gotten married. She had anticipated this moment and looked at him evenly, responding, "I'll call mom and get somebody else if she's not feeling well."

He reached out and hugged her awkwardly. She knew he was handling this in the best way he could, and she was determined not to make this any more difficult than it already was. Across the United States, similar scenes were unfolding.

Shawn knew that something important was happening and studied both of them. Courtney cleaned up the mess Shawn had made while eating and placed him in the sink, which doubled as his bathtub. Other than going to the park, taking a bath was his favorite activity and he soon forgot about the drama unfolding around him as he splashed water with his rubber duck, grabbed the faucet, and laughed. When Shawn had been cleaned and powdered, Courtney put on his best night shirt and placed him on his stomach upon a blanket. This posture forced him to strengthen his neck and shoulders, if he wanted to look around, which he always did.

Rex waited for Shawn to tire himself before lifting him up to his lap. Rex called to Courtney to join them when she finished the dishes. Rex smiled as Shawn tried to unbutton his shirt, and the two were wrestling when Courtney appeared. She took a chair to his right and he turned so that he could look at her squarely. Courtney was touched by the sight of her two men in this tender moment.

"He'll miss you," she said. Rex looked at her sadly, and she added quickly, "We'll be all right."

"I believe you will be, and he's tough and healthy," Rex said, patting Shawn. Hesitating for a moment, he added, "I'm worried that I won't know either of you when I come back, but I'm not much good to you the way I am right now."

"If you take care of yourself, things will sort themselves out," Courtney said.

He looked at her for several seconds and then responded skeptically, "I hope so." His misgivings proved to be painfully well founded.

CHAPTER 3

U.S. Marines

At 4:30 AM, Rex jumped out of bed and dressed quickly. He messed Shawn's hair and kissed his brow, without Shawn stirring. Courtney prepared Rex's breakfast, his last home-cooked meal for a long time. He stepped close to her as she stood over the stove, drew her hair back and kissed her neck. She did not often give him a high grade on warmth, but she always felt safe when he was around. He could certainly protect, if not console.

After taking care of details the day before, there was not much left to be said. They hugged for a minute or more before she slipped out of his grasp and put his breakfast on a large plate.

While Rex was focused and tense, Courtney was sleepy and resigned to the coming change in their lives. He kissed her gently at the door and then left quickly, taking the stairs down to the street, two at a time. From the window, she watched him stride confidently with a gym bag over his shoulder and turn the corner without looking back.

Rex took a bus to the induction center and was directed to a large room with fifteen rows, twelve seats to a row. The room remained approximately half full; men kept entering while others were leaving as their names were called by a big sergeant using a public address system.

Rex was about to experience another chapter in his life. He felt ready for whatever the armed forces had in store for him. The third of four brothers from a hard-scrabble Kentucky mining town, he had battled for food, athletic glory, and a place in the sun for as long as he could remember.

He was a linebacker on his high school team; Coach Felton called him a rover and allowed him to use his instincts to sniff out the ball, rather than assigning him a sector as he did with the other two linebackers. This coaching veteran knew he had a unique ability to always be in the right place.

When challenged by one of the other linebackers' fathers on the freedom given to Rex, Felton explained, "Butler has a gift that he was born with. It's radar, and I can't teach your son radar."

Unfortunately, Rex had not used this gift or dedicated much effort in the classroom to make good grades. He never met a teacher he fully valued, so he developed a disrespect for formal learning. A few teachers saw his potential but were unable to connect with him.

Rex's reflections of his childhood were interrupted by the sergeant barking, "Butler, Rex," and pointing forcefully to his right. Rex stood quickly and walked through a doorway with "U. S. Marines" stenciled above. Without hesitation, he entered the room and into a role that fit him like a glove.

Basic training at Camp Pendleton in southern California was a difficult two months for most inductees because they were easily distracted by a place very different from where they had lived, confused by being given orders in terms they did not understand, and told to do things they had never done or did not want to do. Rex was a drill instructor's dream because he only had to be told once and because he was able to concentrate on the task at hand.

He scored third highest in his 190-man platoon on the rifle range. His ability to focus enabled him to concentrate completely on the target, and accuracy came easily.

In hand-to-hand combat training, he dispatched three opponents quickly before the Drill Instructor stepped in and waved Rex forward. Though the DI outweighed Rex by twenty pounds and had years of hand-to-hand experience, they tossed each other around for five minutes, with neither gaining an advantage.

Breaking free, the DI shouted, "That's enough!" and extended his hand for Rex to shake.

When Rex reached forward, the DI flipped him on his back. As Rex got back on his feet, the DI waggled his finger at the trainees and said, "Our enemies don't fight fair, and you better not either."

All the recruits enjoyed this object lesson, including Rex, whose laugh was his first since being inducted. After dismissing the men, the DI studied Rex as the other recruits filed back to their barracks. Ever on the alert for leaders, he reminded himself to make a notation in Butler's file because Rex had the earmarks of a fine Marine: tough, smart, and close-lipped.

Rex always was by himself; the others respected him but kept their distance because of his smoldering silence. He wrote short letters home weekly and received Courtney's prompt replies, mostly status reports on a thriving Shawn.

Upon the completion of basic training, Rex and a few others were retained at Pendleton to receive non-commissioned leadership training. Because of accelerated personnel needs in wartime, he made corporal in June, 1942, and wore his two stripes proudly.

Rex taught hand-to-hand combat training for six weeks. This experience accelerated his leadership growth, because he did not merely meet Marines from every state but accepted their challenges. The air was thick with testosterone as the training sessions separated the pretenders from the contenders. Rex pushed everyone to their limits; this was not an experience a recruit could finesse. Once again, Rex's quiet intensity helped keep the lid on several potentially violent situations. His ability to anticipate, gained from his football days, enabled him to be in the right spot at the right time. Rex's leadership was apparent to all because he did not overreact, even when fellow Marines around him did.

At the end of each two-week training session, he had the fifteen trainees stand in formation at parade rest. He only spoke for five minutes, pausing between each of the following topics to demonstrate their importance: eating carefully, using alcohol in moderation, paying attention, strengthening the upper body, and writing home. The trainees often blinked at the last topic, because they could never picture this strong, silent man being close to anyone.

Rex concluded his remarks by saying, "Just being skilled and tough will not be not good enough in certain situations. In combat, I would put my money on the man with the best reason for winning."

In one of the three sessions he taught, a husky, brash trainee shouted, "What do you know about combat?"

Rex walked slowly towards the offender, staring at him all the way. He stopped within a foot of the man and said, "You have been here for two weeks. I've treated you and everyone else with respect during that time, partly because you've earned it and partly because I may have to depend on you in combat later on. If we don't respect each other, then we give the enemy an increased chance to defeat us. I'm told that our enemies fight too well to give them any breaks. If you don't respect me, we'll settle our differences right now."

By this time, the man was sweaty and miserable, and the other trainees were not giving him support, which they usually provided against non-commissioned officers. This poor soul probably could not have spoken, even if he had something to say. Rex let him twist in the wind for a full minute and finally shouted, "Dismissed!"

The following morning he and dozens of others received their orders to ship out to the Pacific. Surrounded by Marines speculating anxiously about the implications of this assignment, he walked to the makeshift library and read about the Pacific Ocean and then studied a map of its islands. While others who were shipping out with him, worried endlessly and drank cheap beer, Rex went back to the barracks and crawled into his bunk, figuring correctly that he would need to be rested for what was in store for him.

CHAPTER 4

Troopship

Rex shared an 8 X10 foot room with three sergeants in a crowded, drafty troopship which moved so slowly that he wondered whether he could swim as fast as the ship moved through the water. He did push-ups and pull-ups to maintain his fitness, while most of the Marines talked endlessly in an attempt to ward off their anxiety.

Rex adapted to the food which came in large cans, was transferred to big pots, and finally ladled onto battered trays. He cleaned his plate at every meal, while some chose to eat lightly, mistakenly assuming that the food would have to improve when they reached their destination. Others were seasick and simply could not eat much. One of Rex's bunkmates speculated that he had ingested enough preservatives in the food he had eaten during his military years to pickle a barnyard full of pigs, feet and all.

Rex continued to seek information to prepare himself for combat. He sought the counsel of a grizzled career Marine, Sergeant First Class Doaks, whom he had noticed on deck sizing up everybody and everything.

On their fourth day at sea, he stood next to Doaks on deck. Rex waited a few minutes for things to get comfortable before speaking.

"What do you see that I'm not seeing?" Rex asked.

Doaks turned to look directly at Rex, took a moment to measure his words and replied, "The men are starting to understand what they have gotten themselves into."

"What *have* we gotten ourselves into?"

"We are preparing to fight an enemy which is leaner, meaner, and more experienced than we are," Doaks answered.

"Will we lose?" asked Rex.

"I doubt it. Our leaders won't let us fail, and we will probably outthink the Japanese. Besides, our heroes want to live and theirs are proud to die."

Rex would like to have heard more, but Doaks stood and departed abruptly. Rex was left to ponder what he had been told. He had learned the pain of losing in sports; this grief was far greater for him than the gratification that came with winning. Regarding the ability to think clearly, Rex had often proven this skill under pressure.

Finally, he was not in this war to be a hero, but to help America survive intact. There were soldiers on the ship who already had planned a speech for the medals they expected to earn. Rex simply wanted to do his job and return home. Some craved hero status; Rex did not. He hoped to rejoin his family and be the man that he knew his wife and son deserved, but doing his part in the war effort was something he had to do first.

Rex well understood the line oft-repeated by his fellow Marines that if they traveled many more days at sea, they would return to where they had started, having circled the world. Rumors had the ship going to Guadalcanal, but no one seemed to know much about this place, other than it was the largest of the Solomon Islands.

What was not known by most of those onboard was that

Guadalcanal was an island ninety miles long and twenty-five miles wide, comprised of mountains as tall as 8,000 feet and rain forests that could not be penetrated without using a machete. Also unknown was the fact that the Japanese did not have a large presence on the ground in Guadalcanal; they were spread thin because they had dedicated so many troops to New Guinea. The downside was that the Japanese did have massive naval operations near the island. No one could have imagined that this beautiful nature preserve would be the site of some of the most brutal battles in WW II, fighting which would turn the war in favor of the Allies.

CHAPTER 5

Guadalcanal

As the ship approached the island at night, strong rain and wind whipped the region; the foul weather proved to be a break for the Marines because they were able to disembark without drawing fire. In fact, the Japanese were totally unaware of their arrival until noticing the American ships moving into open water on their way home. The Americans hit the beaches and moved slightly inland, before settling in for the evening in the midst of a rain forest, which served as excellent cover. The latticework of tents and rain gear kept the marines reasonably dry, as they ate their canned rations and cleaned their weapons.

Instead of the smaller rifles carried by most Marines, Rex had volunteered to carry the bulky Browning Automatic Rifle. The BAR would only be assigned to someone like Rex, who was strong, agile and nervy. Rex was powerful enough to swing this weapon from side to side while laying down a field of fire, nimble enough to jump over bodies and other obstacles while moving forward, and bold enough to draw heavy fire from an enemy desperately trying to knock out the soldier responsible for carrying an automatic weapon. Rex particularly liked the option of placing the BAR's bipod on the ground, which would allow him to continue shooting even if wounded.

During BAR training, Rex was challenged by a drill sergeant, who bated him by asking, "You're doing pretty well in *training*, but do you think you can keep your wits about you in combat?"

After this kind of question, the DI had become accustomed to trainees puffing up and making bold statements. Rex, who knew a rhetorical question when he heard one, simply returned the DI's challenging look and stood mute with the heavy BAR comfortably in his grasp. Somewhat shaken, the DI blinked and turned his attention to the next trainee.

Rex cleaned and assembled the BAR expertly, loaded it with ammunition, and clicked the safety on. He checked with the three members of his squad he could find after the offloading confusion and made sure they had a loaded weapon, before returning to his sleeping bag. Just before dawn, their position was overrun by screaming Japanese soldiers. Several Marines responded poorly because they did not have a loaded weapon and panicked by running away from the assault and into a clever ambush.

Meanwhile, Rex fired more than 100 rounds, changing positions every few seconds to keep the nearby enemies off-guard. Though there were thirty or more Marines dead or dying, the Japanese began retreating, discouraged in part by Rex's automatic fire.

Rex had been shot twice, once in the shoulder, and once in the thigh. Neither wound was life-threatening, nor was he losing much blood. As Rex began helping others more seriously injured than he was, one of the enemy soldiers who did not buy into retreat mode dropped from a tree and stabbed Rex in the back of the neck. Rex used his remaining strength to disable the soldier with his elbows and strangle him, before passing out.

CHAPTER 6

Manila Military Hospital

WW II was over for Rex almost before it began. He awoke in a drug-induced stupor and inventoried the damage done to his body: the thigh and shoulder wounds radiated stinging sensations. The shoulder was particularly sore, but he felt time would take care of this problem. His neck, encased in a rigid brace, was another matter. Rex could not move his neck and his upper body had an unnatural feel.

After being hydrated by a busy nurse, he looked around the sick bay at the seven other beds, all filled with injured soldiers. Three had head injuries and a fourth had apparently been blinded, among his other wounds. Two had multiple wounds, including a baby-faced soldier in the bed to Rex's left.

"I'm Josh from California. I'm a PFC and have some pesky wounds and damage to my back."

"I'm Rex from Chicago and a corporal. Something's wrong with my neck. I hope they fix it soon so I can go back to my unit."

Josh looked at him and laughed bitterly, saying, "No one in here is going back to their unit. You don't see anything but wheelchairs, do you?"

"What day is it?" Rex asked.

"Thursday," Josh replied, "but aren't you more concerned by what week it is? You've been unconscious for the entire two weeks that I've been here."

Rex blinked and discovered that he had been in a coma for sixteen days. He also learned that he was in a large military hospital in Manila. Rex had no luck in trying to get information regarding his medical condition from the nurse, who told him he would have to speak with the doctor. Despite Rex's repeated requests, it was another thirty-six hours before a tired, fifty-something doctor appeared.

"I'm Doctor Marshall, and you'll be seeing me often for the next ten days or so, Corporal," announced the physician. "We are watching your leg and shoulder wounds for signs of infection. Of greater concern is your neck injury. We suspect nerve damage and do not have the ability to treat that problem here. We will fly you back to the states as soon as your leg and shoulder stabilize."

"Who's we?"

"There is a team of four of us. We will visit you tomorrow as a group. For now, I will change the bandage on your wounds and give you a shot."

"Why four of you?"

"You're a hero, Corporal. You took on a whole Japanese platoon and ran them off. You're a cinch for a Silver Star and have an outside shot at the Congressional Medal of Honor. Meanwhile, a bunch of senior officers want you repaired and looking good, and what they want, I provide."

"Am I going home?" Rex asked.

"By way of Walter Reed Army Medical Center in DC. You will have months of rehabilitation there."

"Can I speak with my wife?"

"We will try to patch you through later this evening, but right now I need to work on you. After I finish with your leg and shoulder, three doctors will join me to treat your neck. This is going to take a while. I hope you didn't make other plans."

Rex replied sarcastically, "10,000 comedians out of work..." "And you got me," finished Dr. Marshall with a laugh.

After ninety minutes, Dr. Evers and two other doctors joined Dr. Marshall and, while cautioning Rex to remain still, sawed the cast from Rex's neck. The pained looks exchanged by the doctors told Rex all that he needed to know; his neck was seriously, perhaps permanently damaged. Though he had been warned not to move, Rex tried to roll his head to the right on the pillow but was unable to move his head at all.

The doctors walked into a corridor and exchanged views in an animated fashion for several minutes. Finally, Dr, Marshall returned and said, "Remember the ten days I talked about? Think three or four. We are going to cushion that neck for now and then encase you in a stronger support in the form of a cast before your flight."

"What's the rush?"

Dr. Marshall studied Rex intently and, looking over his shoulder, closed by saying, "I'll get back to you on that one."

Early the next morning, two technicians entered Rex's space and jerry-rigged a telephone hook-up. Though the reception was poor and Rex was warned that it was likely to cease at any time, Rex and Courtney managed a brief conversation.

"Hello, Courtney. I'll be coming home soon, but I'll have to spend some time in DC first."

"When will you be home?" she persisted. "I'm not sure," replied Rex.

"How are you feeling?"

"My leg and shoulder are all right, but my neck needs fixing. How's the baby?"

"Shawn's not a baby any more. He points at your picture, but he doesn't understand…" At that moment, the signal broke down and, despite furious efforts by the corpsmen, could not be recaptured.

The following seventy-two hours were a blur of shots, bandages, ointments, and pain before he was bundled onto a large airplane, which was primarily devoted to cargo.

CHAPTER 7

Walter Reed

Sedated on the flight, Rex regained consciousness four times, ate ravenously after awakening, and nodded off again. He was handled professionally in the difficult task of getting him off the plane, onto a Gurnee, on and off a bus with special accommodations, and into Walter Reed Army Medical Center. He was taken into a bay housing three other injured military veterans and fell into a sound sleep, thoroughly exhausted by the trip.

His roommates, a fellow Marine and two soldiers, introduced themselves. While Shawn was sleeping, a doctor had removed the stiff cast and replaced it with one that was somewhat pliable.

Communicating with his wife this time was much simpler, and he was able to speak with her for ten minutes on a clear line. After telling Rex that she had already spoken with hospital administrators, Courtney told him that she and Shawn would be visiting as soon as Rex was "well enough."

"I'm well enough now," Rex protested.

"You haven't spoken with the doctors yet, have you?" "I've been sleeping most of the time," he conceded. "Rex, you need at least one, maybe three operations."

Recovering quickly from this jolt, he immediately considered that Courtney might not have the money for her travel. "Courtney, can we afford…"

"Don't worry about the money, Rex. Your military checks have been sent to me, and Mr. Waxel, the grocer, insists on paying for our travel."

"I have some newspaper clippings which says that they plan to give you an award when Shawn and I visit. A colonel came to our apartment and told me that the details for this award are still being sorted out. Rex, what did you do that has everybody so excited?"

"I did what I was trained to do. I shot my rifle and protected my fellow Marines and a few soldiers. Other than that, I am not sure. There was a lot going on, and after I got shot a second time, things got fuzzy. Some officers have been here to see me, but the doctors shooed them away. They are supposed to come back tomorrow."

"Rex, I'm worried about you, about us," Courtney said.

"Let's get me put back together first and then we'll work on us."

That was not exactly what Courtney wanted to hear, but she had to accept this reasonable request for now. She continued to have an uncomfortable feeling about their marriage, a discomfort that went far beyond Rex's injuries.

After his first operation, he spoke again with Courtney. "I tried walking today, but I kept lurching forward. The doctors explained that I have some nerve damage that they will not be able to fix completely. They also said that they will operate again to fix things they discovered during the first operation."

"I'm clean, well-fed, and doing light exercises." Then he added, "I want to come home."

Her heart jumped when she heard those words, thinking that

perhaps there was a chance for them. Lending further weight to this possibility was the fact that he was talking to her, not opening up completely, but making an honest attempt to communicate.

He concluded by saying, "On this medal business, they are going to give me a Silver Star. They apologized for not recommending me for the Medal of Honor, but said there was just too much confusion at the time to get a clear picture of what happened." He did not add that most of the combatants died during the incident.

Rex asked, "Have you spoken with my family?"

Courtney replied, "Yes. Your mom hasn't been right since your dad died. Your sister is taking care of her. Your brother, Jerry, told me that he might be able to come to DC for your award ceremony, if he can get the time off from work."

"The nurse is here and I have to do my exercises," he concluded. "Take good care of Shawn."

"You know I will."

Rex was as good a patient as he was a Marine, doing what he was told and a little extra, but his neck was not responding as well as he had hoped. By contrast, the doctors were pleased with his progress. In the words of one, "If there ever was a patient who deserved a miracle and made me feel badly for not being able to provide one, Rex Butler is that patient. His tolerance for pain is incredibly high. He is the toughest, most determined person I've ever treated."

A fellow doctor laughingly agreed and said, "When I grow up, I want to be like Corporal Butler."

CHAPTER 8

DC Trip

Shawn and Courtney went to Union Station in September, 1942. Though not yet two, Shawn looked inquisitively at everything and everybody. He inspected the big buildings in Chicago's Loop while riding in a taxi cab, an expense Courtney justified because of the four bags, some containing Rex's belongings that they were taking on the trip. Shawn was fascinated by the stopping and starting of the cab and quickly made friends with the congenial driver, Christopher, who showed Shawn how he drove.

The driver asked Courtney where they were going, and she explained the purpose of the trip. Strongly patriotic, he was quite interested when Courtney spoke of the medal ceremony, and he asked which medal Rex was receiving. When she told him that Rex was receiving the Silver Star, he turned his head abruptly, almost causing a collision.

"He is being given a great honor. Your husband is a brave man. Did you know that the Silver Star is the third-highest military decoration that can be awarded to any member of the armed forces in combat?"

"What are the top two?" asked Courtney.

"The Congressional Medal of Honor is the highest and the second is the Distinguished Service Cross."

"Do they always make such a thorough investigation of people like my husband before they make an award?" she asked.

"I'm afraid General MacArthur made it tougher to get an award because he recently gave a Silver Star to a Navy officer, who was an observer and only a passenger on a plane, in New Guinea. The phony was a political hack named Lyndon B. Johnson, whose plane didn't even draw enemy fire, though he claimed it did," he said with disgust.

Courtney explained the circumstances of Rex's award, drawing an appreciative nod from Christopher, as he pulled in front of Union Station. Getting the attention of a policeman who was directing traffic, he stepped outside the cab and explained Courtney's situation. The policeman tipped his hat to Courtney and pointed Christopher to a reserved spot. The driver grabbed all the bags and accompanied Courtney into the station and directed her to the check-in line.

Excusing himself, he caught the attention of a manager and again explained Courtney's circumstances. The manager nodded and brought her and Shawn to the front of the line. Courtney was already holding the cost of the cab fare and a healthy tip in her hand, but the driver was having none of it.

Smiling broadly, he said, "This is my way of saying thanks. I'll brag about this for months."

He exchanged a lively handshake with Shawn, who threw in a broad smile. Courtney waved as the driver moved toward the exit.

"Well Shawn, it looks like we can go anywhere at no charge if we keep meeting the right people."

Shawn was already reinforcing his learning from the cab ride by pointing to a picture of a car on a magazine being held by a man waiting for a train. The man noticed Shawn pointing to the picture and said "car" in a loud voice. Shawn shook his head in disagreement and responded "cab" in a clear, equally loud voice.

Looking at Courtney and smiling, the man gave up, saying "I don't think I'm going to win this one."

Courtney laughed and moved Shawn along, but slowly enough so that he could absorb his surroundings. He pointed to wildly colored hats on women, saying "Daddy" when he saw men in uniform, inspecting occupied wheelchairs and their occupants, watching two little girls skipping rope, and stepping carefully on lines in the tiled floor. Upon first seeing a train, he jumped up and down, giggling and waving his little hands in the air. As they moved towards the train and he discovered that they were actually going to board, he was frozen into silence. Rarely did things overwhelm him, but the train succeeded in doing so, however briefly.

After Shawn collected himself, he insisted on climbing the tall steps to the passenger car on his own. When a well-meaning young man tried to help him, Shawn turned and stared him down. Upon reaching the floor of the passenger compartment, Shawn looked back to his mother who pointed left, and Shawn went on ahead. Shortly afterward, Courtney called for him to stop. He waited for his mother, and she pointed to their row. Scrambling into the window seat and looking through the glass, he smiled contentedly and soon fell into a brief sleep.

Wisely, Courtney had brought several magazines with colorful pictures and shared them with Shawn. If he was careful turning the pages and repeated the names of objects and body parts in a magazine accurately, Shawn was allowed to keep the magazine and place it in a bag that she had bought for him. On the few occasions in which he got careless or distracted, she put the magazine back into a bag she was carrying. When that happened, he was unhappy but did not complain; Shawn was already learning that his behavior had consequences.

He enjoyed the dining car and ordered the meals in typical Shawn fashion. Having observed that diners pointed to their selections on the menu, he pushed his menu at Courtney until she understood that he wanted her to identify what he wanted to order. Courtney knew that Shawn wanted potatoes with every meal. The first time their waiter, James, came by for their order, Shawn thrust the menu at him and pointed at the roast beef and potatoes entrée. The waiter looked at Courtney, who nodded in agreement.

Turning back to Shawn, James said, "Very good, sir."

Shawn asked his mother to explain other sections on the menu, and this sequence was repeated for all four meals, much to the amusement of nearby diners. James had learned that Shawn would not give up his menu until leaving the table, at which time Shawn insisted on handing the menu back to James, while each returned formal bows.

When the train was pulling into DC, Courtney told Shawn that the trip was over and that they were going to see his dad. Upon leaving, Shawn jumped ahead, scrambled down the stairs backwards, and stood near the train, looking everywhere for his father. Courtney collected him and did her best to tell him that they had to go the hospital before he could see his father. Failing to communicate this message, she then told him that they were going to take a cab. Shawn brightened at this prospect.

The DC cab ride was every bit as disappointing as the Chicago ride was rewarding. The driver snapped at Shawn, chain smoked, handled the baggage roughly and sniffed rudely at the generous tip Courtney gave him. She could not help but smile when Shawn stuck out his tongue at the driver after they got out of the cab in front of the hospital. Courtney was pleased that he did not accept poor treatment without standing up for himself and her. She moved him quickly away from the exhaust fumes, as the driver sped away.

CHAPTER 9

A Butler Reunion

Despite his interest in seeing his father, Shawn stopped and studied the immense facing of the administrative center and was awed by the sheer size of this mammoth facility. He noted every detail at each bureaucratic stop that he and his mother made as they moved through the system, ever closer to his father. Finally, they entered his room, accompanied by a tired but pleasant nurse.

"Rex, you have visitors," the nurse said.

Rex, who had been sleeping, was unable to turn to see his wife and son, but waved with his right hand to position them in front of him. Courtney stepped forward to hug him, as the nurse warned her softly to be gentle with his neck and left shoulder. Courtney carried on a short conversation with Rex, while nurse Ann, who was captivated by Shawn, had placed the toddler on a little wheeled cart and was pushing him around the room. At an opportune moment, she pushed him next to Rex, and the two spent at least a minute studying each other.

"Sojer," said Shawn finally, pointing to a uniformed sergeant, visiting a patient across the room.

"Very good, Shawn, and who am I?" asked Rex, pointing to himself. "Daddy," responded Shawn with a shy smile.

Courtney lifted Shawn so that he could touch his father, but Shawn devoted his attention to the bandages, touching them softly and exclaiming "Owwee" as he patted each dressing. Rex nodded in agreement, and then counted the three owwees.

Shawn pointed and said, "One, two, three." He jumped off the cart and moved quickly to the bed next to Rex's and pointed to the two dressed wounds of the Marine and said, "One owwee, two owwees," while pointing at the young, heavily sedated marine, who managed a smile, despite his pain and grogginess.

By this time, a nurse captured Shawn to prevent any more wound counting, although everyone seemed pleased and energized by his presence. The nurse wisely steered Shawn to Rex's locker, which occupied Shawn for much of the thirty minutes remaining of the visit. He tried walking in Rex's shoes and wearing Rex's hat. His curiosity was boundless, and he came back repeatedly to the logos and emblems on the Marine dress uniform, touching them and consigning them to memory. At once proud and puzzled, Rex could not take his eyes off Shawn.

With Shawn's help, nurse Ann pushed Rex and his bed into the bright dayroom. While Shawn investigated the furniture and visited with its occupants, Rex and Courtney talked and furtively appraised each other for changes. Rex thought Courtney looked older because of the wrinkles in her face, and Courtney was somewhat concerned by the fifteen pounds of muscle which Rex had lost. His shoulders looked almost puny, and his eyes were bloodshot, perhaps from the effects of medication. She found his arched neck unsettling.

Ever the provider, Rex spoke of the future. "I don't think I'm going to be able to do my old job. This neck will never be the same.

I'll have to find something else.

"There are jobs all over Chicago, and many of them don't require lifting. You learn fast and vets are being given priorities in hiring. I've been working twenty hours per week and can work more, if necessary. Mrs. Bellrose, the widow who lives near the tracks, watches Shawn. They love each other and both look sad when I come for him.

"We can sort out the money part. I spoke with the lady at the veteran's office and apparently your disability checks will continue for your lifetime."

Rex was uncomfortable with this conversation, but knew that these issues had to be discussed. He realized now that the collateral damages from his neck injury, loss of freedom and control, were far greater than the physical harm. "I need a nap," he said, providing a weak excuse for his inability to accept his plight.

Disregarding his plea, she went on, "Your brother Jerry will not be able to make it. He almost had to quit his job to get the time off, and then his train reservation was taken by a navy officer," she related.

"One last thing. Your medal ceremony is tomorrow afternoon at two, and Shawn and I have to leave the following day. The doctor told me you will be here for two more weeks, and that you will be able to return to Chicago on a train with other veterans. Tomorrow morning, we need to talk about us, Rex. I'll find somebody for Shawn."

She kissed him lightly and held up Shawn so that Rex could mess his hair. Weighing heavily upon Rex was the realization that he could neither lift Shawn as Courtney had just now done, nor did he know if he would ever be able to do so.

As nurse Ann pushed him back to his room, Rex fell into a sullen silence which the nurse could not break, even with compliments about his family. He picked at his food and slept poorly. While the impending medal ceremony would be one of the high points of most lives, Rex was not looking forward to the rituals; he hoped that they would be quick and straight forward.

With the aid of a volunteer driver, Courtney and Shawn returned to the modest hotel room, which was less than two miles away. Shawn fell into a deep sleep immediately, leaving Courtney to sort her jumbled impressions of the visit with her husband.

CHAPTER 10

Preparing for the Awards

Having rested poorly, Courtney woke at sun-up and checked on Shawn, who needed more sleep. After straightening his blanket, she moved to the window and looked at Washington, D. C., which was just starting its day.

Courtney needed to clear her head before meeting with Rex later this morning. She decided to perform a life inventory, starting with Shawn. He was obviously healthy and seemed bright. Compared to most children, he was low-maintenance, but he would still need at least fifteen more years of parenting, which Courtney would gladly provide.

She wondered, however, whether raising him would be a solo venture on her part, or if Rex would join in and be a responsible role model to his growing son. If Rex opted out, Courtney was prepared to be a single parent, an emerging concept in the United States as many young adult males were dying in defense of their country.

If, however, Rex chose to remain with them physically, but isolate himself socially and emotionally, things became immeasurably more complicated. How would Shawn react to years of contending with a brooding, dismissive male? What kind of adult would he become after years of living in these circumstances? Was it fair for her to force Rex into making this decision, given his physical condition?

Perhaps most important of all, was she strong enough to force Rex to make this choice, now or later? If not now, she realized that once he came back to the apartment, splitting would become even more difficult, without lingering emotional turmoil.

Courtney prepared herself for the awards day and then roused Shawn, who woke quickly and smiled broadly. After a change, she helped him get into dressy pants and a jacket with Marine colors, an outfit which she bought him for the trip. Shawn was beaming and knew that he was looking good.

While waiting for a table in the hotel dining room, a handsome Marine in line behind them noticed Shawn's colors, caught his eye, and held a salute. Ever the mimic, Shawn caught on quickly and presented a smart salute, holding it until the Marine broke it off. After smiling at the Marine, Shawn turned to inspect the dining room, but maintained the rigidly erect posture which he had just learned.

Courtney turned to the young Marine and said, "Thanks. He really appreciates it when people treat him like a grown-up."

"He has the makings of a fine Marine."

Courtney had to work hard in forcing a smile in response to the intended kindness of this fine young man. The Marine sensed her discomfort and apologized for offending her, though not sure what he had done.

"We're visiting his father here," she explained.

To short-circuit the awkwardness of the moment, the Marine looked at Shawn and said, "He's all dressed up."

My husband is getting an award today." "At what time?"

"Two o'clock."

The Marine immediately went through a list on the clipboard he was carrying, until he came to two o'clock. "There are only four ceremonies at two o'clock," he stated.

Courtney reached over and pointed to "Corporal Butler, Silver Star" on his list. Already displaying admirable posture, the marine, visibly impressed, straightened up even further.

"Please don't stand any straighter because Shawn will try to do the same, and I'm afraid he will snap," she laughed.

The server appeared and walked Courtney and Shawn to their table. Shawn continued to walk in an exaggerated, upright posture and waited for his mother to be seated, as he had seen other servicemen wait for women they were escorting. When the server gave Courtney a menu, Shawn extended his hand for one also. Without missing a beat, the server handed Shawn his menu and left the table quickly, suppressing a laugh.

When he returned with two pillows for Shawn to sit on so that he could be even with the table, Shawn pointed to his selection with which Courtney had helped him. The server took his order as though not-yet-two-year-olds ordered from him every day, and earned an appreciative smile and nod from Courtney for playing his role flawlessly.

Children grew up faster in war time, but that would not have made any difference to Courtney. By seeking growth experiences for Shawn, big and small, she vowed that Shawn was going to be prepared to, not just survive, but thrive. Courtney freely acknowledged that some day he would not need her and would fly free. She was resigned to this development as long as he was on the road to reaching his potential.

After stopping in a restroom and changing Shawn, she walked him to a makeshift play school, designed for mothers in Courtney's situation. After signing in and providing information, she appraised the facility and the staff, almost all volunteers. Satisfied that this site was a more than satisfactory arrangement, she was going to say goodbye to Shawn but noted that he was already being shown the ropes by a cute blonde girl, perhaps four years old. Since Courtney was not needed, she made her way to the exit, turned and exchanged waves with the supervisor, and went to meet Rex.

CHAPTER 11

Ultimatum

Courtney walked slowly to Rex's room, still unsure how things were going to unfold. She sensed correctly that each marriage, no matter the length, had a mere handful of key moments, and that the impending conversation was one of those moments. She decided that she had to speak with Rex before the awards ceremony, an event which Courtney knew was bound to change their lives.

She approached Rex's nurse in the doorway of his room. Smiling at Courtney, nurse Ann asked for Shawn and was disappointed when Courtney explained that he was in day care and that she needed to have a private talk with Rex. Recovering quickly, the nurse suggested that she could push Rex's bed into the far corner of the room. After kissing Rex briefly, Courtney helped the nurse move the bed.

Not wanting to have others overhear, Courtney sat as close to Rex as she could and still be able to look into his eyes. From Courtney's posture and tone of voice, Rex knew that the next thirty minutes would be important, but he was not sure why. Was she leaving him? Was there somebody else? Was there something wrong with Shawn?

Rex was not a person who spoke when confused; he let situations present themselves to him. Taciturn by nature, he became even more close-mouthed under uncertain circumstances.

She began, "In part because you wouldn't let me in your world before you enlisted, Shawn and I have become particularly close, Rex.

I judge everything I do by what is best for him."

He was paying rapt attention but was not about to say anything. She looked at him in frustration and knew that she was going to have to do all the work, if this conversation was to be productive.

Courtney continued, "He's too young to be afraid of you, and I don't want that to happen. You've been far away, physically and emotionally. Now that you have come back, with some injuries that we can deal with, we need you to love us, to learn and grow with us, and to emerge from that remote emotional hiding place which you constructed for yourself long before you became a Marine."

She saw him wince momentarily at the reference to a hiding place. Courtney was all but certain that Rex assumed incorrectly that she was questioning his courage. After all, one of the reasons she married him is that she knew he had never hidden himself from anyone physically and feared nothing. Now she was asking him to face his staunchest foe, himself. If he would only reach out by asking, "What do you want me to do?" she would be more optimistic about a successful resolution to their problem, but he did not, could not, and would not.

She plunged forward, "Being without you, I've learned that I'm lonely for a well-rounded adult companion. I will no longer tolerate your silences. Expecting you to do a U-turn and become a loving, caring partner to both of us all at once is unrealistic, particularly when you factor in the additional rehab you will need.

"I'm suggesting that we do things this way. When you return home, I want you to keep a journal of Shawn's progress each day. I want you to make references to ways in which both you and I have helped him learn and grow. I'm hoping that by keeping this journal, you will move close to him and pull me closer to you at the same time. Even if I get the short end of this bargain, I will accept it if you become close to our son and give him the love and attention he needs from his father. What do you say? Do we have a deal?"

His neck injury permitted him to make a shallow nod only, just as the nurse came by and said that it was time for Rex to eat lunch and prepare for the ceremony. Courtney went to pick up Shawn, again walking slowly and trying to assess her marital relationship. Speaking with Rex was like talking with a wall.

CHAPTER 12

Silver Star

With the help of a colonel's staff, the nurse had arranged the room for the award ceremony. The three other patients were pushed into a corner of the room but still were provided good vantage points. Rex's bed had been placed in the center of the room. Courtney had planned to be in the room by 1:45 PM, but it was slow going with Shawn, who insisted on saluting everyone in uniform. At 1:55, they entered the room and were directed to stand behind Rex. Shawn stopped and saluted General Adams, who was standing at the foot of Rex's bed, holding his salute until the surprised senior officer returned the courtesy. Everyone smiled carefully except the General, who realized he had been upstaged. He agreed with W. C. Fields about the dubious value of small children.

Everyone stood at attention as a three-member chorus sang the national anthem beautifully. Shawn, of course, demanded that his mother put him down so that he could stand at attention with the adults. After the chorus finished, the General began speaking, and Shawn, escaping Courtney's grasp, darted to a position at attention next to General Adams. Ready for Shawn this time, he lifted the child gently and placed him on the bed so that he could see his father.

"We are here today to award Marine Corporal, Rex Butler, the Silver Star," Adams announced. "It is possible that Corporal Butler is entitled to a higher honor, perhaps even the Congressional Medal of

Honor, but we were unable to document the full circumstances surrounding his bravery because the fighting he engaged in was so intense.

"The Marine Corps began fighting for this country in 1775. It is possible that no Marine has ever fought more courageously in such a compressed time frame than this man. We assemble here today to honor a splendid warrior.

"We are also pleased to have Corporal Butler's wife, Courtney, and his son, Shawn, whom we have *all* noticed by now."

Everyone smiled and General Adams relaxed since he had taken control of the room with light humor. Shawn was sitting ramrod straight, looking from his father, who had not said a word, to the medal which the General held in his left hand. The senior officer spoke for another five minutes, providing the details of Rex's brave acts and then lifting the medal so that everyone could see it, before moving around the bed near Rex. While Shawn crawled up the bed to be near his father, the general placed the Silver Star carefully around Rex's neck. Courtney moved to Rex's side, and Shawn touched the medal gently, sensing that it was special. Cameras flashed and the General asked Rex to say a few words.

He looked at the Silver Star for a long moment and in a deep voice, looked at his roommates and said, "I'm privileged to have served with many like these three fine men."

Turning slowly to nurse Ann standing in the doorway and extending his hand respectfully towards her, he stated, "With fine people like you taking care of us, we can't lose this war."

Directing his attention to Courtney and Shawn, he added, "I'm glad my family could be here."

Looking directly at General Adams, Rex concluded by saying, "I appreciate this gesture, sir, but you didn't have to give me a medal to convince me that the country is behind us. The other Marines I've served with understand that. While it looks like my fighting days are over, if you will continue to train and support others, as you have me, things will work out in our favor."

Despite his injury, Rex gave the General a smart salute, and Shawn joined in returning it with the twenty military officers and enlisted personnel in the room. Knowing that the ceremony was over, Shawn ran over with his arms outstretched to be scooped up by nurse Ann, a greeting which made her day. Learning at every opportunity, he prodded her to take him to the nurse's station and show him the materials and instruments in the cabinets. When she had to go back to work, nurse Ann returned him to Courtney, who had just finished speaking with Rex. The two women hugged and, of course, Shawn got in on the act.

The trip home was uneventful, with both Courtney and Shawn sleeping most of the way. She went to work the following morning and they fell into their old routine. Recreating the awards ceremony each day, she used a St. Christopher's medal to put around Shawn's neck, with Shawn coaxing Courtney to make a formal statement first. When finished, she was careful to remove the medal from around his neck and to put it out of her son's reach, so that he would not choke himself.

During the next few months, she prepared the apartment for Rex's homecoming. She had been contacted by the Department of Veterans Affairs, and a special needs chair was delivered two days before Rex's return.

A VA representative looked at the apartment and was satisfied that the restroom would meet Rex's demands, without additional construction. The rep joked that this visit was his easiest stop in several days, conveying the message that Rex's situation was manageable and that he was relatively fortunate. Wishing Courtney the best, he smiled at Shawn, who had dogged his every step from the moment he had entered the apartment. The VA representative then stooped to shake hands with him, and Courtney knew that Shawn would be shaking every available hand for a long time.

CHAPTER 13

Rex's Return

Courtney rearranged her work schedule to be home for Rex's return. She cleaned the already well-cared-for apartment and had used her ration stamps to purchase meat and butter. Shawn enjoyed handing the stamp booklet to the butcher and grocer and watched closely as they removed the stamps. Though he did not understand the transaction, he pretended he did, and the shopkeepers played along, when not too busy.

Shawn benefited from being ahead of the wave of the boomers who would be born after the war. Busy men and women would take precious time to explain things to him, often recreating moments of years ago with their own sons, now off at war. He took full advantage of these opportunities.

On the morning of Rex's return, Shawn looked at his mother quizzically when she dressed him carefully in a new shirt and pants. When she said "Daddy," Shawn's posture straightened immediately and he saluted Rex's picture. Shawn fidgeted for hours and listened carefully for sounds of his father among the various sounds of the city outside the apartment. Courtney could not stand his restlessness and eventually prodded him through the door and onto the front steps.

In full dress uniform, Rex rode from the train in a staff car, exited the vehicle gingerly, and turned to salute the captain who had accompanied him from Union Station. Courtney and Shawn waited on the steps, with Shawn joining in with the salute. Courtney and Rex kissed somewhat awkwardly and with their son leading the way, Rex negotiated the stairs to the second floor. The driver brought in the luggage and asked if there was anything else. As Courtney shook her head no, Rex looked lost as he inspected the three small rooms, noting the two inches of mail and journal waiting for him.

Rex asked unsteadily, "Where do we start?"

Courtney replied, "It's a nice day. Let's walk the neighborhood and go to the park. Are you hungry? Do you want to change?"

Rex shook his head no to both questions and moved toward the door. Courtney's heart jumped as he reached to hold Shawn's hand. Misinterpreting the gesture, Shawn shook and released the hand. Rex pointed Shawn to the steps and Shawn scrambled down the stairs and then waited for his parents to descend. Courtney had insisted that Shawn hold her hand at all times on the streets; there was simply too much commotion on the street to turn him loose. Shawn reached for his mother's hand and then his father's.

Out of respect for the uniform and Rex's disability, other pedestrians stepped aside as the three of them ventured down the sidewalk. Rex noted that some greeted Courtney and Shawn by name; most nodded to Rex respectfully and several introduced themselves. Shawn pointed at stoplights, cabs, and dozens of things, wanting to see if Rex understood, and eventually Rex started naming the items, while Shawn did his best to repeat after him. Following a drink from a water fountain, Courtney and Rex sat on a park bench while Shawn went over to the monkey bars and brought back a little red-haired boy, three or four years old, who introduced himself as Paddy.

"Sojer," said Shawn, pointing at Rex. "Soldier," said Paddy quite clearly.

"Medals," added Shawn, pointing at Rex's decorations.

Paddy moved close to Rex, clearly wanting to touch the medals, but not wanting to get swatted for being intrusive. Pleasing Courtney with his gentleness, Rex took Paddy's wrist and moved his hand to the medals. The boy's eyes got big as he ran his fingers over the decorations. When finished, Paddy took backward steps but continued to stare at Rex's medals, including his Purple Heart.

While reviewing plans to visit the veterans' hospital and discussing three job possibilities for which Courtney had phone numbers, the couple sat and used the remainder of the time to become reacquainted. After an hour, Shawn, with his eyes at half-mast, drifted back to the park bench.

"Somebody needs a nap," said Courtney.

Rather than argue, Shawn dropped his head on Courtney's lap. Rex stood and gathered Shawn on his right side, the good side. Courtney held her breath as Rex wobbled as they walked slowly back to the apartment. Shawn fell asleep immediately, and Rex stopped minutes later at the foot of the stairs. Because of the pain, he gave Shawn to Courtney, so that she could carry him upstairs. She took their son without a glance or a word, not wanting to embarrass Rex.

Courtney was encouraged but not surprised when Rex followed up on the jobs the very next day, and he was soon offered a job at all three. Though he would have to take a bus to travel to a distant factory and despite the fact that the position did not pay quite as much as the others, he took a job at a plant that made military uniforms. Rex was burdened with a strong case of survivor's guilt and felt compelled to stay as close as possible to the war effort.

Capitalizing on his leadership training, he was given a job supervising a crew of women who customized uniforms and setting delivery schedules for transport by trucks and trains. Rex impressed Mr. Adams, the plant manager, with his ability to follow through on details and the respect which Rex received from all who worked with him. Everyone was aware of Rex's medals, but he did not speak of his military exploits, thereby increasing the already high esteem in which he was held.

On the third day, Mr. Adams called Rex into the main office and asked him how things were going. Rex nodded affirmatively.

"You've worked ten hard hours each of your first two days. Feel free to cut your days short if you get tired or if your shoulder is bothering you."

Looking pained, Rex just stared at Mr. Adams, who shrunk visibly in his chair. It was clear to Mr. Adams that he had offended Rex, and Adams was struggling for a way to end this matter, which could not even be called a conversation because Rex had not uttered a word.

"Keep up the good work," said Mr. Adams in closing, as he turned to make a telephone call.

Rex left quickly and returned to his duties, leaving Mr. Adams somewhat chastened. What Rex did not share with anyone was that his neck stiffened at the end of each work day and that he was not sleeping well. In the early morning hours, he walked the apartment, stopping often to gaze at his son, who slept like a stone.

The only time he took away from work over the next two years was a twice monthly visit to a VA hospital. There was not much they could do for the nerve damage to his neck, except to give him vigorous massages. Time passed quickly for the Butlers, since Courtney was busy working and housekeeping. Shawn was growing and learning rapidly, and Rex had a job which filled most of his waking hours.

Like most families, the Butlers did not have much time to assess the quality of their familial relations. Such considerations were put on hold, since the very survival of the United States was at stake. There was a sense of unity throughout the country. People who heretofore did not know their neighbors became acquainted with them and even helped one another. Craftsmen and accountants traded favors or simply helped someone in need, with little chance of the favor being repaid. Ethnic barriers began falling, language obstacles were surmounted, and child-rearing was often shared.

Shawn was fascinated each evening as his parents would sit in rapt attention around a large vacuum-tube radio, listening to announcers depict the ebb and flow of war. Overwhelmed by the words, he directed his attention to the impact upon his parents.

Shawn had little difficulty deciding whether the Allied Armed Forces had experienced a good or bad day. If good, his parents would go outside and visit with neighbors, with Courtney doing most of the talking. If bad, his dad would withdraw unto himself, and his mother would sing along with songs on the radio in an attempt to lighten the mood. With more enthusiasm than rhythm, Shawn joined in song lyrics such as, "Over here, over there," while marching through the apartment.

The Butler family went about their business, while widows seemed to sprout all around them. Military staff cars carrying bad news to anxious families were easy to spot because, by this time, most passenger cars had been parked permanently on side streets, due to lack of repair parts. Almost all available metal was devoted to the war effort.

The word on the street was that we were not the only country with brave, capable soldiers and smart officers, and that if we hoped to win, we would have to out-produce and out-supply our enemies.

After three years of war, then, every adult saw himself or herself as an important cog in our country's war machine.

Accounts of shooting and bombing were described on the radio and in adult conversations; children's games on streets and sidewalks, and in parks, often reflected these activities. Most youngsters had toy guns which helped them imitate battles depicted in magazine and newspaper pictures.

These same children went to movies glamorizing war, which was almost exclusively a male preserve. Men fought in distant places, and women, besides holding families together, worked in nearby hospitals and factories. Everybody was important in the war effort, and all were treated that way.

CHAPTER 14

Nick Brown

Courtney took Shawn to the local park three or more times each week, even in the winter. His mother had concluded that Shawn could learn much about the world by studying changes in the park. He made friends easily there by listening carefully to people of all ages and learning to respond appropriately. People reacted positively to his inquisitive look and polite manner.

At age three, while playing kickball with two of his park friends one spring day, he noticed a little boy sitting on his mother's lap on one of the park's many benches. Waving to the other players to continue playing, Shawn went to the boy and gestured to him to join the game. The little boy looked questioningly at his mother.

"Go ahead, Nick."

Nick joined the game and struggled at first, hesitating to make contact with the other boys in scrambling for the ball. With encouragement from Shawn, however, he was soon able to perform acceptably. After the game ended, Shawn walked Nick back to his mother, Mrs. Jane Brown, who was a slender 5' 7" with a ready smile. She wore her black hair in tight curls.

"This is Nick Brown," said Mrs. Brown, standing and pointing to her shy son. "What's your name?"

"Shawn Butler," he responded confidently, before giving his mother a hopeful wave. Mrs. Butler, who had been talking with a group of the other mothers, walked over and introduced herself. The two women talked easily, while Nick showed Shawn his stamp collection. The Butlers and Browns thus began a friendship which was to last all of their lives. During the years that followed, Shawn was fascinated by the many things with which Tim and Jane Brown enriched Nick's life, including a hamster, a small piano, and an aquarium. At age five, when Nick played a passable *Twinkle, Twinkle Little Star* on the piano, Shawn clapped enthusiastically. This applause from Shawn was the highpoint of Nick's life to that point.

In return for Nick sharing his learning experiences, Shawn made sure that his new friend was not excluded from any activity. It was clear to others that if Nick was not welcome, then the popular Shawn would not participate. While most little boys sought out friends with similar interests, Shawn and Nick realized that their many differences made being friends more interesting. Neither fully understood each other, but both were dedicated to trying.

Most children change "best friends" every few years, due to changes in geography, hobbies, schools, and growth rates. Shawn and Nick had a bond, though, that transcended external influences. Nick often looked puzzled or lost, while Shawn was laser focused on the here and now. Nick planned and Shawn executed, and each had confidence in the other's judgment. Nick would arrange the day's activities and Shawn would make sure they happened. On the few occasions when they were apart and Shawn was called upon to plan, he would ask himself, "How would Nick plan this activity?" Without

Shawn, Nick would ask himself, "How would Shawn do this?"

As small boys, they frequented each other's homes and always were on their best behavior as guests. On one occasion, Courtney heard noises down the hall and commanded, "Clean that bedroom before you two start playing!" She laughed uncomfortably to herself when she discovered minutes later that Shawn had gone outside to the mailbox and that Nick, assuming she was talking to him, had started to clean the room.

On a rainy day after their kindergarten class, when the boys returned to the Browns' home sopping wet, Jane brought out a mop and was cleaning the entryway where the boys had taken off their coats. She was having trouble getting the mop head to remain fastened and went into the kitchen to answer the telephone. Shawn, knowing that adults dislike being told or shown by children how to do things, had let her struggle but seized upon the interruption to reverse the mop head and anchor the screws properly.

When Mrs. Brown returned, she noticed that the head had been adjusted and was working fine. Jane knew that Nick would not even have noticed the problem, much less been able to fix it. When preparing to leave, Shawn was putting on his coat when Mrs. Brown held up the repaired mop head, looked at Shawn and smiled. Shawn gave her a coy wink. As was his custom, Nick missed this exchange completely because he was lost in thought while planning their next activity.

CHAPTER 15

Sidewalks & Libraries

In cities like Chicago, sidewalks are much more than a level means of moving with good traction from one place to another. Among their many uses, these surfaces provide a platform for playing hopscotch, riding tricycles, pitching pennies, or meeting informally.

As a pre-schooler, Shawn used them as a canvas for his art. He loved the feel and smell of the brightly colored chalk which he used to draw animals, playmates, and trees on the concrete. When his parents would co-exist in silence, Shawn would often wander outside and lose himself in depictions of the world around him.

Shortly after his fifth birthday, he was busy drawing on the corner sidewalk one July day when four tough ten-year olds, led by Vinny, stopped to inspect his work. Since he had already seen these guys in action, Shawn was frightened and looked on sadly, as Louie started to use the soles of his tennis shoes to smear a chalk lion of which Shawn was particularly proud. Vinny stepped in quickly and punched Louie's right arm.

"Back off, you dope. This kid is an artist. You think you can draw this good?" he challenged Louie, who was trying to rub circulation back into his aching arm.

Vinny picked up a piece of orange chalk and handed it to Louie, gesturing to him to start drawing. Louie's companions started laughing as it quickly became obvious that he had little artistic skill.

Finally, Vinny stepped in and beckoned Louie to hand the chalk to Shawn, gently and respectfully. Before leaving, Vinny patted Shawn on the back, telling him "If anybody tries to push you around, come and get me. If I can't whip the guy, my brothers can. For now, keep drawing, kid! You're OK."

Early on, Shawn learned that if he were good enough at doing things, important people would take notice and give him respect. He also knew that being more skilled or smarter than most was the best way to gain approval in his world because he certainly was not going to get much encouragement from his father. After displaying some initial interest in his son, his father became absorbed in his job. The daily diary of Shawn's progress had been discarded long ago.

A strong visual learner, Shawn acquired the habit of attaching symbols to his life experiences. In his sidewalk triumph, he decided not only to leave the smeared lion, but to spend an hour of his best work drawing a bigger, better lion next to the original. So that his work would not easily be missed, Shawn brushed out his other drawings, leaving only his two lions and Louie's feeble attempt.

As Shawn headed home, he heard Vinny and his friends coming down the sidewalk. They stopped to inspect Shawn's work.

"Hey, Kid!' Vinny yelled.

After Shawn turned, Vinny poked his friends and led them through a deep bow in Shawn's direction. Shawn smiled, waved, and then hurried home. Vinny's gesture had lifted his spirits.

His mother greeted him when he entered the house and noted his pail of chalk, asking if he needed more. Shawn said that he had enough for now but asked if his mom would take him to the library after supper, inventing an excuse to separate his mom and dad, for a few hours at least. Since his mom knew what he was doing, she avoided eye contact but gratefully agreed to take him.

Mrs. Courtney Butler was a tall redhead whose once considerable beauty was fading fast in the midst of household tension. She saw no good way out of a marriage into which she had entered hastily. Rex emerged occasionally from his mental hiding place but retreated all too quickly. She worked twenty hours a week as a grocery store clerk, a job which she neither liked nor disliked, but simply endured.

Courtney's self-appointed mission in life was to see that her son became everything that her husband was not: ambitious, educated, and clever. Above all, she wanted her son to avoid taking life's blows head on. She knew if Shawn did not define himself quickly and firmly that there were many people in this world all too eager to do it for him, and not to his advantage. Even if he became manipulative and artful in the process of learning to be clever, she felt the risk was worth the reward. She did not want her son to become a chump, which is the way she pictured herself.

After supper, on the walk to their local library, Courtney and her son approached the corner featuring Shawn's artwork. Two older neighbors, the Grimshaws, who knew everything about everybody, were standing there admiring Shawn's art. Courtney exchanged greetings with these pleasant senior citizens.

"Whom do you suppose drew this?" teased Mr. Grimshaw, knowing Shawn was the artist.

"It certainly could not have been anyone from this neighborhood. We don't have that kind of talent on this block," Mrs. Grimshaw teased back.

Mrs. Butler enjoyed the praise, being truly happy only when sharing Shawn's victories. She smiled broadly and nudged a beaming Shawn towards the library, which stood adjacent to the local park. Chicago's library-park combinations were splendid legacies of the collective vision of early city officials.

As Mrs. Butler and Shawn approached this fine, old library, she noticed that he looked upwards, as always, to the statue of Socrates above the entrance. Like most parents, she was encouraged to see her son looking forward and upwards. She was proud of the manner in which her son imparted a best-case scenario when possible and a symbol to every conceivable activity. Mrs. Butler felt that these habits gave Shawn both class and a sense of identity. His steady optimism was a welcome counter-balance to her uncertain view of herself.

As they entered the library, Shawn smiled at the two librarians, who returned his smile and threw in little waves, which were reserved for a favored few. Librarians from big cities of the 1950's, Chicago being no exception, were dictators of the highest order. Gang members, accomplished athletes, and the toughest of street punks all became tongue-tied under the withering gazes of women city librarians. For years after many neighborhoods became dangerous, city libraries remained the quietest and safest buildings in the city.

Since Shawn had noticed that Miss Jones and Miss Abraham had not made many friends among the library patrons, he was determined to get on their good side, because he might need their help later on. He had learned that you could never have too many friends.

Miss Abraham was legendary because of the time she looked through a window and saw a boy push a girl to the ground outside the library. She bolted through the front library door, and the fifteen-year-old boy took off on a dead run. She chased him for a time through a nearby park before grabbing the first available bike. She then pedaled casually behind the boy for a mile or so when the boy fell exhausted to his knees. Before returning to the library, she returned the bike and walked the boy to his home. When his mother answered the door, she nudged him through his doorway, glared at the mother, and cast a disrespectful hand in the direction of the boy, snapping, "Needs work!"

At that time, if you had a run-in with an authority figure, meaning any responsible adult, then you suffered their wrath. If the incident came to the attention of parents or guardians, then you were disciplined a second time. Children quickly learned that the phrase, two-for-one, did not just apply to department store sales but also to discipline with a double whammy.

Shawn and his mother had been in the library two months before when two muscular sixteen-year olds began fighting. Knocking over a large bookcase, this evenly matched skirmish went on for two or three minutes before the librarians appeared. Showing no fear or hesitation, each librarian took a bloodied boy by the collar and escorted them quickly to the exit. The boys were a mixture of embarrassment and fright as they were told by name not to come back for one month. After descending the library stairs, the boys departed in opposite directions, without a thought of resuming their battle.

Inside, an older teen-aged boy was trying to turn the bookcase upright by himself but was struggling, so Shawn put his thirty-five pounds to work alongside of him. Standing on two of the hundreds of scattered books, Shawn tried to get some leverage for this task. Despite the older boy's discomfort, he smiled at Shawn and then barked at four or five other children standing nearby to assist.

Pointing at Shawn, the boy told them, "If he can help, so can you."

With the additional children pushing, the bookcase was dollied to its original position. The others then wandered off, but Shawn and the older boy stayed to gather the books. Miss Jones came on the scene and directed the boys through the task, using hand gestures. When they had done what they could, Miss Jones, a woman of few words but a great communicator, waved both arms over her head, indicating that their part of the job was finished. Looking at each boy, she nodded her head in approval, high praise indeed from this formidable woman.

Many observed that the strength and resilience of Chicago in the post-World War II years through the early Vietnam era were largely due to women city workers and Catholic nuns; few dared to argue that point. These women sought no rewards or praise but simply insisted upon keeping order in their corner of the world. They tolerated neither foolishness nor laziness because of their firm belief that a good work ethic would help our neighborhoods and our country prevail. With these women working inside our country and our troops fighting bravely overseas, the United States packed a powerful one-two punch.

All women were spurred on by radio and newspaper accounts of the size and strength of the enemy forces. This contest had no foregone conclusion, and most women relished the challenge.

Intuitively, women sensed that Americans were more of a threat to ourselves than other countries were to us. You did not need dishes to eat at their kitchen tables, because the tables themselves were so clean. Many used soap, water, and a scrub brush to clean the cement slabs which fronted their entryways. Grime was the enemy and must be defeated before bed time. Their only public displays of emotion were teary eyes at church during the holidays. In any event, these women did their part every day to push Chicago, and by extension, the entire country, forward. They paved the way for Rosie the Riveter, a cartoon figure of a strong, capable blue collar working woman, who became the print metaphor for women's activism in World War II homefront support.

Before heading for the library exit, the older boy tousled Shawn's hair. Shawn rejoined his mother, who again marveled at how capably her son had performed in an emergency. When the going got tough, Shawn was able to focus completely on the task at hand. He was also learning quickly what to do and when to do it. His keen sense of the appropriate and his good timing would subsequently serve him well.

CHAPTER 16

Young Shawn and Nick

Like many Americans not serving in the military during the latter half of the war, the Butlers did quite well, saving money and watching the tide shift in favor of the United States. When hostilities ended in 1945, our fighting men and women returned in hordes over the next year. Most needed housing, utilities, and education, while all needed clothing and food. Our veterans wanted things immediately, as they tried to catch up for the years spent in uniform. The baby boom was on, as they rekindled their marriages or married in large numbers and had children quickly. Shawn's 1940 birth put him in the enviable pre-boomer category with children whose lives had already begun when the veterans returned. He had a head start.

Shawn attended St. Genevere's, a Catholic elementary school on the city's blue collar, northwest side. The Butlers bought one of the compact brick bungalows, which were the only single-family housing option for miles in any direction. These well-kept homes on quiet streets were ringed on all sides by busy avenues and spliced by a railroad track which transported freight, 24-7. The homes were overshadowed by the area's many factories, plants which ran for two or three shifts, generally six days per week.

Courtney had learned of these affordable, available homes from Mrs. Brown, mother of Nick, Shawn's friend. The Browns had moved into an identical home a few months before, two blocks away from what was now the Butler residence. Tim Brown, Nick's dad, was an engineer for Hall Printing Company, an Air Force veteran, and an extrovert. While Tim and Rex merely tolerated each other, Courtney and Jane had become close friends; their relationship became even stronger in their new neighborhood.

Shawn and Nick were delighted to be close to one another again and spent much of their free time together. The mothers were used to either having both boys or neither at their lunch table on non-school days. Shawn insisted that Nick play baseball and football, which Nick agreed to do only if Shawn would read and discuss books that Nick selected. Nick gained confidence as he acquired passable athletic skills. Mr. Brown encouraged and prodded the boys in their pursuits, occasionally taking them to political speeches in Bughouse Square.

Entering into this arrangement somewhat grudgingly, Shawn soon saw the many advantages of becoming acquainted with issues and background information provided by assorted books and informed speakers. At seven or eight, he was mature enough to realize that there were hundreds of thousands of talented young American boys, who wanted to occupy one of the four hundred roster spots on the sixteen major league baseball teams. He understood that his chances of success in that arena were slim.

Already one to appreciate an advantage, Shawn liked his chances better in a nation with a seemingly inexhaustible appetite for the leadership skills of men and women smart and confident enough to move a company or the country forward. History and current news interested him as a basis for making good decisions.

Shawn quickly saw the advantages of being one of a few who saw the big picture rather than being like most people who contented themselves in accepting an obstructed view. Shawn observed that most of these obstructions were self-imposed and vowed to eliminate them from his life whenever possible.

Nick was more than willing to sketch scenarios for Shawn's consideration and support him in his quest to play a major adult role. The boys would read newspapers and magazines and second-guess the President, governor, mayor, and school administrators. They would critique commercials, such as Coca-Cola, and emerging companies, like Xerox and IBM. For years, they tracked the evolution of commercial air travel from its military origins.

When asked, Mr. Brown eagerly participated in their discussions, using his engineering background to support or refute the boys' conclusions. From Mr. Brown's participation, Shawn learned the importance of supporting his arguments with hard facts and of stating his positions in crisp sound-bites. Both made sure to include Nick, who always had something worthwhile to say and who was unfailingly considerate to his dad and best friend while doing so. In air travel discussions, Nick foresaw airplanes flying private citizen passengers, Mr. Brown designed a reasonably comfortable passenger compartment, and Shawn sketched an economically feasible regional airport system to move passengers along the Northeast corridor.

Their discussions reflected the optimism that gripped much of the country during the post-war years. Since the United States had already defeated the toughest opponents in the world, it was in can- do mode.

The country's energy and opportunities were boundless, and the Browns and Butlers were riding the crest.

Rex did not engage in these discussions, but every so often he asserted himself as a father. On one occasion, a rough little kid, Neil Yattone, took Nick's bike and stored it in his backyard. Nick explained the situation to his father, and he, Mr. Brown, and Shawn walked over to retrieve it. Mr. Yattone, a used car salesman, came out of the house, stopped Mr. Brown and told him forcefully that Neil had bought this bike from another child.

"That's not true. I bought this bike myself," said Mr. Brown. As he turned to go, Mr. Yattone shoved him and grabbed the bike.

Shawn ran home and explained the situation to his dad, who walked purposefully down the block to the Yattone home. The situation had deteriorated still further by this time and Mr. Yattone had Mr. Brown, who was already bleeding from his nose, pinned against a tree.

As Rex approached, Mr. Yattone, a burly man with a mass of chest hair sticking over the top of his T-shirt, turned and noticed something in Rex's eyes which frightened him. Rex had developed the habit of cocking his head at an angle, to reduce pressure on his neck. This strange slant and his naturally stern gaze had a hypnotic effect upon Mr. Yattone. As Mr. Yattone let Mr. Brown go, Rex grabbed Yattone by the throat suddenly and placed him against the same tree.

"Whose bike is it?" Rex asked softly. Not getting an answer, he warned, "Don't make me ask you again!"

Rex relaxed his grip slightly and Yattone nodded toward Mr.

Brown, who retrieved the bike and stood next to Nick.

"Apologize," commanded Rex, in a voice so subdued that only Yattone could hear.

"I made a mistake," responded Mr. Yattone reluctantly.

"Good enough?" Rex asked Mr. Brown. "OK by me," responded Mr. Brown.

On the way home, Rex accepted Mr. Brown's handshake, but refused to discuss the matter, feeling that combat, big or small, was not a fit topic for conversation. Shawn walked along with his father, sharing the same feelings with his mother that when with Rex, you felt alone but safe. Ever the learner, Shawn noted that you did not have to humiliate an opponent or shed his blood to make your point. By leaving Mr. Yattone some measure of respect, Rex defused a potentially dangerous situation with little fuss. Neil Yattone never spoke another word to him; Shawn was fine with that.

CHAPTER 17

Post-World War II Chicago

Chicago's Catholic school children outnumbered their public school counterparts until the 1980's. From 1946-54, Shawn Butler and Nick Brown were two of 2,000 enrollees at St. Genevere's, with its three- story school, priest house, nuns' quarters, and asphalt-covered, fenced playground. There were forty-plus students per class for Shawn and Nick, but the classes two or three years behind them approached sixty per classroom. The boomers were on the move!

Classrooms were quiet, orderly places. All the teachers were nuns who did not suffer fools gladly. They held grudges against misbehaving students and often had them expelled. It was commonly believed by postwar Catholics that the road to hell went through public schools. Being sent to a public school was a Catholic family embarrassment in a culture in which this type of humiliation was one of the worst things imaginable.

Most nuns tested rigorously every Friday morning and returned test papers promptly after lunch. In their bulky habits, which made them look like linebackers, they moved quickly and powerfully down the aisles, rationing words carefully and missing nothing that was said or done, either in front or in back of them. They were credited with having X-ray vision and a rear-view mirror.

Speculation ran wild as to what the nuns kept under their habits; some guessed weapons and radios, while others supposed food and pets. The sisters did little to dispel the mystery. St. Gen's pastor, Monsignor Brennan, visited the school once a week, sweeping into a classroom without warning, invariably disrupting a nun's carefully prepared plans.

Every aspect of the church was male-dominated, including the schools. This message was not lost on the children, and many very capable girls were discouraged from even dreaming about attending De Paul or Loyola, strong Catholic universities which trained engineers, physicians, and lawyers on their campuses. Each had campuses in the Loop, so named because of the public transit elevated train tracks which encircled Chicago's downtown.

Increasingly, some young women were courageous enough to consider going away from home to attend one of the state colleges, such as DeKalb State Teachers College, sixty miles west of downtown Chicago. Most girls, though, were simply shuttled into a homemaker role, regardless of their potential. The freedom and activism that women enjoyed during WWII was negated by childbearing and homemaking, as the men returned and shed their uniforms.

This was the social backdrop in which Shawn and Nick lived and learned. Childhood disputes were settled quickly with fists and few harbored long-term grudges. Many boys carried pocket knives, but it was understood that they were not to be used as weapons in fights. Some older rogue teens, however, carried switch-blades: these knives snapped open with the push of a button and were designed to slash. Between vigilant parents and nuns with noses for trouble, few switch-blades were ever carried to school, much less used there.

Most households, Catholic and non-Catholic, had one or more guns, which had either been used by our soldiers or our enemies in the war. Returning veterans did not want their children handling these weapons, having learned all too well the lasting damage they could cause. Nearly all rifles and pistols were ornamental, not functional, because their owners generally did not have proper ammunition to load and fire them. Often the barrels had been plugged to prevent shooting. Besides billy clubs (night sticks), police officers carried snub-nosed pistols, while each station house stocked rifles; few urban citizens had rifles with suitable ammunition.

The fire department and the hospitals worked with the police in saving lives; this synergy was a residue of the solidarity through which the United States had won the war. Most city workers were aware that their counterparts in police, fire, sanitation, schools and other city and county offices had also served overseas; this common bond of military service trumped petty concerns and prompted participants to resolve matters amicably and improve the city. All public agencies supported public and Catholic schools, not necessarily in that order.

The social environment which enveloped Shawn and Nick was safe, patriotic, hard-working, and optimistic. Children had chores, with boys toiling outside the home and girls on the inside. Everybody was expected to live according to three sets of rules: those established by parents for home conduct, all criminal and civil laws, and church doctrines.

With few exceptions, Catholics went to Mass every Sunday and Confession at least twice a year. People worked hard and respected the property of others. Marriages, good and bad, tended to last forever, in part because civil divorces were difficult to obtain but mostly because the Catholic Church disallowed them. Generally, Chicagoans were well aware of the numerous rules which governed their existence and lived with guilt when they stepped outside these narrow boundaries.

Without pay other than an occasional hot cocoa in the winter, children were assigned by their parents to care for the exteriors of the homes of the many neighborhood military widows, who never again used a lawn mower or snow shovel. For four years, Shawn cut the grass and bushes of Mrs. Oysterhaus, a widow with striking gray hair and a tight smile. He also removed her snow when he was no taller than the shovel itself. One January day, he rang the doorbell to let her know he would be shoveling. A man came to the door and asked what he wanted. After Shawn explained himself, the man identified himself as the widow's son and told him that she had died the previous evening.

"Will you shovel the snow anyway? I will pay you." "Sure. I do good work."

This big man in a nice suit and tie got a kick out of Shawn's attitude, took a twenty dollar bill from his picket, and extended it to him. At a time when the monthly Butler mortgage payment was only

$66, Shawn was speechless, because he had never even touched a bill of this size.

"Go on. Take it. You've helped my mother for a long time." "I can't, sir. That's not the way we do things around here.

"I'll accept a dollar for the work today," Shawn said tentatively.

Putting the twenty back in his wallet, the widow's son extracted a ten dollar bill and placed it in Shawn's hand, saying, "You drive a hard bargain, kid. Now if you'll excuse me, we each have things to do."

Thanks to the nuns, Shawn knew when he had been dismissed and went outside to shovel. The man finished his paperwork and went to the front window to watch Shawn remove the last of the snow from the sidewalk. Though Shawn had already been paid, doing the job well was apparently more important to him than his pay, and Shawn inspected his work critically before heading home. From this verbal exchange, Shawn had learned the importance of fairness, courtesy, generosity, and a sense of humor.

The widow's son had learned some things, too. Talking to himself, he said, "If this is the kind of youngster we turn out during war years, maybe our country should fight again soon. That boy has character. He already understands lessons that some of us adults will never learn."

CHAPTER 18

Prowling the City

After reading and playing, the two friends often prowled their neighborhood and later traveled to every corner of Chicago's 300 square miles. In the city at that time, people of all ages were safe anywhere in the daytime and in most places in the early evening hours. The boys enjoyed the many mysteries of discarded items in the alleys and scavenged for pop bottles which they could return for deposits of two or five cents per container.

The boys would bring carrots for the horse which pulled a cart driven by a junk-picker, who shouted "rags and old iron," while collecting rags for sale and sharpening knives for homemakers. Shawn watched the picker carefully as he swapped items and services with the women who drifted into the alley in response to the picker's call. The bearded man would read the customers' body language and trade accordingly.

Never did he ever see the picker pay cash for an item. The boys once found a beautiful old mirror, polished the brass carefully, and waited for the picker. They needed a dollar to go to a Cubs game at Wrigley Field and felt that this mirror was easily worth that much. Shawn pointed out the manufacturer's name and date of construction (1893) of the mirror etched in small print on the back. Both agreed Shawn would do the bargaining and that Nick would stand near the wagon so that Shawn could see Nick's gestures but the picker could not.

"What do you have there, boys?" asked the picker as he brought his horse to a halt.

"We have a fine mirror, which I'm going to give to my mother," Shawn lied.

"Let's have a look," said the picker, climbing down from the wagon behind his old horse.

Removing a cardboard covering with a flourish, Shawn turned the mirror to face the picker, so that he could see his reaction. The man jerked his hooded eyelids upwards involuntarily for a brief moment before regaining his composure, but Shawn already had learned all he wanted to know: the mirror was of interest to the scavenger.

"Mirrors of that age aren't worth much, and your mother probably won't like it," declared the picker.

Shawn did not respond but simply began rewrapping the mirror. The picker turned towards his wagon and asked the boys over to look at some of the old items he was carting. Nick stayed where he was and Shawn gave the items a quick, disinterested glance, before turning to leave.

"What do you want for the mirror?" "We want five dollars."

"Five dollars," laughed the picker. "I don't often pay money for items. I'd rather swap, but I will give you a dollar."

"I know how you do business," replied Shawn meaningfully, looking the picker in the eye and gaining newfound respect. "For a dollar, I'd rather give it to my mom."

Shawn turned to leave, giving Nick, who looked shocked at

Shawn's refusal, a wink.

"Make that two dollars," offered the rag picker. "Cash, right now," snapped Shawn.

The picker dredged up a paper dollar, a fifty cent piece, and several smaller coins and Shawn handed the mirror over carefully. The boys left with Shawn keeping a straight face and Nick looking relieved. As they got two blocks away from the picker, they grabbed each other's shoulders and danced around, smiling and giggling at their success. Shawn gave Nick the paper dollar for his share, with Nick protesting that Shawn had done most of the work.

"I'll always split evenly with you, Nick, because there will come a time when my razzle-dazzle will get us into trouble. When I overplay our hand, we will need your level head and common sense. You're my insurance policy," assessed Shawn.

A few years later, the boys went to a Chicago Cardinal professional football game in Comiskey Park on the city's South Side. Despite being across the street from a highly respected engineering school, Illinois Institute of Technology, and a short drive from one of the world's finest educational institutions, the University of Chicago, the surrounding streets were mean. The boys understood that they had to stay on public transportation and return home immediately with the departing crowd after the game. Shawn again looked for opportunities, no matter how long the odds, and noted that there was little chance that the boys would succeed in catching and keeping one of the sturdy footballs, which the teams kicked into the stands for extra points after a touchdown was scored.

Nonetheless, Shawn coaxed Nick into waiting for the extra point kick after the New York Giants scored a touchdown on the stadium's south end. Shawn had noticed that Pat Summerall, the Giants' place kicker, hooked the ball in pre-game warm-ups, so he and Nick waited on the hooking side and the ball came their way. Nick was quickly pushed out of the way, but Shawn kept his position by grabbing one of the metal braces marking the seats, and the ball caromed off at least three hands before Shawn caught it on a dive. As he regained his footing, he was surrounded by at least two dozen older kids who wanted to take the ball from Shawn.

Nick sized up the situation quickly and ran to get help from two nearby policemen. The bigger of the two officers broke through the mob and escorted the boys to the exit. Seeing that the tough kids were still following, the policeman walked them to the Wentworth "street car-bus," a smooth-riding vehicle electronically propelled along metal tracks encased in the street's pavement. Shawn shook hands with the policeman before boarding the bus, and the two boys made it home without incident, though the gang chased the bus for a few blocks before giving up.

Riding the high of owning a real NFL football, called the Duke, they went to each home and showed it to their fathers and then played catch until supper. Rex did not say anything but patted each boy on the back, while Mr. Brown smiled broadly and joined in the excitement. Shawn made sure to explain to both fathers that without Nick, the bigger kids would have taken the ball from him.

CHAPTER 19

Wrigley field

Shawn and Nick went to see the Chicago Cubs play baseball often, either walking or paying the seven cent fee to ride the Chicago Transit Authority's buses to Wrigley Field, which was four miles away. In the late forties and early fifties, the boys seldom had the thirty-five cents to sit in the bleachers or the princely sixty cents to sit in the grandstand, so they waited until the seventh inning when the gates were opened and watched the last few innings. Frequently, they stayed after the game, staked out a grandstand aisle, picked up newspapers and scorecards, and were given a small, yellow pass to come back the following game day. Often arriving early for batting practice, the boys would scramble for foul balls hit into the grandstand or balls hit into the bleachers, with Shawn doing most of the work.

At a time when baseball was increasingly played under the lights to accommodate working fans, baseball at the Friendly Confines of Wrigley Field was exclusively a daylight affair, remaining that way until 1988. Shawn was aggressive in seeking autographs, and Nick was skilled at cataloging them in their shared collection. They knew all the players by position, visitors and Cubs alike, in the National League. The umpires learned to recognize the boys and would give them packages of gum which Mr. Wrigley provided as gifts for the umpires.

Another advantage of having the team close by was that many of the players lived in the neighborhood. The Cubs' best player in the early fifties was Andy Pafko, who lived on the block next to Shawn. If the boys did not go to a game, they always listened to the contest on the radio. When Pafko did well, as he often did, Shawn would shout congratulations to him as he walked from the bus after a game. Invariably, he replied with a heartfelt thank you, urging Shawn to "Say hello to your old man!"

Because salaries were modest, several players, including Pafko, worked in the factories along Fullerton Avenue during the off-season.

There were no cushy public relations jobs for athletes at that time, and players worked assembly line jobs or loaded trucks. Most baseball players stayed in shape by working in these plants and paid their bills by their winter blue-collar routine, which lasted until spring training started in the Southwest or Florida in February.

The boys watched some of baseball's greatest players and teams in the 1950's. Shawn and Nick enjoyed the 1952 Brooklyn Dodgers, arguably baseball's all-time best team. They were intrigued by Jackie Robinson, a former UCLA halfback and a terrific infielder, as he broke baseball's color barrier. Perhaps due to his football background, he had a distinctive running style, more of a shuffle than a sprint. His extra-base hits were a treat, because he would accelerate as fast as necessary to arrive at the next base safely.

In the last portion of that decade, the boys marveled at the extraordinary pitching ability of Sandy Koufax, also of the Dodgers, a team which had moved to Los Angeles. He threw so hard that he made the baseball look more like a golf ball when it approached home plate. The classy Koufax's overpowering pitching was all the more remarkable, since he weighed no more than a seemingly delicate 170 pounds and spoke so softly he could barely be heard.

After 1945, when they had won the National League pennant, the Cubs were a mediocre team for twenty years but still were able to hold a loyal fan base, mostly children during the week and adults on the weekend. Though they lost many more than they won, when the flag over the bleachers heralded a win that day, pedestrians would cheer and motorists would honk and wave.

The Cubs engendered an optimism that permeated all aspects of the city's north and west sides. Housewives who did not know their elbow from third base made it a point to know if the Cubs had won or lost on any given day. From April-September, radios could be heard echoing throughout the two-fifths of the city north of Roosevelt Road.

The White Sox, who played on the South Side, usually lost most of their fans by July Fourth, except for the rare occasions when they were contending for a pennant. Infrequently, Shawn and Nick visited aging Comiskey Park to see Mickey Mantle of the Yankees and Ted Williams of the Red Sox; otherwise, they stayed at Wrigley.

The Chicago Bears also played in Wrigley Field, beginning their regular season in early September and ending the twelve-game schedule around Thanksgiving. During that era, there was no Super Bowl and only the one playoff game between the two conference champions to determine the NFL champion. By early December then, professional football was done for the year, and fans' attention turned to the college bowl games played during the Christmas holidays.

The boys attended almost every Bears' game, but never saw the first half of any of these contests. Tickets cost between three and six dollars, a princely sum. The Bears' management could not handle the rush for food and drink at halftime, so they opened the stadium gates to allow fans to frequent nearby bars or to buy food and drink from street vendors. Using stubs passed to them from fans inside Wrigley who were not venturing outside at halftime, the boys were able to enter and watch the second half from whatever vantage point they could find, often locating a spot behind the visiting team's bench. In doing so, they learned the art of being nimble and the skill of getting lost in plain sight so that the ushers did not roust them.

Occasionally during the winter, the boys would pass Wrigley and look at each other sadly because there was no place more lonely to them than Wrigley Field during the off-season. Without fans inside and out, the stadium showed its age badly and reminded Shawn and Nick of their neighborhood's many widows.

Shawn viewed winter Wrigley as a cemetery. He used it as an incentive to accomplish something in life, because the stadium was a clear reminder that time runs out quickly. As a teen-ager, he measured life by Cub seasons, not in years. Shawn had overheard seriously ill people say that they hoped to live for at least twelve more months, because they were sure that next season was certain to be "the Cub's year."

Just as the Cubs inspired loyalty because they kept coming back to compete, Shawn was inspired by Nick's reliability and knew that he was one of a kind. He had difficulty separating the Cub logo and

Nick's loyalty. Nick and the Cubs were intertwined in Shawn's view, with each giving meaning and substance to a city full of opportunities. With Nick, the Cubs, a strong father, a loving mother, and a little effort on his part, a fine future was all but guaranteed.

CHAPTER 20

Grammar School

As the boys moved through the eight grades at St. Genevere's Catholic school, their friendship grew stronger. Shawn was a leader on the playground and athletic field. He looked directly into the eyes of his classmates and sensed whom to tease, push, or exclude. Nick was never far away and seemed to blend into his surroundings.

Shawn locked horns initially with a few of the nuns who taught him, but he became savvy enough to build working relationships with them. His adjustment problems were non-existent with Nick close by. Nick would cock his head to the left when Shawn was pushing his luck, and Shawn would dial things back. When Shawn was on the right track, Nick would move his head and shoulders forward, and Shawn would proceed.

Shawn was a solid B student, who could have done even better if he did not spend so much time manipulating his environment. He made almost perfect grades in math due to strong computation skills. His writing skills were painfully direct. He did not take time to edit his work, and his writing-related school work suffered as a result. He noted the criticism and suggestions on his test papers, and he never took the remarks personally. As school became more challenging, Shawn learned to gauge the rhythm of the educational process and to stay in step with it. Not only was he adept at playing the system, but he enjoyed the challenge.

Nick was an A student and a teacher's dream. He paid attention, never caused trouble, and understood difficult concepts the first time through. If a nun was feeling that she had perhaps not explained a lesson well, she made herself feel better by calling on Nick, who always understood the questions and generally knew the answers. He was bored by rote school work which came easily to him and intrigued by complexities and abstractions, which permitted him to operate in gray areas which he found comfortable. His writing was precocious because he was at ease with his own thoughts and spent so much of his life between his ears.

There were three years when Shawn and Nick (never Nick and Shawn) had different teachers. On walks to and from school, Shawn described his problems, and Nick either offered solutions or gave Shawn a tilt of his head, indicating that Shawn either was being unfair in analyzing the problem or that the problem was of Shawn's making.

In fifth grade, Terry McDermott, a cocky, muscular son of a policeman, challenged Shawn's leadership during recess one day as Shawn set up a dodge ball game. "You always want to run things and boss people around. You don't know squat," shouted Terry, as he advanced on Shawn menacingly and threw a long, looping right hand which Shawn ducked easily.

Shawn knew he was being tested and reminded himself to be calm, as he kicked an off-balance Terry squarely on the inside of his right leg. Terry went down hard and regained his feet unsteadily. Terry swung again, missing badly, and Shawn spun him around and pushed him into the chain link fence which bordered the playground. Terry then attempted a clumsy tackle which Shawn easily avoided before starting to laugh. His laughter was a cue for the large crowd which had gathered, to join in the amusement.

Shawn then motioned a frustrated, puzzled Terry to sit at one side of a picnic table, while Shawn took a seat opposing him. Shawn beckoned Nick to set the boys' arms for a wrist-wrestling bout. Shawn gave a fine effort in a contest which he lost, before standing and shaking Terry's hand. For good measure, in managing what could have been a difficult situation, Shawn tweaked Terry's impressive right bicep, drawing more laughter and cheers for both boys.

Intuitively, Shawn realized the importance of leaving an opponent some measure of self-respect. In the bargain, he was able to give everyone reason to be comfortable. His classmates had enjoyed a good show, his leadership was strengthened still further, no one was hurt, and Shawn had allowed Terry to save face by acknowledging his opponent's superior upper body strength. From that day forward, the two combatants were close friends.

The consulting Nick did for Shawn was painless and interesting. Shawn valued his opinion on school matters, since Nick was able to anticipate test questions by listening and watching. When the discussion turned to sports, the roles were reversed, and Nick invariably followed Shawn's suggestions regarding which sports to pursue and what positions to play.

One of the sports highlights at St. Gen's was an annual seven-man touch football game on the first Saturday in October, pitting the Catholic school eighth graders against Spaulding's public school eighth grade, coached ably by a local attorney, Daniel Billings. The Catholics had won the previous two years, and Mr. Billings, not used to losing, had been training five talented skill position players twice per week during the summer, giving the public school a considerable advantage.

Father Delaney, coach of St. Genevere's, held a brief try-out for the team on the first Saturday in September and conducted practices on September's remaining Saturdays for the fifteen players chosen. The priest knew better than to cut Nick, a marginal player who shied from contact, because he might have lost his quarterback, Shawn, in the bargain. Shawn and Tommie Lupinski, a tough Polish iron worker's son, were both talented athletes; Shawn was clever and passed the ball well, while Tommie was an excellent runner and fierce blocker, who went on to be a high school star good enough to receive a college scholarship. Terry McDermott was also a terrific blocker, who particularly liked playing with Shawn. Father Delaney built his offense around these three and felt ready for game day.

Saturday, October 5, was rainy and windy, with just a hint of the frigid winter sure to follow. The two-handed tag game was played in an open area in Kelvyn Park with towels staked in the ground on each goal line. In two-handed tag, the referee would blow the whistle and stop play when a defender put two hands at the same time on the player with the ball. The sidelines were marked by the park maintenance men. Women and girls were not forbidden from attending, but all understood that this activity was distinctly male.

Two officials, a Catholic policeman and a non-Catholic fireman, stood at mid-field waiting for the coaches and captains. The portly Father Delaney, sporting rain gear appearing big enough to cover the entire sixty-yard playing field, and Shawn, his captain, met Coach Billings and his captain, Eddie Enstrom, a fleet six-footer, for the coin flip. Shawn, who at that time was proud of his five feet, five inches, felt like he was standing in a hole across from Eddie. Coach Billings correctly called heads and elected to receive, and Father Delaney chose to play the first half with the wind at St. Gen's back.

On defense, Shawn played safety and shouted instructions to his six teammates as the plays unfolded in front of him. On the public school's well designed first play from scrimmage, Enstrom went to his left as a decoy. When Shawn noticed what was happening and shouted to McDermott to move to the other side of the field, it was too late and a Spaulding player took a short pass and ran down the sidelines until Shawn put two hands on him, three yards short of the goal. Two plays later Spaulding scored a touchdown and Enstrom ran around left end for the seventh point.

St. Gen's gathered themselves and kept the game close into the fourth quarter, trailing 46-41 with four minutes left and in possession of the ball. Shawn, Eddie, and Terry were exhausted, having played both offense and defense, while Spaulding had the luxury of substituting freely because they had fifteen skilled players, while the Catholic school's talent pool fell off rapidly below their top three. Nick had played sparingly and was glad of it, realizing he was outclassed. Father Delaney called a time-out in an attempt to give his big three a chance to catch their breath. "What do you think,

Shawn? Is there a play we haven't called? We need a surprise!"

"Yes, father. They are squeezing the three of us," he said, "but if we stay in the middle of the field, I can roll right and throw the ball back across the field to Nick. He should be wide open."

"All right," said Father Delaney, looking doubtfully at Nick, "but run one play first to set it up."

"Yes, father."

Shawn handed off to Lupinski for a short gain and then looked at Nick in the huddle and smiled, "It's your turn."

Shawn took the snap, rolled right, stopped, and threw a beautiful spiral across the field to Nick who had managed to escape coverage. Nick had grown six inches in the past year, and his legs were like those of a young colt, weak and unsteady. In addition, he had just been fitted for glasses and had not quite gotten used to them. As Nick took a step towards the pass upon which he was unable to focus clearly, he stumbled into the ball. Rather than catching it, he deflected it to the nearest defender who caught the carom with a graceful dive, and Spaulding ran out the clock.

As St. Gen's players left the field dejectedly, some were grumbling and giving Nick dirty looks. Shawn ran ahead to get in front of all the players and stopped them by holding up his arm. "If any of you have anything to say about the way the game turned out, say it now!" demanded Shawn.

To let the other players know that Shawn also spoke for them, Terry and Tommie flanked Shawn with their jaws set aggressively. With Nick standing to one side in misery, the rest of the team dropped their eyes and did not say a word, before slinking off. Shawn gestured Terry and Tommie to move on, signaling to them that he would console Nick by himself, before turning and waving good-bye to Father Delaney.

"I stink and I let you down," Nick said softly.

"The only way you can let me down is by talking like that. You'll always be my best friend, unless you turn into a whiner," Shawn scolded him. "Now, let's talk about something besides football. Have you noticed the way Ann O'Hara looks at you? I think she likes your style, big guy!"

Nick blushed deeply and the healing began.

CHAPTER 21

Post-World War II Years

The Butlers prospered along with a thriving country after the war. Rex's physical condition continued to deteriorate because his neck did not respond to treatment. He took long walks to tire himself, so that he could sleep at least four or five hours before waking, cramped and in pain.

On the other hand, his job was going well; uniforms were needed for many occupations. Being a careful observer, he was able to make suggestions which improved efficiency and led the way to expansion. Using words sparingly, Rex was respected by employees at all levels and became an indispensable contributor to his company's prosperity. Though a puzzle to his superiors because of his seeming lack of interest in being promoted, he was promoted anyway. If you wanted something done well, you assigned the task to Rex.

With the help of Mrs. Grady in caring for Shawn, Courtney was now working full time in Sloshner's clothing store in the booming Six Corners shopping district on north Cicero Avenue. Mr. Sloshner would have liked to have made it strictly a family operation, but neither his daughter nor his son wanted any part of the grueling retail business.

Courtney impressed the owner with her customer service approach; she did not hurry shoppers and never tried to talk them into buying an item. Since Mrs. Sloshner was in failing health and needed his attention, her husband counted upon Courtney to hold the business together. He gave her regular raises and delegated to her all tasks, big and small, including the critically important pricing of merchandise.

Courtney agreed to come in early each day but insisted upon going home at five o'clock to fix supper and be with Shawn. Mr. Sloshner stayed home with his ailing wife until late in the morning, while Courtney opened the store. If she had an early morning problem she could not resolve, she called Mr. Sloshner at home. The owner closed the store by himself at seven o'clock before going home.

Rex frequently worked late, returning to find his wife and son talking excitedly about events in their lives. For the most part, he had shut himself out of what could have been a healthy family triangle, but did realize how important the mother-son relationship was for each of them. He was content to be an appreciative but passive spectator.

After putting Shawn in bed one evening, she was surprised to see Rex blocking her way with a pleading look on his face. "What is it, Rex?

"It's my turn. I want to talk and enjoy you as Shawn does." "Sit down with us and see how it goes," she replied.

"Fair enough," Rex agreed.

Shawn was listening and smiling himself to sleep. So began a building process that grew over the years into the basis for a stable marriage, nothing that was going to spawn music or movies, but communication that moved three fine people ever closer.

Around them, the country was growing rapidly, and veterans worked particularly hard to meet the demands of that growth. Most veterans did not spend much time thinking about complex world-wide military and political matters, because they had spent big chunks of their time defending their country and now were playing catch-up in building their lives and providing for their families.

Working fifty hours or more per week, many were also taking college courses, courtesy of the GI Bill. As a group, veterans were honest, hard-working, patriotic, and family-oriented. They were too tired to steal, as the joke went, and too proud of their families to embarrass them.

The exception was the group trapped by alcohol abuse; this group spawned the term, functioning alcoholic, because many drank as aggressively as they worked. Local taverns, often on street corners, generally did a booming business. Rex worked harder than most and only had one drink each evening to wind down. Hard work was held to be a virtue, and WW II veterans defined themselves by their ability to work long hours productively to support their families. No longer lugging shoulder packs and rifles, their upright posture conveyed their confidence and their fitness.

The extraordinary success that our country enjoyed for generations afterward was accomplished in no small measure on the strong backs of this sub-population in the twenty years following WW II. The Korean War (1950-53) was an aftershock of WW II and resulted primarily from faulty armistice provisions. Many of our WW II vets re-enlisted for this brutal struggle or simply had remained in uniform. The country was not so much divided in its support of the Korean "police action," as they were confused by our motives and those of the United Nations and China.

Shawn followed the war in the newspapers and spoke with Nick about deceptively romantic sounding names such as the 38th Parallel, the DMZ, and the Yalu River. Mr. Brown had traveled throughout the world and provided an excellent resource for Shawn and Nick in their discussions.

As the Korean peace accord was signed, Shawn and Nick were considering high schools. Kelvyn Park High School was close by and a reasonable public school option, except for those parents who wanted their children to continue their Catholic education. St. Ignio had a dicey inner-city location but a great reputation for academics and discipline built around the Jesuits, while Fenwick bordered on suburbia and was strong academically, led by Dominican priests. St. Patrick's was in a good neighborhood on the northwest side, and the Christian Brothers who taught there made the school better than the average Chicago Catholic high school academically.

Since it was a foregone conclusion that the boys would go to the same school, Courtney suggested that the families get together to thrash out a solution. The Browns agreed to host the discussion on a Friday evening.

The two boys and their parents assembled in the Brown's comfortable living room, sitting on either side of a chalkboard that Mrs. Brown had borrowed for the occasion. She had Nick prepare the chalkboard with the name of four high schools, Kelvyn and the three Catholic schools, one in each quadrant and asked Shawn to take notes. Courtney had gathered the literature available on each school and they circulated it, so that each of the six had a chance to skim the contents. Mrs. Brown selected parents to lead a discussion on one of the high schools. Courtney looked quickly at Rex but he displayed no emotion, which did not surprise Courtney.

What did surprise Courtney was Mrs. Brown asking Rex to describe his school, Kelvyn, first. Without hesitation and while looking straight ahead, he began his summary.

"Kelvyn is a good public school, paid for by our taxes. We could save money that we would spend for Catholic school tuition at the other three schools. The teachers are certified, come to work on time, and do not leave until the students are gone. Most of the students who go on to college from Kelvyn begin their work at Right or one of the other junior colleges. Our sons could walk to school and already know the neighborhood. If they chose to live in the area as adults, Shawn and Nick would benefit from the contacts they would make," Rex said in closing.

"Any questions," asked Mrs. Brown.

"How important do you feel missing the religious training would be?" asked Mr. Brown.

"If we have raised our children properly, it wouldn't be important at all," Rex replied.

"Would you go to school there if you were fourteen again?" asked Courtney.

"In a heartbeat. The service taught me to find a way to deal with everyone and also that I could learn anywhere."

Mr. Brown asked, "Don't you feel our children could benefit most from learning in a school full of serious learners?"

Rex answered, "I feel our children can learn best in a little world that is like the big world in which they are going to live later on."

Looking at everyone, Mrs. Brown announced, "Since there are no further questions, let's break for refreshments."

The group stood and talked for ten minutes before Mrs. Brown called them back into session. Mrs. Brown (Fenwick), Courtney (St. Patrick's), and Mr. Brown (St. Ignio) gave their presentations, making brief, pointed comments. It was obvious that the women favored any Catholic school and that Mr. Brown leaned towards Fenwick. The adults engaged in a brief discussion, with the two boys paying close attention.

Finally, Mr. Brown turned to Rex and challenged him, "What is your choice?"

"It doesn't make any difference what my choice is. I'm not going to high school, but they are. Let's hear what they think."

All eyes reverted to Shawn as they expected him to talk in what all knew was a critical moment in this discussion. Shawn, who had been on the edge of his chair, settled back, folded his hands, and stared at Nick.

"I'm interested in what Nick has to say," said Shawn.

Nick was obviously tongue-tied by this turn in the discussion. He looked about frantically as if hoping to be thrown a rope so that he could pull himself to safety. No rope was thrown.

Finally, Shawn encouraged him still further by saying, "Come on, Nick. I've known you since you were just out of diapers. You always make good decisions because you are smart and dead honest. What should we do?"

Ever the diplomat, Nick responded in a firm voice, "We're lucky to have parents who value our opinions. I went into this with an open mind. You have each described a school that I would like to attend." He hesitated for a moment before delivering his recommendation, asserting that "Because we would probably learn to help poor kids in tough situations, my choice is St. Ignio."

All looked at Shawn to gauge his reaction. "St. Ignio it is" confirmed Shawn. The men shook hands, the women hugged, and the boys drifted outside to check signals.

CHAPTER 22

Freshman Year

Like most St. Ignio High School boys, Shawn and Nick boarded Chicago Transit Authority buses every school morning for the trip to the city's near southwest side. Shawn generally bought a newspaper through an open bus window from one of the paper vendors who worked the corners of most stop light streets. He read about how Chicago was being run and by whom, while trying to grasp the issues. By contrast, Nick studied textbooks non-stop as they rode, except when Shawn needed help.

Shawn played freshman football and was elected class vice-president. He spent a portion of his time trying to outwit the Jesuit system in place and decided it was best to speak succinctly, respectfully and fearlessly. The priests sensed apprehension and treated those who exhibited it harshly, in an attempt to build men. The only mistake worse than being afraid was sarcasm, which was a habit you broke quickly unless you enjoyed having your life made difficult.

Shawn enjoyed football, as much for the chance to lead, as the opportunity to polish athletic skills. The three freshman coaches used him to bring rogue players into the fold and to prepare for big games.

A fine Polish linebacker and receiver, Alex Dombroski, had been having anger management issues related to his father's heavy drinking. He had been ejected from the first freshman game for grabbing a referee by the shoulders. In the locker room the following

Monday, Alex was shouting at a big lineman for no apparent reason. Attracted by the noise, Coach Highsmith came out of his office and was about to get in the middle of his two players, when Shawn stepped in front of him and looked questioningly at the coach. Highsmith nodded and returned to his office, while Shawn moved to a seat on the bench next to Dombroski.

Speaking loud enough so that everyone could hear him, Shawn said, "Alex, I need your help. The team is not playing well and needs a leader. I have tried doing it by myself but I've been coming up short. I want you to look around and see who is not doing his best. Then, come to me and we'll try to improve things. Will you work with me?"

For the next few weeks, Alex was so busy inspecting others that he did not have time to cause trouble. Meanwhile, the other players were determined not to be selected, and their play improved. After the second game, which they won handily, Coach Highsmith was singling out players in a team meeting for their contributions. He was about to praise Shawn, who gave a brief nod in Alex's direction.

Highsmith caught the cue and praised Dombroski instead, after which the players joined in a rousing ovation. That was the end of Alex's poor behavior and he became one of the ingredients of a fine freshman season. Thanks to Shawn, Dombroski morphed from a problem to a solution, Shawn gained another supporter, and Coach Highsmith received credit for the team's improvement.

Meanwhile, Nick ran cross country and joined the chorus. The choral group was a natural for him because it allowed him to support others and, because of his height, to stand in the back row out of the limelight. He had an acceptable baritone and took cues and tips from Mr. Bartels, the choir director, with respect.

Nick ran number three on the freshman cross country team. In races, he found a comfortable spot mid-pack and then cruised on the outside as he picked off fatigued runners. The two St. Ignio runners who ran ahead of Nick dueled each other in practice and races; they often ended their runs on their knees, gasping for breath. By contrast, Nick recovered quickly and showed few signs of weariness. Mr. Samuels, Cross-Country coach, tried various means of getting Nick more involved but had no success. The coach had Shawn in his study hall and called him aside one day to speak with him about Nick's situation.

"He could be a great runner, if he would try harder. Will you talk with him?"

"I will, if you insist, but he is good at deciding things for himself," replied Shawn. "You can't make him want something. He has to decide that winning races is important to him."

"I'm supposed to be helping young people reach their potential," insisted Mr. Samuels.

Shawn said convincingly, "For now, maybe this is all he needs or wants. The other kids like him, don't they?"

"Yes, except for a few who envy how easy he makes running appear," laughed Coach Samuels.

He waited for Shawn to speak; though only thirteen, Shawn knew when to keep quiet. Before turning to leave, Mr. Samuels said with little conviction, "Maybe time will change things."

Each knew that this was not likely to happen. Competitions for Nick were not with others but rather against his own standards of excellence.

Shawn and Nick met at the end of the day when their athletic schedules permitted. Occasionally, another boy would join them for the bus ride home, but others soon realized that the impenetrable bond between the two boys made a third person uncomfortable. Few joined Shawn and Nick a second time.

In these private moments, Nick often took charge. Shawn often was excited at the end of the day and wanted to discuss what he had experienced. The boys engaged in these discussions until the westbound bus reached Western Avenue, at which time Nick would raise a textbook above his head, indicating that it was time to review academic matters. At that time, Shawn asked Nick's opinions on instructors and tests, and Nick made suggestions. When they exited on Cicero Avenue and waited for a northbound bus, they talked professional sports, girls, and family issues. From the time they boarded the next bus, Nick insisted on absolute quiet and devoted his attention to his reading. Shawn had no choice but to follow suit.

Shawn found the routine to be helpful in disciplining himself academically. By organizing his homework on the ride home, he was able to complete it earlier in the evening, thus making time to talk with his mother and occasionally his father before going to bed.

He asked his father to attend a freshman football game, which was to be played in a city park near the high school. On the day of the game, his father did not mention anything, and Shawn thought he had forgotten the invitation.

When the game started, Shawn had his hands full in a spirited game with St. John's freshmen. There were no grandstands, so all spectators stood on the sidelines, grouped around their teams. Late in the game with the score tied, Shawn completed a nice pass to Dombroski, who was tackled hard by three opposing players. Despite his size, Alex was knocked head over heels and was about to take a nasty fall into a group of St. Ignio mothers, when Rex stepped in the way, caught Alex by the shoulders and set him casually on his feet. It happened so fast that many nearby were not even sure it had happened. After a long look over his shoulder, Alex returned to the huddle.

Other than tightening his lips to fight the pain in his neck, Rex had not changed his expression. A player's father who was standing nearby reached over and slapped him enthusiastically on the back in an effort to congratulate him. Rex turned and left the field immediately as he experienced excruciating pain from this well- intentioned but misguided swat. With tears streaming down his face, he waited for the bus.

The well-played game ended in a tie. Though there was no shortage of game-related things to discuss, most of the buzz surrounded the man who caught the player and prevented injury to the mothers. Though Shawn had not seen the topic of discussion, he was not surprised when told his father was the hero. His father seemed to do whatever needed doing without a fuss.

When Shawn returned home two hours later, his mom and dad had already eaten. Shawn looked at his father seated in his easy chair and said, "I heard you were at the game, dad."

Rex stood, came over to Shawn, and squeezed his shoulder, conveying in a single gesture that he was pleased with the way Shawn had played, proud of his leadership, and not at all anxious to discuss the Dombroski matter. Shawn tried to remember when his father had last touched him as he savored the tingling in his shoulder.

Football season ended before the regional cross-country meet in which Nick ran as a freshman, thus Shawn was able to see Nick compete for the first time. The two-mile event was held in Riis Park on the hilliest course in Chicago in a city which is, for the most part, pool-table flat. Nick did not notice Shawn, who by that time had joined Mr. Brown, until the runners were assembled at the start. Shawn smiled and nodded at his friend, and Nick returned the greeting with a shy wave.

The other runners looked around nervously at one another, while Nick looked calmly into the distance; Shawn knew he was mapping the race in his mind. When the race began, there was jostling as the runners jockeyed for position. Nick ran easily on the edge of the pack and continued to look to the horizon, before ascending the first hill. Shawn turned quickly and ran to the finish line, one-half mile across the park. Mr. Brown trotted slowly in Shawn's wake, anxious to see the completion of the race.

Ten minutes later, Shawn had positioned himself beyond the finish line and in full sight of Nick, who was running almost evenly with the tightly bunched lead pack of eight runners but remaining outside. Three of the lead runners, including St. Ignio's two top runners, were tiring and dropped in back of the top five. Nick saw Shawn raise his arm slowly; in response, Nick began a kick, while uncharacteristically churning his arms vigorously. One of St. Ignio's runners in the pack was distracted by Nick on the outside and fell, dropping out of contention, leaving the other four and a fast-closing Nick to cross the line in a blanket finish. Shawn grabbed Nick and lifted him off the ground, and Nick asked to be released so he could cool down.

After a lengthy discussion by race officials, Nick was awarded fourth. Shawn did not see it that way and started to argue with them, but Nick gently steered him aside and said quietly, "There will be other races."

Mr. Brown nodded his approval, as much for Nick's handling of the situation as his son's fourth place regional medal. Shawn's already high estimation of the Browns was pushed higher yet, as he received another lesson from Nick in how dignity should always trump achievement. The Browns understood some things that most people never even considered. In case Shawn had missed the point, Nick reminded him quietly, "The race took only eleven minutes, but I will have to spend the rest of my life dealing with the way I conduct myself today."

CHAPTER 23

Off-Season Training

The years at St. Ignio's passed quickly for both boys. Each mentored and tutored needy elementary school students from schools near St. Ignio. Both Nick and Shawn were highly prized by Father Alex, who praised Shawn for "interacting so successfully and quickly with all students" and Nick for "getting great mileage out of a few words" and "being a powerful learning model."

In the classroom, Shawn made a B average and was elected captain of the football team at the end of the football season in his junior year. He played quarterback, running the ball cleverly and passing adequately. Shawn, however, was unable to throw the ball further than forty yards, in a sport that had become increasingly pass-oriented. As a result, opposing defensive backs played close to the line of scrimmage and punished Ignio runners. Unless a change was made, St. Ignio's approaching football season, Shawn's senior year, was destined for mediocrity. Shawn could not let that happen.

He had noticed a raw-boned sophomore with a slingshot arm, Danny Kames, who played quarterback on the practice team. Danny had trouble learning all the plays but was a fine runner who appeared to get bigger and stronger every week. In early May, Shawn and Nick waited for Danny after school, outside the front entrance to the school.

"Hey, Danny, I want to talk to you," said Shawn.

Since Danny knew the team captain usually handled problems, Danny took a step backward and looked frightened. "What's wrong?

What did I do?" stammered Danny.

"Relax. What you *did* was show everyone what great skills you have! How would you like to play first string quarterback next year?" asked Shawn.

Danny was at a loss for words, and Shawn took him by the arm, motioning to Nick to follow. "Let's get a coke," said Shawn firmly.

Over bottles of the original six-ounce coca-colas, Shawn told Danny that he would like to teach him the team plays on North Avenue Beach three evenings a week during the summer. Nodding his head eagerly, Danny explained that he would be working construction with his uncle, but that he could get there by 6 PM on week nights.

The boys practiced in the beautiful park across Lake Shore Drive from the beach. The steady hum from the traffic was in cadence with the player's footwork as they choreographed their skills.

Shawn used the only rainy summer evening of practice as a test of Danny's resolve, but he was there early and never said a word about the weather. During the workouts, Nick waved his long arms in front of Danny, as the new quarterback threw passes to Shawn. Then Nick would run effortless laps around the field as the two players worked on executing the running plays. A grateful Danny learned quickly and was soon throwing perfect spirals up to sixty yards, while perfecting his handoffs and footwork. All three boys did pushups and situps at twilight, swam parallel to the shore, and talked briefly before going home.

Before the first practice in August, Shawn and Danny stepped into

Coach Fenton's office, not speaking until the hard-nosed coach acknowledged them. "What is it?" the coach asked.

"Coach, I think we have our quarterback," stated Shawn. "What are you talking about? You're the QB."

Shawn countered by pointing at Danny, "He's better than I am. He's four inches taller, thirty pounds heavier, and throws the ball harder and further."

The coach said, "He doesn't even know the plays." "Yes sir, I do," interjected Danny.

"We'll see about that," said Fenton and waved them out of his office.

Danny was about to respond but Shawn grabbed him by the shoulder and pushed him through the door. "Talking won't convince him. He needs to be shown on the field. Just remember all that you learned this summer and you'll be OK."

Practice began with the two quarterbacks trading snaps with the first team. Since this procedure was obviously acceptable to Shawn, the other players did not question the arrangement.

Coach Fenton stopped Shawn after the second day of practice, stating, "He's doing well and he can sure stretch the defense with that arm. What are we going to do with you?"

"I'll back him up and play special teams. I also know all the plays for the slot back position if Monroe gets hurt," explained Shawn. A slot back is a receiver who catches short passes and tries to make big yardage after the catch. Shawn had good hands and set up his blockers nicely, so the position suited him.

CHAPTER 24

Shawn's Senior Season

With Fenton's capable coaching and Shawn's encouragement, Kames blossomed. When they lost their second game of the season, Kames threw a bad pass and a defender ran it back for a touchdown. Neither the coach nor Shawn made an issue of it, and Kames' confidence grew as St. Ignio won four of their first five. Shawn had helped establish a fine special teams chemistry and mopped up for Monroe when the game had been decided.

During the week before the sixth game, a crucial battle with a talented St. Liam team, Monroe had an appendicitis and Shawn moved into the starting lineup at slot back. Largely because they had thrown the ball to each other all summer, Shawn was able to catch seven of Kames' passes in helping win a close game.

St. Ignio played into the final four of the Chicago Catholic League playoffs and was pitted against St. Orem's, a perennial power. Shawn had many aches and pains, while realizing that he had at most three more football games to play in his life: two to win the Catholic League Championship and one more in playing the Public League winner.

The Catholic-Public game was played in Soldier Field on Chicago's lakefront and drew 60,000 spectators or more each year, affording all an opportunity to see two fine teams. Another angle to this game had the mackerel snappers (Catholics were forbidden to eat meat on Fridays) playing teams who had many players not attending church on Sunday, as Catholics were required to do.

The Catholics had an advantage in the title game, because they were allowed twenty days of spring practice to none for Public League teams. Catholic schools used these precious practice days to install additional plays and to have their players learn a second position, a big advantage in a high-injury sport.

In the late 1950's, Catholic schools were full, despite the tuition costs, and public schools were not, in spite of their tuition-free operations paid for by tax revenue. The gulf between the two groups was huge. Catholics were strongly pressured to date and marry other Catholics; mixed marriages (Catholic & non-Catholic) were fraught with various complications, including the contempt of strict Catholics. Non-Catholics typically did not suffer the depth of guilt experienced by Catholics, who were governed by rigid church laws.

St. Ignio had a required Sunday Mass at the school's chapel for the players on game day. If you were a starting player and late, you did not start the game. If you missed Mass altogether, you did not even suit up for the game.

Shawn was ten minutes early for Mass on game day. Trying to reduce the tension, he poked and bumped his way through his nervous teammates who were standing outside the church. Many scrambled to seat themselves near him during the service.

Despite his bumps and bruises, Shawn was eager to play a top-drawer team. He also had many special team players depending upon him. Shawn had to be positive and energetic, if he expected others to be. During team meetings and practices, he noticed that these players often looked his way for signs of weakness or dissatisfaction and would not have dared let them see any.

When Mass ended, Father Morgan asked Shawn if he had anything to say. He stood, looked slowly around the room, and spoke emphatically, "We have all been raised properly, taught well, and coached effectively. If you have some doubts about your ability to play at this level, sometimes I do, too."

Hearing him confess to being less than supremely confident puzzled his teammates. Shawn quickly added, "Whenever I feel that way, I look around me and the feeling quickly disappears, because I trust and believe in you, every one of you. I hope you feel the same way, because if you do, we will play well today." A murmur of agreement swept through the church as the boys exited.

The game was played in St. Orem's stadium, a hostile environment with cow bells and noisy fans. St. Ignio kicked off with Shawn trailing the play as usual and directing his teammates to the ball by yelling instructions. By the time he neared the Orem kick return man, Shawn's teammates had already knocked him to the ground. As Shawn eased up at the whistle, he was blindsided by 220 pound Marty Steinbrenner, an Orem special teams player who was also their finest linebacker. Shawn had never been hit that hard before and he walked off the field unsteadily, with Steinbrenner taunting him. The referees missed what should have been a penalty, a late hit, much to the displeasure of Ignio's coaches.

The game was scoreless in the second quarter when Steinbrenner intercepted a Kames pass and, instead of trying to elude Shawn, tried to run him over. Shawn was able to make the tackle but needed help as he hung on desperately.

This was the first chapter of a lifelong competition between the two young men. Steinbrenner, mean to the core, just could not accept Shawn's composure and leadership qualities. While the burly linebacker had to threaten his teammates to get them to do anything, Shawn's mates looked to him respectfully for instructions.

Kames played well, but two of his long passes were dropped and he was unable to elude Orem's fine tacklers. In a game marked by great defense, Orem built a 10-0 lead and held it into the fourth quarter, when Ignio's offense finally caught fire. At the end of a long drive, Shawn caught a short hook pass and spun, apparently to fall to the ground. Steinbrenner, in his haste to crunch Shawn, dove prematurely and Shawn sidestepped him and scampered down the sidelines, carrying a tackler into the end zone. Steinbrenner arrived too late to make the tackle but in time to stomp on Shawn's right hand as he lay on the ground. The referees threw a penalty flag this time as Shawn left the field to seek attention for his injury.

Ignio missed the extra point, and Orem recovered the ensuing onside kick and was able to run out the clock. As the teams engaged in the often hypocritical ritual of congratulating each other by shaking hands at mid-field, Steinbrenner made it a point to grab and twist Shawn's hand, which he had stepped on during the game. Disengaging himself without looking back, Shawn simply shook his head and figured logically enough that Steinbrenner was a person he could easily avoid. Over the years, he came to realize how wrong he could be.

CHAPTER 25

College Choices

Shawn and Nick loved high school, and the years passed swiftly. The two families shared Christmas together at the beautifully decorated home of the Browns in their senior year. After dinner, all six stood near the ten-foot blue spruce and enjoyed the moment. No words were necessary because they had all the ingredients for a perfect evening: a great setting, an excellent meal, good health, close friends, two boys destined for success, and financial comfort.

To avoid spoiling the evening, they agreed beforehand not to discuss college plans; instead, the families convened two days later at the Butlers' home for this purpose. All six sat at the kitchen table and Shawn initiated the discussion.

"It's time to talk about college. Before we begin, I want to thank Nick for keeping me on track academically. Some of his good habits rubbed off on me, but right now, he's a better student than I'll ever be."

Nick blushed and Mrs. Brown messed his hair. Rex and Courtney laughed and then the room grew quiet, because most knew what was coming.

"I would love to go to the same school as you, Nick, but I don't want to hold you back. Where do you want to go to college?"

Both families knew that Nick had visited Lakewestern, known as the Harvard of the Midwest. Sitting north of the city on Lake

Michigan, the school enjoyed an excellent academic reputation and its employees grasped the notion of customer service long before this concept became fashionable.

Nick had asked Shawn to visit the campus with him on an August Sunday just before classes began. Of course, Shawn was glad to oblige, because his friend asked so little of him; besides, Shawn was curious about how things were done at this fine institution.

As they exited the bus on the Chicago city limits, each was struck by how ordinary the homes were as they made their way to the campus. By contrast, the LW campus was beautifully landscaped, the buildings carefully tuck-pointed, and the playing fields perfectly manicured.

Nick was content to think and roam for the first ninety minutes to get a feel for the campus, and Shawn was patient in letting him do so. Nick observed carefully the students who had returned for the fall term. He wanted to see how comfortable they were with each other (very much so), if they respected each other (without exception), and how they were attired (casual but clean). He also noted some loners, like himself, who seemed to be thinking as they walked, and saw himself fitting comfortably into this setting.

Finally, Shawn grew bored and waved Nick into a men's gym used for intramural sports, where they shot baskets for ten minutes and then went outside to watch the LW football team scrimmage in preparation for the coming season. Shawn felt a little stirring when he watched the practice, but the size, speed, and strength of the players confirmed his decision not to play college football.

The library was closed, so they ended their day by having a sandwich in the Student Union. Shawn noticed the glint of excitement in Nick's eyes. In early November, Nick returned to the campus with his father and loved the campus, even in a light rain.

Nick realized he had taken a full minute in reflecting upon his LW experience. Finally, Nick said "I'm torn between Loyola and LW. The Jesuits will forgive some of my tuition at Loyola, but LW has offered me a partial academic scholarship. I feel as though I owe the Jesuits something, but I don't think that's a sufficient reason to attend their college. Because of its diversity, I feel I have a better chance to become a responsible adult at LW. I'm still sorting majors, but that's where I want to go, if they'll have me."

Nick looked painfully at Shawn, hoping he had not offended him, but Shawn replied with a quick wink and a smile. Shawn said, "Nick has LW and suburbia written all over him. The world is a bigger place for him than it is for me. I love this city. If I can't see, smell, and taste the air, I get suspicious. If I don't have to be careful crossing a street, I figure something is wrong. If there's no line for carry-out food, I assume the place is being robbed.

"I want to attend Right Junior College and graduate from Chicago State. Later on, a city law school, perhaps Kent, looks good, probably on the GI Bill. Nick and I agree that going into the military seems like a good idea. I like the Marines, and he favors the Air Force."

Nick surprised everyone by interrupting, "Though we are going to travel different roads, Shawn and I are going to remain close friends and are likely to form some sort of partnership as adults. People rally around him in the present, and I'm often able to see how things will turn out in the future."

Shawn joined in, "Sure, he can see years ahead, while he trips over his own feet in the here and now."

Everyone, particularly Nick, laughed long and hard. The adults were left with several questions, which they would ask their own sons in private. For now, each boy had a plan which made sense.

CHAPTER 26

Honors Banquet

Nick was on his way to graduating third in a formidable class of 280 college-bound, Catholic men. With Nick's help, Shawn would finish twenty-first and was admitted as a marginal member of the Honor Society. At the prestigious spring banquet held on the gym's basketball floor for honor students, the Butlers and Browns sat at a table with two other families. The boys had been expressly warned not to wear their sports letter sweaters, being told in person and by mail that this was an academic evening only.

In the reception preceding the formal dinner, Shawn took his parents to meet the mothers of the two honorees whose fathers had passed. His parents quickly understood what he was doing, with his mother saying all the right things to the widows, while his father was sympathetic and listened to the widows politely.

Nick looked lost for a moment but soon found himself in the company of four classmates who also lived deeply within themselves. The parents of these introverts were greatly relieved to discover that their often distant sons were not one of a kind in their school. For them, the evening was a success before the program began.

The Jesuit dean of discipline and former Marine chaplain, Father Callahan, directed the crowd of one hundred to their chairs with a single, deafening clap. He set the tone for the evening when he explained that this event was to honor parents "who qualified for sainthood by putting up with their offspring." The thirty male students in attendance quickly understood that they were just props and sat back to honor their parents.

Father Callahan had done his homework, indicating that in attendance were the parents of 112 children, including the thirty being honored. Among these parents were two medical doctors, three dentists, ten engineers, three lawyers, and others who had distinguished themselves in various ways. He went on to say that there were seventeen fathers and two mothers who had served in the military. Included among the service decorations, Father Callahan noted four Purple Hearts, six Bronze Stars, and one Silver Star.

Shawn stole a glance at his father, who did not bat an eye, as the group buzzed with the Silver Star reference. If his father had anything to say about it, this would be the last Silver Star mention of the evening. Again, Shawn noted how much he had learned from his remarkable father, without words being used. Looking at the Browns, Shawn knew that they would not consider divulging Rex's secret. The chaplain concluded his remarks by extending a well-received compliment, explaining that they had made instructing their children easy, because they had done their parenting job so well.

Each of the thirty honor students was introduced individually in reverse order of their class rank. Shawn and Nick clapped loudly for each student. When the initial response was weak for two unpopular students, Shawn looked accusingly at nearby students and the parents who were not clapping, and they instantly applauded. When it was Nick's turn at number three, the generous applause was as much for

Shawn's close relationship with him as it was for Nick himself. Shawn's leadership crossed age and gender lines. An underdog always had a chance when he was present. Courtney was so proud of the way Shawn conducted himself, that she became teary-eyed.

After the formal portion of the evening, Shawn asked both sets of parents if they could stay for a while and they agreed. Shawn motioned to Nick and they hastily intercepted three or four parent- nerdy son combinations who were about to leave. As usual, Shawn did most of the talking, explaining to parents how smart their sons were and how these students made everybody work harder because of their dedication. Nick followed Shawn's lead, filling in the gaps and chatting with the parents.

Shawn encouraged the parents and sons to stay and visit, telling them that there were others who wanted to meet them and then steered his classmates to make these meetings happen. Heading back into the gathering, the parents beamed and the students were grateful for having been shown appreciation by perhaps the class's most popular student and his well-mannered friend.

After thirty minutes, parents and students alike were talked out and drifted towards the door. Father Callahan, who had noted the contribution of Shawn and Nick, stood near the exit and shook hands with everyone. As the Butlers and the Browns approached him, the priest shook Rex's hand and pulled him out of the flow of departing people.

Father said softly, "Semper Fi. I see you're not wearing your decorations this evening, Corporal Butler."

Rex looked deeply into the priest's eyes and gave a tight smile. "I never do. Besides, I'm outranked tonight," Rex replied as he nodded in Courtney's direction.

Father Callahan turned to Courtney and surprised her by saying, "You've done a wonderful job with Shawn. For our students here, we tolerate a few, honestly enjoy most, and are downright fortunate to have an exceptionally fine human being once in a while. Shawn falls into the lucky-to-have category. He understands more about how to get people to do the right thing than some of us who have taught all of our lives. He brings out the best in all of us."

Father went on, "You both appear healthy. If you have more sons, there will always be a place for them at this school. Thank you for coming this evening."

He turned to the Browns and said, "Classy behavior at any age is a treasure. Nick has it in abundance. He is more polished than most of his classmates and has a broader perspective. You must be fine people to have raised such a decent, centered young man."

He shook hands with the four parents and moved on to praise other students. Father Callahan's praise was uniformly appreciated because it was obvious that he was well acquainted with the students and that he was undeniably sincere. Nick joked days later that his father's posture had improved since meeting Father Callahan, whose Marine bearing was always ramrod straight.

CHAPTER 27

Pre-College Job

Shawn and Nick made it a point to spend as much time together as possible during the summer before starting college, including working the same job. Nick would have been content to sell ice cream locally, but Shawn insisted that they get out of the neighborhood and become acquainted with parts of Chicago they had not yet seen.

The boys reported each morning to an intersection along South Cicero Avenue, from which they were transported by van to apartment buildings and homes to deliver soap samples, a task for which they were paid ten dollars a day. Shawn spoke with the boss and arranged it so that he and Nick could work together on the same streets, with each taking a side. Shawn wanted to look after his friend, knowing that Nick would likely daydream and put himself at risk in neighborhoods where visitors were not always welcome.

Things went smoothly for three weeks until a sweltering Wednesday when Nick stepped around three tough teen-age boys who were sitting on the steps leading to a dingy three-flat apartment. One of the boys pulled a knife, which shone in the sun. As soon as Nick approached the small entrance to the building, the three boys pushed him into the entryway and slammed the door. Shawn, who had observed the incident as he emerged from a building, turned to a resident whom he had just given a soap sample and asked her to call the police. After she assured him that she would, Shawn ran across the street, while wrapping his jacket around his left arm to ward off possible knife thrusts.

The three boys had Nick pinned and were in the process of stealing his wallet when Shawn bulled his way into the cramped entrance, catching everyone by surprise. He grabbed the wallet and shoved Nick outside. The boy with the knife slashed at Shawn, who blocked the thrust with his wrapped forearm. The knife cut through the jacket and drew blood from a superficial wound.

Meanwhile, Nick had grabbed a large broom and when Shawn stepped outside, Nick jammed the broomstick through the door handle, closeting the trio in the entryway. Shawn and Nick knew when it was time to run and they were well on the way back to the soap sample intersection of the day before the three boys could exit the entryway by getting someone to remove the broom handle. Nick saw a police car but Shawn shook his head no to Nick and they kept on running, choosing to avoid further trouble by not returning to the scene of the confrontation. Shawn figured that he was lucky to have escaped with a slight wound and that pressing charges might spawn a batch of more serious problems.

After sorting things out with the soap sample boss, Shawn and Nick were excused for the day. On the bus ride home, Shawn questioned his friend, "What did you learn today?"

"I need to pay closer attention to the world around me." "Is that all?" Shawn prodded.

"I think so," Nick replied tentatively.

"An equally important lesson is that not everyone has our best interests at heart. If you don't understand that being right, fair, and decent is often not enough to guarantee success in dealing with people, then you are not going to be able to watch my back as we engage in increasingly complicated situations. There are many out there who will hurt and even kill us without losing a minute of sleep."

"I'm starting to understand. I wonder if my mom will let us go back tomorrow," Nick said, hoping that Shawn did not want to return to work the next day.

"I am going to go home with you to state our case," Shawn stated firmly in a tone that did not invite debate.

The boys watched the end of the Cubs game on TV and waited for the Browns to come home. When Mrs. Brown returned first, Shawn said, "We need to speak with you and Mr. Brown about something. There is nothing wrong, but it is reasonably important."

Mrs. Brown was anxious to know what was going on but realized that the boys were growing up and should be treated as at least junior adults. She decided to be patient and wait for her husband to return.

When Mr. Brown arrived, the four of them took seats in their comfortable living room. Shawn began, "We had an incident today and we want you to know exactly what happened. Nick, will you describe things as you remember them?"

Nick thoroughly explained the matter, and both boys answered several questions from the Browns. Nick's parents were deeply concerned but not frantic, largely because of the calm manner in which the boys were describing the situation.

When the Q & A was over, Shawn spoke slowly, "Here is what I propose. I suggest we meet our commitment and deliver our samples for the rest of the summer job, which is only five more weeks. If we start backpedaling from our current obligations now, it will become easier to do the same thing the next time the going gets tough. Nick and I will face tougher challenges in life and have trouble overcoming them, if our instinct is to take a step backwards. I promise you that we will continue to look after each other."

The group was silent for a minute before Jane Brown spoke, "I need some reassurance that the potential communication between you two is constant. Shawn can't be watching Nick at all times."

Shawn anticipated this objection and said, "How about if we each carry a whistle?"

"I would feel much better if you did," responded Mrs. Brown. "We will, mom," assured Nick.

"Could you do something else that makes you less vulnerable?" asked Mr. Brown.

"We could each carry a pocketknife," replied Shawn.

Both Browns nodded somewhat uncertainly and they agreed to allow Nick to continue. Again, Shawn had settled a complicated matter, while respecting all involved. This skill would be invaluable in his adult years.

CHAPTER 28

Summer Romances

Shawn and Nick had not made much time for girls in their busy lives. Girls were attracted to Shawn because of his complete confidence and to Nick because of his seeming disinterest. The boys had some idle hours during the summer and decided to test their wings, using double-dating as their mode of operation.

Sally and Amy were good friends who lived in a twelve-unit apartment building at the end of the block on which Nick lived. Sally was 5' 8" and physically mature, extroverted, with auburn hair which gave away her Irish lineage. Amy was 5' 4" and still blossoming, with a quiet nature and beautiful green eyes which accented her jet black hair. Newly turned seventeen, both were rising seniors and inseparable. They attended Algonquin, a well regarded girls Catholic high school.

The pairs had seen each other many times but never spoken. Shawn suggested a walk to Nick one evening after supper on a day in which both had worked. He purposefully led Nick to the apartment building in which the girls lived. Fortunately for the boys, the girls were standing in front of their building.

Shawn steered Nick towards them and said, "Hi. I'm Shawn Butler and this is Nick Brown."

"I'm Sally McMahon and this is Amy Petruzzi," said Sally.

Shawn and Sally did most of the talking and they eventually

decided that the four of them would meet at this same spot and walk to a movie theater at 7 PM on the following Saturday.

On the walk back to his house, Shawn said, "I like Sally. You don't have to guess what she is thinking. I believe we'll get along fine. What do you think of Amy?"

"She seems nice," Nick replied vaguely.

The boys met at Nick's house thirty minutes before their dates. Shawn wore a light green knit shirt and had shaved successfully. Nick wore a navy blue button-down shirt and had gotten a short, somewhat uneven haircut.

Not anxious to put themselves or the boys through a grilling by their parents, the girls were waiting outside. As the boys approached them, Sally stepped forward and grabbed Nick by the hand, leaving Shawn looking at Amy. He recovered nicely and took her by the hand, making a friend forever in Amy in what could have been an awkward moment. Amy realized that Shawn saw himself with Sally, but Shawn was determined not to be disappointed. Besides, Amy's eyes were so trusting that Shawn could not and would not do anything but give her the fine treatment she deserved.

The four teens walked up Fullerton Avenue towards the show, which was a mile away. Leading the way, Sally also led the conversation in a pairing for which Nick was sorely overmatched. Shawn did his best to draw Amy out but received mostly smiles and blushes for his efforts.

In 1958, television was just taking hold, while movie theatres were still going strong. The foursome walked to the *Bijou*, a 500-seat venue which generally filled on Saturday nights. Nick planned their arrival fifteen minutes early so that the foursome could find seats together.

After four previews, a cartoon, and a seven-minute newsreel, the audience settled in for the award-winning *Witness for the Prosecution*. This big screen production featured three of film's most famous performers: Marlene Dietrich, Tyrone Power, and Charles Laughton. Sally favored Nick, her date, over the film and did her best to get him to respond to her charms by rubbing his shoulders and kissing his ears. Amy was visibly uncomfortable with her friend's aggressiveness, but Shawn calmed her down by holding her hand gently.

On the walk home, Amy surprised Shawn by making several perceptive comments about the relationships portrayed in the movie. He had underestimated her intelligence simply because she was cute and shy and vowed not to make that mistake again in sizing up other women. He found her complexity and insights remarkable. For all his skills in a man's world, Shawn realized that he had much to learn about women. Not many would grant him the unqualified acceptance that his mother did. Shawn realized he would have to earn women's respect.

Much more comfortable on the way home, Nick used his height to assert himself and was able to hug back the relentless Sally and get her laughing. Nonetheless, Nick vowed to date someone less formidable the next time.

During the following week, Shawn and Nick talked at length about the evening and what they had learned. Both agreed that in the future it was critical to determine whose date was whose. Nick also promised himself not to wear a button-down shirt if there was to be wrestling involved; the buttons had scraped his neck. The boys had been thrown off balance by their dates but were able to treat the evening as a learning experience, in large part because they were able to bounce their impressions off one another.

CHAPTER 29

Right Junior College

Shawn set aside one day before classes began at Right Junior College to make a dry run by simulating a school day, which included riding a Chicago Transit Authority bus to and from the college. A veteran bus rider, like most city kids, he looked on vacant seats for newspapers to read or simply enjoyed looking out the windows at the fast-paced city traffic. The bus deposited him in front of the school building, and he tried both entrances before deciding upon the best one for future use.

Right had only one block-long building, a sprawling three-story brick structure with wide hallways from end to end; it was thirty years old but in excellent repair, thanks to costly but highly efficient union labor. The hallway lighting was marginal but the classrooms and offices were well lighted. Half of the classrooms faced a busy boulevard, while the other half looked onto a quarter-mile cinder running track, which encompassed a football field. Modest but sturdy brick residences loomed beyond the field. Children in these homes knew that their parents would only leave these homes feet first and that they themselves likely would live and work within twenty miles of their childhood residences.

Shawn used his schedule to direct him to each of his classes. He had booked himself solid between 8 AM and 1 PM three days per week and soon realized he would have to step lively through crowded hallways to make each class on time. Walking into each of his classrooms, he tried to determine the best vantage points.

When he stepped into his 10 AM Economics classroom, Shawn was greeted by a tall, friendly teacher, who boomed, "Come on in and look around. Take a syllabus if you like. I'm Dr Wagner."

Accepting the instructor's firm handshake and the syllabus, Shawn introduced himself and added, "I'll bet I'm the only one who visits in advance."

"You would lose your bet. I get at least four such visits each semester and I've noticed that everyone who stops by for a preview seems to excel. I'm expecting good things from you, Shawn Butler," concluded Dr. Wagner, before returning to his tasks.

"Thank you, sir," replied Shawn over his shoulder as he exited.

Entering the library, he startled a thirty-something librarian from central casting with thick glasses and drab, though probably comfortable, shoes. Shawn apologized and turned to leave, but the librarian invited him to stay, indicating that he could not check out materials yet but was welcome to read newspapers and magazines or simply walk around. He was tempted to decline but looked at the woman and saw that her attempt to be friendly came with great effort. Shawn thanked her, skimmed reading material for thirty minutes, and then shook her hand while asking her name. Andrea Russo dropped her eyes and flushed, though she was clearly pleased. He made a mental note to make her smile at least once a week.

As he passed through the cafeteria, Shawn looked at the vending machines and smiled at the workers preparing for the first day of the fall term. All were too busy to speak with him, but no one was unfriendly. Shawn noted that he would be eating in the early afternoon, if at all, in the school's cafeteria.

Standing near the football field, Shawn saw the dedicated players heading to practice early. Two players whom he had played against in high school spotted him and alerted the head coach. All three waved him over but he simply waved back, without moving. Hesitating a moment, he turned and re-entered the building. He had learned valuable lessons playing football, but it was time to move on. After a stop at the bookstore where he was able to purchase used, discounted books because he was an early bird, Shawn boarded a southbound bus which carried him home. By virtue of this preview, he already had a slight edge on most students, who would fight the crowds for the next week. He looked for an advantage in all situations and was willing to invest time, energy, and money to gain leverage.

He made a solid "B" average during his two years at Right. He fashioned a reputation for speaking up forcefully in class during a time when few challenged authority. He gained considerable respect when he confronted an English teacher, Mr. Spenser, who had missed two weeks of class and tried to make up this lost ground in a hurry.

At the end of the first class upon the instructor's return, Shawn stood and said, "I'm Shawn Butler and I believe there are some things you are not taking into account. Most of us have at least three other classes. You have assigned three papers and a test on a book to be read, all in the next two weeks.

"Remember, we were available while you were sick. Many of my classmates have families (several nodded their heads), while others of us work demanding jobs (more nods).

"While we all appreciate your wanting to have us catch up quickly, your proposed schedule is unfair to us. Please adjust your schedule so that we can handle our other responsibilities and get the most value from your well-planned assignments."

Rather than considering Shawn's reasonable request and making a compromise, Spenser flashed anger and began to berate Shawn. At this, the entire class stood in hostile silence behind Shawn in a show of solidarity.

The instructor wisely backed off and agreed to post an adjusted timetable by 4 PM that afternoon on a bulletin board outside the classroom. Since Mr. Spenser had five English classes, he had to adjust the schedule for all of them and Shawn's fame grew. A by-product of this incident was that the newly hired Mr. Spenser moved more closely in step with most of the hard-working Right instructors, who received respect from students because they were fair and honest with their students. Pretentiousness did not play well on either side. Educational institutions, states, and our country were working in unison, buoyed by a cooperative spirit. Posturing was not at all fashionable.

CHAPTER 30

Jerry Diminico

In response to the Spenser Showdown, a wag named Jerry Diminico created the phrase, "The Butler did it." Jerry was a short, amiable Italian with a big mouth, who coaxed Shawn into running for class vice-president. Shawn's biggest laugh of the year came when ten students surrounded Shawn in the hall and promised him that they would each get him four votes, if Shawn would simply muzzle Jerry for at least two days. Evidently, his noisy, non-stop campaigning was driving everybody crazy. Shawn thanked the students and worked things out with Diminico. With "The Butler Did It" slogan and Jerry as his campaign manager, Shawn won easily.

Diminico was one of eight siblings, each louder than the next, who lived near the junior college. Shawn loved to visit Jerry's home because everybody hugged, argued, and ventured strong opinions, often at the same time. Jerry's five sisters all liked Shawn, and each made it a point to mess his hair or hug him when he visited. The smell of tomato sauce hung in the air perpetually, and Mrs. D graced her roost with a smile that would not quit.

Mr. D owned a thriving nearby restaurant which gave full meaning to the term, "family restaurant." The Diminico children stormed in and out, serving, cooking and clearing in constant motion. They pointed and waved rudely to each other but then fawned over and spoiled the customers. The patriarch had been known to stop customers when exiting, if they even looked unhappy. Mr. D wanted satisfied customers because they meant repeat business.

One of Mr. D's rules was that there was to be no family arguing in his place of business; he insisted his brood settle their problems at home. The business made money, but he could have made more if Mr. D did not send a big container of food each evening with Jerry to the homeless males in Belmont Park. Mr. D had continued this arrangement for four years.

One evening, there were more men waiting for food than usual, and it was clear that there was not going to be enough for full helpings for everyone. Jerry was trying to arrange a compromise when two men began fighting. Homeless does not mean defenseless, and these two were well matched and tough as nails. Jerry jumped up on a table and let out a roar.

Everyone froze and Jerry said simply, "My father said if there ever came a time when his food was going to cause a problem, then he would no longer provide it. If we can't work this out now, then this will be the last meal my family will bring to you."

It was against his nature, but Jerry knew he had to be quiet and let the men decide. The men looked at each other and began moving to stifle the combatants, but no intervention was necessary. The fight was over and the dispute was settled amicably.

In early spring, Shawn brought Nick with him one Saturday evening to a mixer at Right, knowing that Jerry would be there. Shawn wanted to find out how the two would interact, since they were polar opposites. It did not take him long to find out.

Jerry was holding court in his booming voice as Shawn and Nick entered Right's gymnasium, the mixer site. When the band began to play a slow song, most in the throng around Jerry drifted towards the middle of the gym to dance, leaving Shawn to introduce Nick.

Sizing up Nick's button-down shirt and wing-tip shoes while shaking his hand, Jerry quipped, "If I want to buy some insurance, I'll give you a call."

Nick surprised Shawn by responding, "If the sound system breaks down, I'll come and get you."

All three boys looked at one another for a long moment and then burst out laughing. Nick and Jerry sensed that Shawn wanted them to get along and both dedicated themselves to making whatever accommodations were needed.

Jerry had no plan beyond graduating from Right and decided to shadow Shawn in his enrollment at Chicago State College. He respected Shawn deeply and figured that anybody else's plan, particularly Shawn's, was better than no plan. When Jerry explained to Shawn that no Diminico had ever received a four-year college degree because they "were too busy," Shawn understood. When Jerry told him what he had in mind, Shawn pointed out how important grades were in the transfer process. Jerry knuckled down, made B's in two tough courses during the summer, graduated in August, and enrolled immediately with Shawn at CCC.

Shawn, who had graduated in June, came back for the August graduation ceremony to honor Jerry. Fewer students graduated in the late summer; consequently, the graduation throng was much smaller.

No one, however, could blame the Diminico family for the sparse attendance. They filled four rows of ten with siblings, aunts, uncles, and cousins, with Shawn, the only non-family member, sitting happily with his hair badly mussed in the midst of this high-voltage group. They spoke with their hands, whispered loudly, laughed uncontrollably, and wiggled incessantly.

The college president called each graduate by name, as the students fidgeted in line at the right and moved slowly to the center of the stage. As Jerry moved close to having his name called, the family buzz grew louder. When the president announced, "Diminico, Gerald Anthony," the family went wild, hugging, kissing, jumping, and yelling. Despite himself, the president laughed, stepped back, and waited a moment for things to calm down before introducing the remaining graduates.

CHAPTER 31

Joan Conley

Jerry introduced Nick to some of the girls he knew, and Nick found Joan Conley to be particularly interesting. She was 5'9" with short brown hair and serious green eyes which always seemed to be looking at Nick. When Nick timidly asked her to dance to a slow recording by Elvis, she looked at him doubtfully, but took his hand and accompanied him to the gym floor. He held her stiffly, but she got him to loosen up and they got through the next few minutes passably.

When rock and roller Jerry Lee Lewis began singing about "great balls of fire" in manic tones, Nick pointed to two vacant chairs and she laughingly agreed. As she sat down, Joan mentioned that she had not seen him around Right, and he told her about his first year at LW.

"I'm majoring in Business and hope to work downtown," he told her. "I like the architecture and Lake Michigan."

"Where would you live?" Joan asked. "I've heard apartments are quite expensive near the lake."

Nick was trying to impress this charming creature, but did not know how. At the same time, he was sure he would not make a positive impression by telling her that the very thought of moving away from his parents terrified him. Instead, Nick spoke vaguely of spending a few days walking in the Loop during the summer to investigate housing opportunities and then wisely switched the discussion to her. He discovered that Joan was an only child and lived with her parents in an apartment on a boulevard two miles due south of Right. For the next thirty minutes, they exchanged observations on the pros and cons of life without siblings. The dance was winding down and Joan said that she owed two friends a ride home.

"Did you drive?" she asked.

"No, I'm riding with my friend, Shawn," Nick replied.

"Care to ride with me?" Joan asked. "I want to see the look on my friends when they see that I finally met a boy, whoops sorry, I meant man."

"Sure. Let me tell Shawn," said Nick, blushing and laughing at the same time.

Shawn turned up at that very moment, smiled at Joan after having the situation explained to him, and asked Nick to give him a call the next day.

"You may have to walk him to the door," Shawn warned Joan, before departing.

"What would you two do, if you didn't have me to tease?" countered Nick.

With that, they all headed towards the exit. Joan's two slightly chubby and super-cute friends, Debbie and Jane, talked incessantly, often at the same time. They sat in the back of Joan's father's Buick Century sedan, flanking Liam. It was difficult to tell whom Liam was with because he had almost disappeared into the upholstery between these two quick-witted, fun-loving young women.

Joan paid close attention to her driving but allowed herself a laugh when her friends said something particularly clever or outrageous. It was obvious that these two had picked Joan as a friend because Joan was so different. At the same time, the mutual respect was apparent. Joan checked on Nick often enough to assure herself that he was comfortable. On his part, Nick was lost in plotting his next move, so that he could see her again.

Joan dropped off her friends, one at a time, waiting for her passengers to enter their front doors safely. Nick gave her directions to his home and they drove in silence for a few minutes.

"Do you like movies?" asked Nick suddenly. "Very much," responded Joan, smiling.

"I have to stay on campus next weekend, but I'll be back in two weeks. Would you like to go to a show on Saturday, week after next?"

"Sure."

Nick sat back in his seat, looking quite pleased with himself, before Joan reminded him that he would need her phone number, which she gave him and which he committed to memory. Joan also told him that she could drive again, if necessary. Nick told her he would try to arrange things with his parents to use their car.

Because Joan realized that Nick was overwhelmed by events of the past two hours and needed some time to reflect, she decided not to extend the evening by talking further. Joan bid him a soft good-bye, touching his arm gently. She then waited for him to enter his front door and smiled as Nick gave her a small, shy wave. Joan knew he was not yet in her league, but she saw potential in this shy young man.

Wearing a goofy smile, Nick drifted by his parents, who were seated in the living room, and went into the kitchen.

"Everything all right, Nick?" asked his mother.

"I'm not sure, but I hope so," responded Nick vaguely.

CHAPTER 32

Shawn's Love Life

While Nick wanted the stability of a steady female companion, Shawn viewed dating a variety of young women his age as a learning experience. Nick had a deep fear of being alone, while Shawn had a concern that he did not know nearly enough about females to make good decisions involving them.

It seemed that every time Shawn felt he had a woman figured, she would confound him. He found their unpredictability both disturbing and challenging. Still, knowing that he did not know gave him leverage over most of his male peers. Because his dates appreciated that he was trying to understand them, many were happy to explain themselves.

Though he was interested in sex, he did not feel that it was worth the risk. For now, he was content with steamy back-seat necking sessions, often punctuated with laughter. While his male classmates often made enemies in trying to assert their sexuality, Shawn usually made friends.

To complicate sexual activity still further, birth control methods at the time were notoriously unreliable. An unwanted pregnancy did not fit into his plans, and he gravitated towards women who wanted children in an orderly manner, not as a surprise.

Among the dozens of girls he dated and regarded as friends, Molly Jean Donovan, a trim blonde with sparkling blue eyes, surfaced more often than the others. She was consistently denim-clad and sported little make-up. Take me as is or leave me alone, she all but shouted! When Shawn would disappear for a while and then call out of the blue, Molly never badgered him.

Daughter of a policeman, she was a year younger than Shawn and had four brothers with rough edges and bad attitudes. Molly was amused at the ease with which Shawn mingled with them in a home in which other male visitors his age generally did not fare well.

While many of Shawn's dates were eager to leave Chicago, MJ shared his love of the city and hoped to spend her life there. Both preferred riding the CTA buses and elevated trains because of the opportunities they presented to see the extraordinarily diverse mix of urban residents.

They used public transit to go to Soldier Field, Wrigley Field, museums, and beaches. Shawn and Molly shopped on Maxwell Street, where the prices were negotiable and buyers were at risk. Neither took gambling seriously but they enjoyed visiting Hawthorne Park race track because of the characters who were regulars there. This inquisitive pair once went to Arlington Park's track, but the smugness of Arlington's predominantly suburban clientele turned them off.

Shawn liked her because she did not embarrass easily and always expressed interest in what he had been doing. Another trait that endeared her to Shawn is that she treated Nick respectfully; Nick in turn was comfortable around her. Most importantly, as much as they enjoyed each other's company, Molly Jean never needed Shawn. Each prized their independence and did not crowd one another.

Molly's father, Matt, was a lieutenant in the homicide division and king of the hill at work and at home. He was used to putting people off balance and keeping them that way. His pretty wife, Agnes, a formidable person in most circumstances, drifted into the background in her husband's presence.

Matt liked Shawn and even asked MJ when he was coming over again, something he never did with her other male friends. Molly had talked with her mother one Friday before leaving for school, telling her that she planned to ask Shawn to join the family for dinner.

"He is always welcome here, Molly, you know that. Your brothers act better when he is around and your dad likes him because he shows no fear," Mrs. Donovan said.

"And you, mom?"

"He is what your father would be if he was a generation younger.

He listens and is considerate. Best of all, Shawn makes me laugh." Switching gears, Molly asked, "Dad loves you, doesn't he, mom?" "Yes, and I love him. He treats me as well, if not better, than my women friends are treated by their husbands, but often that's not enough for me. Women in your generation have opportunities that ours never had. I don't worry about you taking advantage of your chance to realize your potential. You stand up straight."

There was nothing left to be said so she hugged her mother and hurried off to school. MJ learned a little bit each time they spoke. Her mom was always there for her and didn't miss a thing.

When Shawn arrived at the Donovan house before dinner the

following Friday evening, he and Molly sat in the front room making small talk before Molly joined her mother in the kitchen to help prepare dinner. Shawn insisted upon helping and he wound up tossing a salad. Mr. Donovan entered and did a double-take upon seeing Shawn.

"I didn't know you were a chef," quipped Mr. Donovan. "I'm not. I'm a chef's helper," corrected Shawn.

Wanting to assert control in this situation, he asked, "Are you two going out tonight?"

"Yes, we are going to the movies."

"What are you going to see?" Mr. Donovan asked Shawn.

"I don't know, sir." Turning to Molly Jean, he asked her, "What movie are we going to see? It's her turn to pick what we do," he explained to Mr. Donovan.

Not liking what he heard, Mr. Donovan took the stairs to his bedroom rapidly while still trying to figure out how to gain control. After changing clothes, he descended rapidly into a kitchen now crowded with Molly's four noisy brothers. He walked over to Agnes and asked loudly, "How would you like to join these two at the movies this evening," he asked.

The silence in the kitchen was deafening as everyone looked at Agnes, who turned to Molly, who turned to Shawn, who nodded and smiled. Shawn was smart enough not to interfere in this dramatic family moment. Both MJ and her mother were the two most surprised people in the city, while Mr. Donovan felt he was finally in charge and Shawn realized he was merely a bit player in this drama.

To top off this exchange, Mr. Donovan said, "Will you check with Molly to make sure her show selection is something you would like, dear?"

Completely stunned, everyone sat down at the usually boisterous dinner table. Shawn carried the conversation until the Donovan boys recovered their seldom ruffled composure.

The evening went well as soon as the Donovans realized that Shawn never missed a beat in adapting to a night out with a homicide detective. Shawn enjoyed talking with Mr. Donovan and again proved his ability to handle himself in a potentially sensitive situation. On her part, Molly Jean felt that she and Shawn had done her mom a favor of sorts. Agnes concluded that she had taken a baby step in balancing the passive, one-sided power struggle with her husband. All four were reminded that there did not have to be losers in personal situations, no matter how complicated.

aldermen who did not let their bulk prevent them from attending all community events in their wards. Most of these men had not gone to college and had limited language skills. Seeing themselves as a dying breed, they realized that the party's future rested upon young Democrats who had taken school seriously and understood topics such as cognitive mapping, polling techniques, and the exploding computer field. Boyle stressed how quickly those with legal training and accounting experience moved up in the party's ranks.

After his introduction, Boyle turned to Shawn and asked each what he was going to do after he graduated from college. When Shawn told him that he was going to join the Marines and then attend law school in the city, Danny all but cheered. For his part, Nick indicated that he wanted to enlist in the Air Force and then get an MBA at one of the universities in or near Chicago. Boyle nodded approvingly and then asked several probing questions.

Had Shawn and Nick not mentioned their military service plans, Danny would have asked, because the manner in which men handled this obligation was important politically. In terms of Democratic Party value, enlistments trumped the draft because of the time and commitment involved, while being drafted easily outshone being in the reserves, because the reserves were viewed as a refuge from a tour in Viet Nam. Democratic leaders were expected to stand tall, rather than bob and weave.

There seemed to be no preference between a new member's attendance at any of the city's fine Catholic universities or public institutions, but the party clearly favored those who graduated rather than the many who got bogged down pursuing a degree. Future leaders needed to be among those who finish successfully.

Shawn and Nick were impressed by how much Boyle knew about military service and the city's colleges. Danny mentioned having a degree in political science from De Paul. There were no flies on this round, smiling man, who seemed comfortable as a hybrid in having bridged the gap between the stereotyped alderman and the new breed of Democrat.

Boyle tilted the discussion to their participation, saying "We meet Tuesdays twice a month in the Veterans Hall on Belmont and Western where our group actively supports campaigns. If a member has a problem, such as a house fire or an illness, we pitch in time and money until it's solved. We provide a quasi-insurance policy to active members."

Boyle could see that Shawn and Nick were about to say that school took up most of their time. Beating them to the punch, he stated, "We expect everyone to understand that your schoolwork comes first. If any of our members misses that point in working with you, we will make believers out of them. We want you to finish your degree, for you and for us. Shawn, if you want to open a textbook during our meetings, no one will be offended. Nick, if you can help us in campaigning on an occasional weekend when you're home from school, we would appreciate it. All we ask is that you keep your hand in and learn the members' names. In return, the Party can and will help you in ways than you can't even imagine."

Neither Shawn nor Nick even considered declining this attractive offer that was so reasonably presented. Handshakes and details were exchanged, and the first step was taken in a journey for both men that would color and shape their lives.

CHAPTER 34

Chicago City College

Shawn worked a construction job for a small contractor, Tom Leahy, during the summer after graduating from Right. Leahy was a demanding sort who liked workers to pay attention and take pride in their work. His sons, Bill and Frank, worked for him as did an experienced bricklayer, who also dabbled in carpentry. All four got along fine with Shawn, who more than held up his end.

After a shower and supper, Shawn walked the blocks near the Butler home with his mother and talked mostly about his coming enrollment at Chicago City College, nicknamed Triple C. The only breaks in their conversation came when greeting a neighbor. If Shawn was not acquainted with this person, his mother would take great pride in introducing him, and vice versa.

It was during these walks that Shawn noticed that his mother was becoming weak and somewhat disoriented. Towards the end of a walk in early August, Courtney leaned heavily on his shoulder, while sweating heavily and blaming her condition upon a flu bug. Shawn was also concerned by her slurred speech but his mother, not a drinker, refused to discuss the matter.

Soon after, he attended his orientation day at Triple C, arriving early on a fine September morning so that he could case the campus and make new friends before the classroom grind began. He made two practice circuits of his classes, all scheduled in the morning, and decided that that he could go from class to class easily without being late. Finally, seeking fruit juice, Shawn entered the cafeteria and was immediately greeted by several former high school classmates who waved him over. Shawn's newest academic/social whirl had begun.

His Triple C visibility was accelerated as he asked two questions during the orientation for 1,000 new students, queries which would otherwise have gone unasked. Encouraged by Shawn's boldness, several of his new classmates joined the discussion.

The capable discussion leader and Dean of Students, Dr. Rita Wilson, was grateful to Shawn for his initiative and made a mental note to ask Shawn for his help in the future. This poised late thirties administrator with bright red hair and blue eyes had also made an impression upon Shawn, since she appeared energized by the challenges posed by the students.

He soon discovered that Dr. Wilson was one of the first women activists on the Chicago scene and also a member of the Democratic party. Shawn was curious about the meaning of "doctorate" and he went to the library and discovered that Wilson's doctorate was in political science. She had taken 17 graduate courses, passed lengthy oral and written exams, and written a book-length dissertation on "The Emergence of American Women in Urban College Administration." The librarian informed Shawn that this dissertation was on file and that she could show it to him but that he could not sign it out. She handed him the impressive tract and he read the abstract before handing the weighty document back to her.

The entire doctoral process had taken Wilson almost three years to complete. He looked further into these terminal degrees and discovered the existence of medical doctorates, doctorates of science in education, doctorates of philosophy in literature, economics, and the physical sciences, and doctorates in law. He was impressed by the size of the obstacles presented in these programs and the dedication and time required to complete one. By virtue of his search, his estimation of Dr. Wilson continued to rise.

Most of his Triple C instructors were in their forties or beyond and many were military veterans, who had had their graduate studies interrupted by World War II and/or the Korean Conflict. As he listened to these dedicated people in various settings, they talked of writing theses and dissertations at nearby universities, supported by the GI Bill.

In Shawn's mind, the most impressive dimension of Triple C's fine teaching cadre was the unwillingness of these instructors to complain of the hardships spent in defending their country and the physical and mental injuries suffered while doing so. Even the older and obviously injured stood as erect as possible and never complained, and few would speak of the circumstances of their service. Their heroism and humility was not lost on Shawn.

In a political science class, Mr. Robert Grimes, a distinguished professor nearing retirement, was leading a discussion which drifted into a critique of the military draft for which all U.S. eighteen-year old males were required to register. They then either received exemptions or were called upon to serve two years, generally in the Army. Some chose to "push up" their number through the Voluntary Draft, so that they could meet their obligation immediately. A contingent of six or seven students were making noisy arguments against the draft, and Mr. Grimes was patiently deflecting them.

Finally, Joey Broncato, the most outspoken of this group, proclaimed, "If I am drafted, I will go to Canada."

At this, Mr. Grimes, whose posture was already ramrod straight, managed to grow an additional inch or two. He stood in front of the student and asked, "How old are you, Mr. Broncato?"

"Nineteen," he responded weakly, knowing he had gone too far.

Mr. Grimes slowly and forcefully stated, "As countries go, Mr. Broncato, the U.S. is the gold standard. If in nineteen years, your parents and teachers have not made this point, we have failed you miserably, and on behalf of all of us, I apologize.

"Some of us were privileged to wear our country's uniform. I never considered my service an obligation. When I enlisted in 1942, things were moving pretty fast in a war we could easily have lost. I was surrounded by brave men and women who were not going to let that happen, and they propelled me along with them. Frightened and overmatched for a time, I did not let fear hold me back.

"Our country needed me then just as our country needs you now. If you choose not to answer the call and run off somewhere because you're scared or selfish, do it, but do not sit in this classroom and tell me it's your right. You haven't earned any rights yet."

The silence in the classroom was almost painful, and Mr. Grimes had tears falling from his eyes. With extraordinary timing, the bell to change classes rang and prompted a standing ovation from all but the chastened anti-draft group.

An exhausted Mr. Grimes returned to his desk and slumped into his seat. Broncato led his defeated band to a stop in front of Grimes' desk.

"I'm sorry, sir," said Joey.

"There's nothing to be sorry for. You took a position and defended it. You simply happened to hit a nerve." Making full eye-contact while extending an olive branch, he said, "I hope you decide to join our side, Mr. Broncato. We could use you."

Joey and friends knew when they had been dismissed and retreated quickly. Shawn, who had lagged behind to catch the final words in this powerful drama, had the importance of military service underscored once again.

CHAPTER 35

Chicago City College Drama

Shawn learned other lessons from these modestly paid but unmistakably proud instructors, who lent glowing dignity to the term, public servant. Shawn was a solid "B" student, who again could have done better if he had not been so determined to grasp the big picture in his school settings.

Serving on the Triple C Student Council gave him a good perspective and he repeated student and teacher names to himself, until he knew more people by name than anyone, except perhaps Dr. Wilson. His grasp of community service continued to display itself.

While sitting in a history class on a drab November day, he heard the unmistakable sounds of cars crashing, followed by screams. Without thinking, he immediately ran from the classroom, down the steps, and into the nearby street. Shawn almost collided with an alert security guard who also was heading towards the accident scene. Without exchanging a word, they combined to force entry into the back seat of a vintage Honda and drag two occupants to safety.

Nodding to each other, they ran back to the larger vehicle involved, a badly damaged late model station wagon, which was leaking gas. They looked into the passenger compartment and saw an injured driver in the front seat, which was jammed. The security guard pointed at the Honda and both ran back to look for tools to spring the front seat door. Shawn grabbed a large screwdriver and the security guard found a jack with a flat-edged bottom. With Shawn holding the screwdriver in a crevice between the door's edge and the chassis, the guard began hammering the screwdriver.

Because of the seeping gas, time was a concern. Fire engines could be heard approaching the scene. Finally, the door buckled from the pounding and the guard was able to reach in and grab the occupant, a medium-sized adult male. As the guard and the injured party began to move away from the station wagon, Shawn heard a sucking sound from the gas and instinctively tackled these two from behind. As the three hit the ground, the station wagon blew, scattering flying metal and glass to a radius of fifty feet.

The guard and Shawn looked at each other and exchanged tight smiles, while the injured party looked relieved. Medics soon descended upon them and sat Shawn upon the edge of a fire truck, while the guard and injury victim were secured for a trip to the hospital.

After performing a quick inventory, Shawn doubled back to his classroom, picked up his books and made his way through the chaos to his bus stop. On the ride home, the ringing in his ears stopped. All he had gotten for his pains were a torn pair of pants and some singed hair, which he trimmed with a scissors upon returning to his home. He showered and napped before his mother returned from work.

After making Courtney promise not to mention the incident to anyone but his father, Shawn recounted events of the morning as he remembered them. She listened carefully to his description, interrupting only to determine that he had not been hurt, and nodded thoughtfully. Rex walked in and she gave him a shorthand version.

"Did you do all you could for those needing help?" Rex asked. "Yes I did, dad."

"Is there anything you would do differently, if something like this happened again," asked Rex.

"Not that I can think of."

"Did you stick around to give a statement?" "No, sir."

Rex turned quickly, but Shawn was sure he saw his dad smiling softly to himself and equally sure that his father had no interest in discussing this matter further. His father was teaching him the difference between doing the right thing and heroism. Rex felt that doing the right thing was not proper cause for celebration. If others did not see it that way and chose to seek praise and accept awards, then so be it, but Rex wanted no part of it.

Loving his father was not easy, but admiring him came naturally. His father refused to be compromised or involved unnecessarily, and Shawn was beginning to understand the advantages of these traits.

Walking the halls at school the following day, he acknowledged the compliments directed his way, but he kept on moving to avoid discussion. After the closing bell for his last class, Shawn was gathering his belongings when Dr. Wilson came up behind him. She was wearing a plain pink blouse and a brown skirt which swirled on her as she moved. Rita Wilson was one of those women who made all her clothes appear expensive.

"Have plans for lunch, Shawn?"

"To eat a lot and pay as little as I can," he quipped.

"We have an exclusive gourmet lunch planned for you in celebration of your rescue efforts," she stated. "Your meal is on us."

"Count me in."

"I'll lead the way," promised Dr. Wilson.

Shawn was proud to accompany her. The college's most popular administrator and its latest hero created quite a stir as they picked their way through the crowded halls. She led him into the lunchroom, at which point Shawn stopped her and said, "If this turns into some kind of ceremony, I'm going to pass."

"Relax. This is simply our low-rent way of thanking you for your rescue efforts yesterday. I've asked Alan Brown, the security guard, to stop by and re-introduce himself. Other than that, it's just you and me."

Seated at the front of the massive dining hall, Shawn received a standing ovation from the students, and Wilson prompted Shawn to get on his feet and acknowledge this well-intentioned response. He stood and pretended to quiet the clapping with his left hand, while urging students with his right hand to continue cheering. Everyone laughed, including Dr. Wilson most of all. By lowering his hands, he then encouraged the students to take their seats. Shawn then waved and bowed to the students, before rejoining his lunch companion.

"You're a natural at managing groups, if your hands don't wear out," she observed.

"Maybe I'll be the governor some day," he laughed. "Maybe you will," she responded sincerely.

After assuring Shawn that the driver in the accident was

recovering nicely, Wilson introduced the security guard, who had been waiting. Both men sized each other up, with Alan several inches taller.

"I rendered aid as part of my job. Why did you get involved?" "I'm a student here, so I'm automatically involved," Shawn said. "You could have been hurt."

"So could you, "Shawn retaliated. "Were you scared?" "Damn straight. You?" replied Alan.

"Afterwards. During our little dance, you didn't give me a chance to be frightened," Shawn explained.

"I'll include in my report that both supposedly brave rescuers were scared down to their socks," Wilson observed.

"That's fine with me," said Brown.

"Seems about right," agreed Shawn lightly.

Waving over his shoulder, Brown ran to investigate a loud noise in the entryway. Wilson followed after squeezing Shawn's shoulder, leaving him alone with his food. It was going to be some time before the tingling would go away, he hoped.

CHAPTER 36

Triple C's Graduation

City college graduations have a unique flavor, with its large contingent of first-in-the-family graduates, a liberal dose of language barriers, and readily apparent vestiges of low income. Many of the attendees are at first visibly uncomfortable in a formal setting, but most are dressed in the best clothes they have and display enormous pride in the graduate from their family. Triple C went out of its way to welcome their 3,000 guests, realizing that for older family members, this was the college's only personal chance to say thank you.

Sharing strong people skills and fluency in Spanish, Dr. Wilson and a young male dean floated in the lobby between the registration desk at the entrance to the gym. Though pre-registration was required and only a limited number of seats were available, some giant-size families simply appeared and these two administrators tried to accommodate them.

Wilson often explained to the spokespersons for the mega-families that they would be able to view the graduation from a second floor balcony which had been child-proofed by stacking benches over trouble spots. Though Jerry had warned Dr. Wilson, she did not truly believe it would happen until she saw the Diminicos pull up in a packed, full-sized school bus. This group of sixty strong with at least forty talking at any given time was given its own section.

Walkers, wheel chairs and strollers further complicated

graduation flow and safety in an aging building. Wilson had met with fire department officers two days earlier to discuss contingencies.

At the last moment, she noted that a Latina in her fifties was standing in the corner of the lobby crying and looking miserable. Using her passable command of Spanish in a rapid-fire exchange of information, Wilson learned that Mrs. Sanchez wanted to see her son graduate but had been delayed by a plumbing problem at her home.

With no seating available, Rita took the woman's arm and guided her onto the stage and into the seat reserved for Wilson herself. After nodding to the faculty and administrators close by, she turned and walked to the back of the gym. Wilson glanced over her shoulder and was not surprised that the savvy employees seated near Mrs. Sanchez already had her talking and laughing. Few noticed Wilson's courtesy, but Shawn had. In his estimation, her stock continued to rise.

With no children of her own but inspired by previous interaction with a gaggle of nephews and nieces, Wilson had set up a cry room with clowns, balloons, and squirt guns. In a relatively quiet corner, her younger partner, a father of three, had arranged a room with two nurses, several rented infant beds, and a stack of diapers.

For graduation, Triple C became a combination amusement park, convention hall, and community center. In paper cups for safety's sake, coffee, juice and cola were served after the ceremony; college administrators wanted their visitors to remain after the ninety-minute ceremony and to savor the occasion. By terms of their contract, instructors were obliged to circulate and meet their students' families after the event. All faculty members agreed afterwards that this requirement was one of Right's best.

On balance, the ceremony went well, with only a nasty spill by a female student who had tripped on her gown and a quickly resolved dispute between a husky, older man who insisted on standing in front of another man's children. Most visitors realized that it was a day for proud parents and ratcheted up their behavior accordingly. Triple C hosts and their guests understood that they were part of something bigger than themselves on graduation day.

The warm-up speaker, Mr. Halverson, was a grizzled old dean of students. His job was to enliven the audience so that the commencement speaker, the college president, inherited live lines of communication. O'Malley had been executing this routine since he had been discharged from the U.S. Navy after WW II.

"If you are a Triple C employee and were active military, please stand," O'Malley requested. At least 100 college workers stood and received a strong round of applause.

"If you are one of our guests but not a graduate today and were or are active military, please stand." At least 400 guests stood, and the applause was deafening, with all Triple C employees standing and cheering.

"If you are one of our students graduating today and have been active military, please stand." At least 200 of the graduates stood and the applause shook the rafters.

When things settled down, O'Malley continued, "You didn't think I was going to quit there, did you? If you are a mother, please stand."

At least 800 women stood.

'If you have two or more children, remain standing." At least 100 women sat. He continued this approach until only two women remained standing at eleven children each. Neither appeared in any hurry to sit.

O'Malley sensed a rousing climax, since the audience had warmed to the competition. Waving to Dr. Wilson to bring up the names of the contestants, he discovered he had a Mrs. Andriotti surrounded by her clan and a Mrs. Ryan engulfed by hers. A match made in heaven, this was a classic Irish-Italian conflict, the type which had pitted males from each ethnic group against each other in fights in the streets and neighboring bars for two generations. Before continuing the contest, he introduced each contestant by name, and the crowd quickly caught the ethnic implications.

"You realize that we may be living in the only city on earth where a competition like this could take place without a brawl. Who would want to live anywhere else?" The throng again went crazy.

"If you have twelve or more children, remain standing."

Neither woman budged and the crowd roared. By this time, the women were facing one another, Mrs Andriotti smiling softly with her pudgy, strong arms folded and Mrs. Ryan gazing serenely.

"If you have thirteen or more children, remain standing." The women did not even flinch.

"If you have fourteen or more children, remain standing." At that, both women took their seats, but Mrs. Andriotti immediately bounced back upon her feet and made her way to Mrs. Ryan. O'Malley and everyone else stopped, transfixed by this drama.

"I lost a child. Did you miscarry, dear?" asked Mrs. Andriotti.

"Yes, I lost two." responded Mrs. Ryan.

Mrs. Andriotti beckoned to Dr. Wilson who was standing close by and graciously conceded, "Mrs. Ryan is the winner."

Wilson immediately went to the podium and explained the situation to Mr. O'Malley, who thought for a minute before making a statement. He decided not to mention the basis for the decision.

"These two fine mothers have decided that Mrs. Ryan is the most prolific mother. How wonderful that they could decide this between themselves without lawyers or bloodshed. With mothers like these two, how can our graduates possibly go wrong?"

O'Malley then acknowledged police officers and firefighters before turning over the microphone to the college president, whose job had been made easy by Mr. O'Malley. The president's earnest address was well-received by the attentive audience.

Shawn moved confidently among the students and guests, introducing his parents and the Browns at every opportunity. He could not have been more proud or more comfortable, a mood which changed abruptly when Courtney had to cut the afternoon short because she was feeling weak and feverish. As he rejected her plea for him to stay, Shawn became determined to find out more about her health.

CHAPTER 37

Courtney's Decline

The Browns had another stop to make, so the families had driven separately. Since there were just the three of them, Shawn was able to speak freely. From the back seat of the family's aging sedan, Shawn pressed the matter of Courtney's health. His father drove carefully but was not missing a word.

"What are you not telling us, mom?"

Courtney chose her words carefully before responding, "I went to see Dr. Anderson yesterday morning. He had received the results of some tests run two weeks ago. I have terminal stomach cancer and will be gone by the end of the year."

The silence in the car was painful. Rex gripped the steering wheel harder than he ordinarily did and Shawn shook his head repeatedly, refusing to accept the bad news.

"Can we get a second opinion, mom?"

"Yes. Dr. Anderson encouraged us to do so. To make you two feel better, I will, but I just know the diagnosis is correct."

When Rex pulled into a parking space in front of their home, he and Shawn jumped out of the car and supported Courtney under each arm. Too weak to provide much resistance, she allowed her two men to half-carry her into the house.

Courtney dropped onto the living room couch, saying, "If you two are going to hover over me, I'm going to die prematurely from sheer exasperation. If I need something, I'll ask. Understood?"

Shawn nodded first, Rex followed suit, and that is the way Courtney's last days played out. Rex had the habit of lurking in the doorway, waiting for Courtney to ask for anything. After about a week of that, Courtney said, "Rex, I need a hug."

He complied and after that, she only had to look at him and he would come to her and hug her gently for increasingly long periods of time. Puzzled but pleased, Shawn would frequently walk into a room and find them hugging, without either saying a word. Shawn thought it a shame that it took Courtney's illness to bring the two of them closer together. In some ways, Courtney's last three months were the best months the family had together.

Shawn had visited the local U.S. Marine recruitment office and explained his mother's situation to Sergeant Pauling, who agreed to accept an open enlistment, dependent upon the date of Courtney's passing. Shawn took his physical and otherwise prepared himself for his hitch. On a particularly bad day for Courtney, she had turned in early, allowing Shawn to speak privately with Rex.

"I'm going in the Marines, Dad."

"I figured as much. Have you told your mom?"

"I wanted to talk with you first. Do you think telling her is a good idea?"

"She probably already knows. I'm not sure she could accept you holding back something important from her. The two of you have a bond that is deeper and more complex than her love for me. Tell her ASAP."

"We'll talk in the morning, after you go to work," Shawn promised.

In the morning, Shawn went for a run, and his dad was gone when he returned. He moved to the table to join his mother, who was leafing through the newspaper and drinking coffee.

"Got a minute, mom?"

"I'm down to my last few, Shawn," she laughed. "I'm going into the Marines.

"When do you leave?" "Pretty much when I want to."

"Or when I pass on?" she asked.

Shawn blushed before replying, "Something like that."

"You've never disappointed me," she assured him. "Not once. Do you feel that you have to be a Marine to satisfy your father?"

He hesitated, "Maybe, but I don't think so." "Will you be an officer?"

After being in college, I believe I already understand how officers think. Instead, I want to be an enlisted man and learn how they reason, so that I can lead them later on in civilian life.

"In what capacity?" she asked.

"I don't know. I'll manage a small company or run for office."

"Whatever you do, I'm sure you'll be successful. You look people in the eye, play fair, and don't take shortcuts. With you already a mature adult and your father solid as a rock, dying around here is a piece of cake."

Becoming increasingly flippant, his mother had a knack for getting to the heart of things and ending a discussion, without jamming the words down somebody's throat. They talked each morning until her nap. Shawn spent the rest of his time reading and exercising. When his dad came home from work, Shawn went out with Nick or dated. Sometimes Shawn doubled with Nick and Joan, who were seeing each other and becoming close.

Shawn returned one evening and his father was hugging his mother. Used to it by now, Shawn proceeded through the living room into the kitchen. It took a moment for the tears in Rex's eyes to register. He had never seen his dad cry before. Shawn stepped back into the living room and looked at his father, who simply shook his head. Courtney had passed.

Rex was reluctant to put an obituary in the *Chicago Tribune* and only agreed when Shawn agreed to keep it short. His mother wanted cremation and requested a brief service at their house of which she was so proud. In the obituary, Shawn issued an open invitation to everyone who knew the family to stop by and pay their respects.

Shawn handled most of the details, while Rex did not miss a day of work. On Saturday afternoon at 2 PM, the Butlers hosted a memorial service/open house, expecting no more than a few dozen people. By 2:15, the house was full and dozens more were backed onto the lawn on a perfect September day. More than one hundred of Courtney's friends from the park and the neighborhood attended. Sixty of Rex's co-workers made an appearance; they came out of curiosity and out of respect for this dignified, taciturn man. Approximately two hundred of Shawn's friends from Right and Triple C came to pay their respects.

When Shawn saw how the crowd was growing, he asked Nick to go for additional refreshments. Triple C's Dr. Wilson, a surprise guest, overheard this conversation, introduced herself to Nick and volunteered to help him.

Shawn stood on a chair outside and announced that a brief formal service would be held at 2:45 in the back yard. He then circulated inside and repeated the same message. Looking around, Shawn concluded that their little family had many friends he did not know they had. He had long figured that he was part of something special, but it was nice to have others confirm this assumption.

Rex insisted upon being first on the agenda but refused to discuss his remarks with Shawn. At exactly 2:45, he moved to a central point in the back yard. He clapped his hands once and most of the guests became silent. The few who continued talking immediately quieted down when they glanced in Rex's direction. Everyone immediately understood that Corporal Butler was in charge.

In a firm, even voice, he began. "I am Rex Butler, Courtney's husband. Some of you knew her and some didn't, but you all have come here today out of respect for her, our family, or both. Shawn and I deeply appreciate it. Stay afterwards and enjoy some refreshments, but most importantly, use this opportunity to relate to each other.

"I loved my wife more than she ever realized, but I could never put the words together to convince her completely. Many of you are college-educated, like Shawn, and expressing yourself verbally comes naturally for you. If you have somebody special in your life, talk to him or her, because words are important. Do not ever believe otherwise. Talk even when you don't have much to say because by reaching out you show respect and keep lines of communication open.

"Shawn will speak with you now before Father Dan moves Courtney and the rest of us a little closer to God. Shawn…"

"Thanks, Dad." He paused and looked at everyone, while measuring his words. "My mother often felt uncomfortable in a city where one-child families are rare. I did not feel that way. It meant that there was more Mrs. Courtney Butler for me. She was my mother but also my big sister, counselor, mentor, and best friend.

"I was never spoiled but always loved. She never intruded but was always available. She never portrayed herself as superior to others but refused to bow or scrape to anyone. With apologies to my father, she is the best person I have ever met. Now that she's gone, I choose to cherish the years I had with her, rather than regret the years that have been taken away.

"You will see me laughing before you leave today, even if it hurts, because that is what she would have wanted. My dad in his way and I in mine always tried to please her, particularly since she did not ask for much and never once demanded anything. Father Dan, help me here because I don't have anything else to say."

Father Dan Reilly finished up admirably, stating that "If enough people led the kind of life Courtney Butler did, churches would go out of business." He said, when working with her on a committee three years ago, that "the only occasion when they couldn't find Courtney was when it was time for her to take a bow." Rex broke into a teary smile on that one.

Father Dan continued, "The Butlers understand not just the importance of family but how to build one and strengthen it. When Rex speaks, which isn't often, everyone listens because they know what he's saying is important. When Shawn nudges people in a direction, most comply because they know his motives aren't selfish. When Courtney conversed with others, everyone soon realized that she was trying to help them, not herself. I believe that God took her so quickly because He needed her more than we do."

The crowd broke into applause at this notion and Father Dan opted to quit while he was ahead. Later, Shawn introduced Molly Jean Donovan to Dr. Wilson; both soon discovered that Dr. Wilson knew Lt. Donovan, and the women chatted amiably. Shawn steered them to his father who was capably handling the dozens who wanted to meet him.

"Dad, this is Dr. Wilson from Triple C, who apparently thinks I will make something of myself, if you're patient. Am I correct, Dr. Wilson?"

"You have given yourself the best of it, as usual, but you're close, Butler," she teased.

Rex proclaimed, "I have great respect for colleges. When veterans return, we are emotionally ragged and academically dull. You do more for us than simply say 'welcome.' By reaching out, your institutions help us adjust."

Dr. Wilson turned to Shawn and smiled, saying, "Your dad makes a better case for our services than we do."

Shawn laughed and said, "Dad, this is Molly Jean Donovan, who is not in mom's league yet, but who has great potential."

Rex looked at Molly carefully since he had never heard Shawn compare anyone to his mother. He painfully realized that his son would soon leave home. Rex would then face the only thing he had ever feared, an empty house.

"Where do you live, Molly?" Rex asked. "At Irving and Austin."

Rex continued, "Do you have…"

"Brothers, four of them, "Molly Jean finished his sentence. "Do you know them?" she asked.

"Not personally, but I've…" Rex paused.

"Heard of them," she finished. "Everybody has," she laughed. "It's nice to meet you, sir. Sorry that it had to be at a memorial service."

Rex surprised everyone by continuing to open up, asking to meet her father sometime soon. Molly Jean wondered, "To see how he is surviving my brothers?"

"No. To see how he and your mom raised you. I'm impressed."

She softly said, "Thank you, sir," knowing that she may never again receive a compliment from a tougher critic.

Molly Jean, Rita, Andrea, the Browns, and the Diminicos, stayed for the clean-up, which was made easier because of the willingness of guests to tidy up after themselves. The cooperative spirit engendered during WW II and given a booster shot by the Korean War still had citizens willing to work shoulder to shoulder on tasks, big and small.

Courtney's urn was placed on a living room shelf, and life moved on. Properly honored, she was gone but never to be forgotten.

CHAPTER 38

Nick Brown's Graduation

Nick and Lakewestern were a choreographer's dream for four years. He had compatible roommates throughout his stay in two dormitories. These randomly selected peers respected his privacy and studied as hard as he did. On two weekends, once during Nick's freshmen year and once during his junior year, Shawn stayed in Nick's dorm room when Nick's roommate was gone. Shawn was impressed by the refinement of LW's men and women, and Nick was proud to have a friend who could talk to anyone with ease.

Shawn and Nick spoke several times of Nick's next move. Nick noted how easy it would be to stay at LW for another year and complete an MBA (Master's degree in Business Administration).

"Just because it's easy, doesn't mean that it is the best path for you," argued Shawn.

"There are buddy enlistments. How about if I go into the Marines with you?" suggested Nick.

Shawn wasn't sure that Nick's skin was thick enough for the Marines. Instead of crushing Nick by telling him that, he said, "We need to be learning different skill sets, so that we can sort out complicated situations later on. If we duplicate each other, we may miss some important points. If you stick with your original plan, an Air Force enlistment, you can learn technical skills which we will need later on in business and politics."

"What if something happens to one of us?" asked Nick. "Vietnam is heating up and we're competing in their jungle. They have home-field advantage."

"Then the one of us remaining will have learned varied skills and how fragile our lives really are," responded Shawn. It was clear that Shawn did not want to discuss this matter further.

"I already have the Air Force enlistment packet and will go back to the recruiting office next week," Nick promised, glad in a way to have this matter resolved.

Shawn and his father drove to the Saturday morning graduation ceremony with the Browns and Joan Conley, whose parent's health problems prevented them from attending. Nick and Joan had agreed to delay discussion of marriage until her parents' medical situation was resolved and until he had served at least one year of military service.

Both were quite comfortable with the delay. Joan had just graduated from CCC and had accepted a job teaching third grade at Elbert Elementary School; she wanted to devote most of her energies into learning how to teach. While Nick was at LW, the Browns had become quite close to Joan and helped the Conleys when medical situations flared up. Rather than simply two young adults engaged in a courtship, it was more a matter of two families blending.

The contrasts between the Triple C graduation and LW's were many and varied. To attend the Triple C graduation, you either parked on the adjoining city streets or rode Chicago Transit Authority buses. Triple C administrators assumed that attendees were street- wise.

Going to Lakewestern's ceremony, however, you drove onto the imposing campus and were directed to numerous small parking lots by paid, off-duty police. Plush buses were available for those who did not want to walk the mile or two to the gymnasium, which had been beautifully decorated for graduation. With the exception of a few flowers and flags, CCC's graduation ceremony spared almost *every* expense. Families of the graduates expected the public city college to be frugal with their tax dollars, and their administrators did not disappoint.

There were few big families at LW's ceremony and the guests were almost entirely well-dressed adults. Any enthusiasm was well contained; children in these families graduated as expected. Attendance by many of the parents was looked upon more as a courtesy to LW rather than a celebration of the accomplishment of the graduates. Spontaneity was restricted to the dozen or so pairs of LW students who had gotten engaged while enrolled as students.

The ceremony went flawlessly, as the President told the parents what they wanted to hear: how smart they were for sending their sons and daughters to LW. Every detail from lighting to the processional was choreographed beautifully. A tasty champagne brunch capped the event.

The differences between Shawn and Nick were apparent; Shawn tried to work with everybody, but Nick devoted his energy to the quality of relatively few relationships, while processing the world around him. Compared to Shawn's circle of friends, Nick's was much smaller, but the high regard that Nick and his friends had for one another was obvious. Shawn could not resist smiling when he noticed how proud Nick was of his guests, as he introduced them to his classmates. He had never seen Nick happier.

Nick and LW held up their ends of the four-year obligation. In his wake, Nick left a gentle, tasteful imprint upon the university's fabric.

CHAPTER 39

Shawn's Marine Training

Shawn entered the US Marine Corps in fall, 1962, and was sent to Camp Pendleton in southern California, seventy miles north of San Diego. He loved the beaches, even when dressed in fatigues and backpack. Shawn was in good shape when inducted but still was challenged to meet the rigorous physical demands.

Behind every training exercise loomed the specter of Vietnam. There was not much accurate information available regarding this new country, but there was no shortage of misinformation. Maps were of little help in this pre-Internet era. Wags convinced the gullible that the North Vietnamese were triple-jointed midgets who could wiggle through cannons and hang from trees in ambush for hours on end. Natives were said to be able to cook and eat almost anything that grew in the jungle, a claim which proved to be partially true.

He made several friends during basic training and admired the work ethic and laser focus upon Vietnam. Sleeping on the ground and firing weapons were adventures for Shawn; he had tired of the classroom and was stimulated by the military environment.

His two fist fights during basic were unforgettable. You did not have to be a great fighter in the Marines, but you had to be willing to fight, no matter how smooth your people skills.

The first skirmish came about because Buddy McCluskey, a raw-boned Texas teen-ager who hit like a mule, did not like college kids.

Shawn wrestled him to the ground and used football elbows to get a draw from the onlookers who eventually pried the two fighters apart. The combatants shook hands, wiped off the blood, and held no grudges. Shawn's nagging headache went away after a few days.

His second battle against Amos Johnson, a muscular, six-foot African-American gang member from St. Louis, was more complicated. On the last day of basic training, Shawn had drawn a detail, which kept him out of his barracks until mid-afternoon. Almost all of the 28 Marines on the second floor had drawn passes and gone to town.

Remaining were four Black Marines, including Johnson, who blocked Shawn's path as Shawn headed towards his bunk. Shawn said softly, "I can't fight all four of you, but I will fight you one at a time." Turning to Johnson, he challenged him, saying "I'll fight you first."

Amos turned to his friends and said, "Come on. Let's get him!"

His buddies, who knew and respected Shawn, each took several steps back, and Johnson, caught by surprise at being rebuffed by his friends, dropped his hands, before Shawn hit him hard with a right hand. The two fighters then exchanged an equal number of punches, with a much stronger Amos clearly getting the better of things.

Here is where luck helped Shawn, who had been knocked to the ground for a second time. As he struggled to regain his footing, he tripped over the edge of a foot locker and lunged towards Johnson. As Johnson loaded up a right hand, which could have ended the fight, Shawn threw a desperate upper cut which caught Amos flush, breaking his jaw. The cracking sound sobered Amos' three friends, while Shawn propped his opponent on one of the bunks. Stepping back from Johnson, he looked quizzically at the three Marines, who each shook their head meaning no more fighting, as they tended to Amos. Shawn showered quickly, left the barracks, and returned just before curfew.

The Marines were assigned to different barracks on the following Monday and preparations for Vietnam began in earnest. At one point, Shawn received thirty-three inoculations over a six-day period, four of them anti-malarial. The Medical Corps was unsure of what our troops were going to face, so the variety of shots was the result of educated guesswork on its part.

In advanced training, Shawn was assigned to an eleven-man squad in a 150-man platoon. Sizing up his chances for surviving what he was going to face, he figured that he could improve the odds by gaining the respect of all ten and the unflinching loyalty of one. Without realizing it, the other ten were auditioning for Shawn.

There were two likely prospects, seventeen-year olds from Tennessee and South Carolina, but they bonded quickly and became inseparable. Randall Pettigrew, a 23 year-old graduate of Vanderbilt University, would have made an interesting choice, but Shawn was determined not to choose another college graduate. One of the other Marines, Jerry Alston from San Diego, was doing a poor job of concealing his dislike for military life.

Four down and six to go. Three of those remaining were loners and unlikely to change. This left two African-American marines, Gene Baldwin and Doug Venable, and a latino, Manny Rameres. Shawn and

Baldwin had earlier exchanged a few laughs and seemed to connect. Venable was so serious, it was difficult to determine whether he was studying things intensely or just plain scared. Shawn could not afford to take the chance. Rameres was soft-spoken and home-sick, and his English and Shawn's Spanish were marginal. Shawn ruled him out.

Shawn decided to study Baldwin for a week to see whether pairing with him would work. His subject was a husky six foot two and wore thick glasses. Gene floated through the physical training with ease but barely qualified with his M-1, a mediocre performance which did not bother him at all.

He scored points with Shawn by responding when being teased about his poor shooting, "that he did better in real world situations. Why don't you go down-range about 150 yards, hold up a bottle, and we'll see if my accuracy improves?" he challenged his fellow Marines.

Shawn retorted sarcastically, "Why don't you lend me your glasses so that I can see other planets?"

At this, they grabbed each other's shoulders and put on their tough looks but could not keep straight faces. They burst out laughing and took a giant step towards building a close friendship.

Shawn and Gene circulated among squad members during training days but always seemed to wind up eating dinner and shining boots together. Gene and his two sisters had been raised in a poor home in Louisville, telling Shawn that "his neighborhood was so messed up, that all the homes were on the wrong side of the tracks." He conceded that schools he attended did not get him ready for much of anything. He advised Shawn that he would try to forgive him "for being white."

On the last Friday morning of Advanced Training, the platoon assembled. Used to ignoring redundant announcements, they stood in sleepy silence at parade rest. Sergeant England, a grizzled Texan stood behind Lieutenant Barber, as Barber said softly, "We leave for Vietnam next Monday. Sergeant England will give you the details."

As England stepped forward, 150 marines were falling all over themselves, trying to determine if they had heard Lt. Barber correctly.

"Ten-Shun," England shouted, while waiting for the platoon to gather themselves. "Yes, that's right, you meatheads. For two months, I've listened to you tell anyone who would listen, how tough you are. Now you're going to get a chance to prove it.

"For two days, you will pack and load. Your squad leaders will march you over to the PX where you can shop and call home. On Sunday, we will clean this place from top to bottom. You will sleep on the floors Sunday night and board buses on Monday morning."

The next 72 hours were a blur as Marines moved purposefully in and around their barracks. Impressed, Shawn understood why the Americans won wars: our military is flexible and does whatever needs doing. Exhausted by Monday, Shawn and Gene sat next to each other on a bus and could do little but chuckle, before falling asleep.

CHAPTER 40

Vietnam Tour I

Shawn's first Vietnam tour only lasted six months. He had seen old-time movies as a small child, in which the film was speeded up far beyond normal motion. His overriding impression of Vietnam during his first tour was that everything was done on fast-forward.

The fire fights gained full strength within seconds, and Shawn, though blessed with good eye-hand coordination and superior lateral vision, was hard pressed to keep pace. Shot once in the thigh, Shawn was well laced with adrenalin and he kept running and shooting until the enemy withdrew. His stay in the field hospital was brief and the attention by the doctors and nurses rapid; in fact, he wondered whether he had received aid at all. His Purple Heart was awarded on the spot, but he was anxious to return to his unit, and the award lay unattended and eventually was lost.

He had even learned to sleep in the daylight and always seemed to be chasing a few elusive hours. He ate quickly while squatting, before checking his ammunition, pack, and socks. He and Gene Baldwin inspected each other and did not sleep until things were in order.

Some of the Marines were only 17 or 18 and needed more sleep than Shawn and Gene. Consequently, some squad members found themselves not fully prepared. PFC Pettigrew from Tennessee inexcusably ran out of ammunition, was pinned down and shot twice.

Squad members knew that they would not likely see him again.

The effectiveness of the Butler-Baldwin duo was apparent to all. Lt. Harper, a rare Ivy Leaguer from a military family, spoke with Shawn about being the squad leader, but Shawn suggested Gene, whom he figured would probably be a career Marine.

"I want you as my squad leader and acting sergeant, Butler, but I will promote Baldwin to corporal and the two of you can continue to work together," decreed Harper.

This discussion was over and the arrangement worked well. Squad members understood that if they had a problem with either Butler or Baldwin, they had a problem with both of them. The atmosphere created within the squad was one of mutual respect and restraint. Shawn knew the time to relax was during the day and for the adrenalin to flow was in the frequent firefights at night.

He wrote twice to his father; both letters were solely devoted to accounts of his squad and neither contained complaints, which Shawn knew his dad did not want to hear. His father responded once, reminding him to keep his head down and to look for wires leading to explosive devices. He was touched when his father said that he was keeping Shawn's bedroom clean; this was his dad's way of asking him to come home on leave. Was it possible that his dad missed him?

A letter from Nick reached Shawn two months after he landed in Vietnam. Nick said that he was being trained at Travis Air Force Base in California in the burgeoning computer field. He called it Nerd Central and stated that he liked it as much as he did LW. Nick said he was surrounded by airmen "with vacant looks and dreams of what could be." He went on to say that he was living up to his end of the Butler-Brown bargain by studying computer operations and related technical matters.

Shawn responded by saying that he was learning more about people from all over the world every day. He added that his degree helped him connect with ordinary people in stressful situations. He closed by saying that "his composure and courage were tested constantly." As Shawn wrote this letter, he was explaining his relationship with Nick to Gene.

On the last night of their tours, Shawn and Gene had what each understood would likely be their final conversation. They walked out of hearing distance from the others and spoke softly.

"You helped me in more ways than I can count," said Gene.

"You didn't need much help, and I couldn't have made it without you. I slept and ate better having you around. You were my security blanket," said Shawn.

"You never talked down to me and never interrupted me when I was speaking, even when I had trouble forming my thoughts," explained Gene.

"You never gave me reason to condescend to you. I was always comfortable speaking with you and eager to hear your comments."

"I never felt inferior around you," Gene persisted.

"It's because you're not," Shawn said, making direct eye contact with Gene.

At that, Gene let Shawn have the last word, and they shook hands for several seconds before returning to their bedrolls. This type of bonding was taking place all over the military and was a lynchpin in the civil rights movement taking shape in the states.

CHAPTER 41

A Subdued Leave

Shawn received a shot for his wound before boarding and slept most of the way on the four-flight, two-day trip to Chicago. A doctor had cleared him to go directly to Chicago, making Shawn promise to seek treatment if his leg gave him trouble. The doctor had warned him "not to sit on the stupid bench" if his leg bothered him and to be "smart, rather than tough."

Shawn knew he had been given a break and thanked the physician, whose patient appreciated being treated like an adult. With the doctor's checklist in hand, he hobbled onto the plane.

He was glad to see the city's skyline and limped happily onto the tarmac at O'Hare. Upon entering the terminal, he encountered a surprise reception committee composed of his father, all three Browns, Joan Conley, Molly Jean Donovan, and Jerry Diminico. They engaged in a group hug, with MJ corralling Nick and Jerry and bringing Joan into the fold. Jerry insisted that the hug continue until everybody was smiling, "ear to ear."

Shawn noted that his father was in the center of the hugfest and clearly enjoying himself; he wished his mother was here now but was determined not to let her absence bother him. Shawn and Nick looked at each other, knowing there would be little time for them to talk that evening. Nick flashed him four fingers, and Shawn, nodding affirmatively, was all but certain that the signal meant Nick had four days left on his Air Force leave. Shawn underplayed his role in this eight-player mini-drama, greeting each of the others privately before the group drifted towards their cars.

The plan was to leave the Butlers interact on the drive back to the Browns' home and to have the remaining six join them there. Rex drove expertly and let Shawn open the conversation.

"Is the house presenting any problems?" asked Shawn.

Rex glanced at him briefly without answering, since Shawn knew that Rex prided himself on being able to fix or maintain anything house-related. Other than letting him cut the grass, Rex would shoo him away any time Shawn inquired if he needed help. "Go read something or work out," his dad would usually say.

Switching gears, Shawn asked his father "if he had been scared in combat."

"Every minute in my brief tour," Rex replied.

"I wasn't afraid during combat, but I became more frightened after, and I've had trouble sleeping since. How long does that last?" Shawn asked.

"I still have flashbacks," Rex admitted. "I was a hero with a small "h" and your mother was a Hero with a capital "H. "If you decide to marry, find someone who can deal with your nightmares."

"I'm pretty sure that I will have to go back. I'm dreading it already. Because of you and mom, I never had reason to be afraid, but I am now."

"I can't help you there," Rex conceded. "Some things you just have to work out by yourself."

"I'm thinking of enrolling in law school when I'm discharged. There are several good schools right here in the city. When I am discharged, could you put me up for a while?" Shawn inquired.

"For as long as you want," Rex answered evenly, but was secretly delighted.

Rex stopped for gas to give the Browns a few extra minutes to get organized. Again, his father always seemed to do the right thing, without making a point of doing so.

As the Butlers entered the Browns' home, everyone cheered loudly led by noisemaker-rattling Jerry Diminico, "who was a party animal," as described by Molly Jean Donovan. This label delighted Diminico and he became the life of the party without a serious challenger. Jerry was fed by noise and laughter.

The Browns served soda, beer and three pizzas. Jerry, who had opened a small pizzeria of his own called, not surprisingly, Jerry's, had driven directly to his restaurant and delivered the pies personally.

"The pizzas are delicious, Jerry," said Molly Jean.

"We're trying to attract a lunch crowd, highlighting ravioli and sausage. The dine-in hasn't caught on yet but the carry-out trade for the construction guys is going gangbusters," Jerry replied. "Cops and firemen are also big business for us. I'm only two miles from my dad's place, but we don't compete much. He serves older people.

"I didn't realize how many friends I had at Right and CCC, and dozens have become loyal customers. We are closed to the public on Monday evenings because the Democratic Party has a meet-and- eat every other Monday and I give my employees alternate Mondays off,"

Jerry explained.

The party went well, since there were no age, gender, or ethnic barriers. MJ's parents, Matt and Agnes, stopped by and met everyone. Matt toned down his attitude in deference to Shawn, the guest of honor, while Agnes joined in fully and was clearly enjoying herself. Dr. Rita Wilson also made a late appearance due to evening responsibilities at CCC.

Shawn, jet-lagged and emotionally overloaded, stepped off to one side and became tearful because he was overwhelmed by the support of the people who had come to his party. Dr. Wilson settled alongside Shawn and stood there for a moment before stepping in front of him.

"It's a little much, isn't it?" observed Wilson.

"I had forgotten how thoroughly decent you all are," he responded, in a choked up voice. "You set the performance bar high for me and just assume that I will clear it. I couldn't show my face at a gathering like this if hadn't given my very best, be it serving during a Marine enlistment or doing anything else.

"We're not going to win in Vietnam because we aren't playing to win, but hundreds of thousands of us are going to come back reaching out to others. How bad is that?" asked Shawn rhetorically

She gave him a long, approving look, then worked the room, paying particular attention to Rex and the Browns, before heading for the door, while winking and waving good-bye to Shawn. He always had trouble looking at her because Shawn would swear that he could see sparkles emanating from Dr. Wilson. He wondered idly if she had ever been just a girl, before becoming a formidable woman.

The party was clearly the high point of his leave, though he took his dad to a play downtown and walked along frosty North Avenue Beach with Nick as they made future plans. Shawn visited Right and saw Andrea, the librarian, who jumped up and down when she saw him and hugged him so hard she almost left bruises. Her response was so enthusiastic and genuine that it shocked and pleased her fellow employees and students who had come to view her as semi- robotic. After the manner of his acceptance, he simply had to sit down and huddle with Andrea, who surprised him with her insight and quick wit.

Shawn spent two days of his last week of leave, sizing up law schools. He wore his Marine dress uniform and was allowed to sit in classes and wander the buildings. No one dared to deny any reasonable request from a slightly limping Marine in uniform.

The impressive cluster of law schools made his choice difficult. He visited Clement School of Law because it was run by ex-military employees seemingly for ex-military students. While waiting in Clement's administrative office to visit a counselor, he was resting his elbows on a counter. A counselor emerged and bristled when he spotted Shawn's posture, despite Shawn's three stripes.

"Ten-hut," the counselor barked. "We don't permit anyone to lean on anything at Clement. Straighten up and stand on your own, Marine, if you expect to get your questions answered at this station. Is that clear?"

"Yes sir," replied Shawn.

"Don't call me sir. I work for a living."

Shawn could be excused for not guessing Mr. Roberts' branch of service, since the counselor was dressed in civilian clothes. Had Shawn looked carefully, he may have noticed Roberts' Marine lapel pin.

"Yes, sergeant."

"Come into my office and we'll see if you're worth helping," the counselor shouted, showing off to amuse employees and students.

Because of his tender wound, Shawn was a step slow entering the office, and the counselor closed the door quickly behind them. Laughing, he extended his hand in friendship to Shawn, who realized he had been played. The two sergeants grasped hands tightly.

"I wanted to make sure you hadn't forgotten how to be a Marine," the counselor explained. "You don't want to lose your edge."

Getting down to business, Shawn explained that he was half-way through his hitch and likely headed back to Vietnam for another tour.

The counselor described how a program could be put in place, so that he could hit the ground running upon his discharge.

"We don't have the most prestigious law school in the area but we follow our graduates as long as they need help. For example, a recent graduate began drinking heavily and our advisory committee sat down with him. If you think I come on strong, you should see these guys in action. They told him they were going to rescind his degree and have his license revoked."

"Can they do that?" wondered Shawn.

"No, but he was so scared, he didn't know that and was afraid to challenge the committee. It's been six months and he hasn't been in a bar since, much less had a drink."

Shawn grinned appreciatively and made his decision on the spot. He loved a good bluff and treasured a sense of humor highly. Also, he was intrigued by the school's quasi-military orientation. Clement was too good to pass up!

As Rex dropped his son at O'Hare Airport for the trip to Camp Lejeune, North Carolina, Shawn's next duty station, he exited his vehicle and shook hands formally with Shawn. There was to be no hug this time! He understood his father's message: your leave is over and it's time to revert to Marine mode. "Semper Fi!"

CHAPTER 42

Shawn and Nick Apart

After extensive training at Travis, Nick was assigned to be a computer classroom monitor, assisting in the installation and maintenance of computer equipment and providing tutoring help to trainees on a one-to-one basis. He was also required to edit training manuals and to perform basic repairs. Administrators and instructors appreciated his ability to step in when necessary and to fade into the backdrop when his services were not essential.

In the first few months of his hitch, Nick would like to have had a face-to-face discussion with Shawn, but gradually he substituted a mix of Air Force personnel for Shawn and bounced ideas off them. Nick became more confident as he realized that he was able to communicate complex technical concepts in simple terms and that others, even those smarter than he, generally valued his opinion. Underplaying his hand by speaking only when he felt he had something important to say or when asked a question made him a highly valued team member.

Nick missed his parents and spoke with them by phone at least once per week. On their side, the Browns understood that being separated from Nick was a vital step on his road to maturity. They grew to love Joan, while playing an increasingly important role in helping her parents avoid a nursing home. The Browns were savvy enough not to insinuate themselves into Nick and Joan's relationship.

The two young adults found the distance between them challenging. Joan intrigued Nick with her methods of personalizing their communications, including pictures of Joan surrounded by her young students or flanked by Nick's parents. For his part, he sent pictures of his team working on a computer installation or of Nick posing in portions of the charming city of Fairfield, CA. They ended their phone conversations by saying that they loved each other, but after hanging up, both were able to devote full attention to their job responsibilities. Pleased to have someone special, each was content to let their relationship grow slowly and steadily.

Nick attracted women in uniform because he treated them with respect and was not full of himself, as were many airmen. It was not unusual for Nick to go into town with two or more women or a larger group of men and women. Nick was always welcome because he was well-behaved, honest, and humorous.

Occasionally, women would want more than friendship from Nick. In one instance, Angela Darren, a pretty brunette, suggested that they park her car and "watch the submarine races."

Nick responded that "he already had somebody." When she looked skeptical, he told Angela, "Her name is Joan, and though we are two thousand miles apart, we are somewhat compatible."

"You've never told us about her. Why is that?" asked Angela. "We're trying to build something that will last. Neither of us feel that getting others involved in our relationship will do anything but confuse matters. We don't even confide in our parents much, although we each are close to them," said Nick. "We know we are going to change in the next few years and are waiting to see if the changes bring us closer together or push us apart."

"It sounds as though you two have a good thing going," countered Angela. "Few women and even fewer men are willing to work that hard to make sure a relationship is on solid ground. It's so easy to wing it and then be surprised when a relationship crumbles.

"I'm betting on you two to go the distance, but if you don't, at least you'll know why. Meanwhile, I'm going to be sizing up my dates from a different angle. I have you to thank for that," Angela stated.

"Let's go for a milk shake," suggested Nick.

"OK. Maybe I'll find someone who likes pineapple shakes as much as I do, and we can build a relationship from there," Angela mused.

Nick found his Air Force enlistment to be similar to his undergraduate years and did not feel restricted by the rules and discipline. Chameleon-like, he had a knack for blending. Frequently a designated driver for drinkers and a sympathetic listener to lonely enlistees, Nick served as brother, uncle, friend, and rabbi to his colleagues.

On one occasion in the barracks, an obnoxious drunk, Benny Derwinski, went after Nick claiming that "You think you are better than the rest of us." Benny grabbed Nick by the throat and had him in a bad way before four airmen intervened and surrounded Derwinski.

"He's not as smart as he thinks he is," Benny stated defensively.

James Garren, one of the airmen replied, "He's as smart as he has to be and a good friend to all of us. If you don't understand that, it's your problem. Now that I think of it, he is better than the rest of us and we don't want you bothering him. Is that understood?"

Benny realized he had messed with the wrong guy and nodded weakly before heading to his bunk. Nick's stance as an untouchable was confirmed in this incident.

Many people owed Nick, but he never collected his debts. In the words of one airman whom Nick had cleverly prevented from doing something stupid, "He's the kind of person we all should be. If he ever needed anything, I would want to be first in line to help. Just being around Nick makes us better. He is consistently reasonable, while for most of us, common sense comes and goes."

CHAPTER 43

A Second Vietnam Tour

Camp Lejeune was a blur. Vietnam training had taken on an intensity and focus that strongly resembled the real thing in Shawn's recollection; the props, language training, and non-commissioned officers' tactics were spot on. There was also a distinct divide between those with in-country experience and all others. Vietnam vets tended to band together but curiously did not talk much about their combat stories. Their focus was generally upon the relevance of the instruction they were currently receiving. Training instructors tended to grade the quality of their offerings on the interest displayed by veterans who had already served in Vietnam.

Shawn rested at every opportunity during breaks in training, since he knew of all too many who died because they were not alert when they needed to be. He returned to Vietnam, this time during the peak of a war that by 1967 had consumed southeast Asia. Because Shawn had graded out highly in combat, communicated effectively, and was again super fit, he was assigned to an elite eight-member field unit, Echo Charley (EC). His unit's mission was to gather intelligence data about enemy troop movements and weapon caches.

Shawn did not need to groom a best friend this time, since all eight knew that they were part of something exceptional and were special in their own rite. Taking hold immediately, the mutual respect and willingness to sacrifice for one another ran deeper than in most families. The adrenalin flowed freely when in tight situations, and the ability to anticipate the reactions of the other seven was finely tuned. EC was combat ready and then some!

Shawn served thirteen months on his second hitch and rarely had a day during the first eight months when his unit was not threatened by rifle fire, explosive devices, and/or poisonous snakes. He learned to eat heartily when they met up with larger US forces, to sleep in ad hoc hammocks, and to write letters in the dark.

Trudging through a defoliated jungle, Shawn cleaned himself with fresh water at every opportunity in an attempt to avoid the effects of what came to be known as Agent Orange. Shawn was regarded as "Mr. Hygiene" because he was always encouraging the others to care for their teeth, feet, and hair. When they met other American units, he traded for or bought soap and then pushed the soap off on his squad members, while insisting they use it.

Without much discussion, each squad member gravitated to a specific service role within the squad. Tony, a tough New Jersey kid, provided TLC for everyone's rifles and pistols, while Randy, MS born and bred, prepared food and was laughingly referred to as "The Cook." Ralph, a smooth CN college grad, became the one who carefully picked camp sites, hence the title of "Tour Director." Ralph also handled radio communications for the squad. Mark, a Pittsburg native nicknamed "Trip," was proficient in disarming explosives and disconnecting trip wires, while helping Ralph pick safe camp sites.

Jack, with sniper skills, insisted on positioning himself well outside of the squad group as they slept at night, because he had an excellent feel for sights and sounds far away. On more than one occasion, "Lonesome Jack" had prevented the group from being surprised by an approaching enemy. Chris, a light sleeper referred to as "Old One Eye" because he was said to sleep with one eye open, was responsible for insuring that the snorers in the group were poked or prodded if they were making too much noise. They all understood that "If we can hear you, so can they." No one complained when a frequently exhausted Chris occasionally nodded off during the day.

For eight months, EC gathered information effectively without incident, by being careful and lucky. Shot at often but not hit, never damaged by improvised explosive devices, and somehow eluding serious diseases, the Echo Charley grunts led a charmed life. Inevitably, their luck ran out.

Circumstances conspired against Echo Charley on a cloudy evening. A tight Viet Cong force of twenty men moved in downwind from Lonesome Jack, escaping his notice for a time, and caught Old One Eye in a deeper sleep than usual. The VC had moved within thirty yards of the campsite when Lonesome Jack began firing.

This fire fight was more intense than the average exchange because of the proximity of combatants. Shawn rolled behind a bush and by the time he had fired three clips from his M-14, the enemy force was disengaging, largely due to Lonesome Jack's accuracy with his night visions scope. Leaving Jack to walk the perimeter, the uninjured EC members picked up weapons, ammunition, and food before leaving the area.

Jack and Shawn scooped up the body of Old One Eye, who had

been shot through the forehead; no one dared mention the bitter irony of his ghastly third eye. They dragged his corpse a mile from the campsite. Ralph and Chris, both with non-life-threatening upper torso wounds, were pulled and pushed along gently by the remaining squad members. Ralph, still operating the radio, had requested a helicopter and been given good instructions; the confidence in safe chopper getaways was widespread and always in the back of everyone's mind. What was left of EC, squad members and all, was evacuated quickly.

Echo Charley was no more. Ralph was dead, the two wounded flown to Philippine hospitals, and the remaining five EC members reassigned. On his part, Shawn was handling the short-term stress well, while understanding that the real test of his emotional state would come months, even years later.

A sharp-eyed non-com with decorated experience in the Korean Conflict, Sergeant Dirks, saw Shawn coordinating the support of the EC wounded. Dirks asked the sergeant major if he could have Shawn assigned to his supply depot and his request was granted immediately. Now a supply clerk, Shawn's last five months were spent on-call with weird hours, good food, and a dry place to sleep.

On the day of Shawn's departure, Sergeant Dirks took him aside and told him, "You're a good Marine, kid, and you'll be successful in anything you try as long as you don't let someone else hurry you or make your decisions. I'm not going to thank you for doing your job well, because that's what you're suppose to do, but I *did* notice," he added, with what was as close to a smile as Shawn could remember.

Shawn came to attention and held a salute until Dirks raised and dropped his right hand. "Semper Fi, Sergeant!"

"Hoo-rah," responded Dirks.

On the first leg of his trip home, Shawn gazed wistfully out the airplane window at the jungle, pristine and life-sustaining for centuries but now ugly and toxic. At CCC, he had discovered that our planet will not last forever. In an introductory environmental education course, he learned that, individually and collectively, we all exhaust a portion of the earth's life and that the greedy and/or foolish use a disproportionate share.

Sadly, he concluded that he had been part of an undertaking which had dramatically hastened the earth's demise and that his environmental account was in arrears. He had some making up to do!

CHAPTER 44

Shawn & Nick Reunite

Since Shawn and Nick had enlisted for four years during the same month, they were discharged within two days of one another. Shawn returned to Chicago first and rung his father's doorbell after dark, because he had given up his key. Rex shook his hand, gave him a careful look, and then went back to the kitchen. As Shawn followed, Rex pointed to a stack of mail, lifted up a cup of stew, and handed it to Shawn. While sitting and waiting for the stew to cool, Shawn gazed around the plain, squeaky clean kitchen.

"It's not necessary to look any further, Shawn. Your mom's not here. I check every day," paused Rex. "Wherever she is, your mother is applauding you. She always did."

Shawn gulped, "You made it easy, dad. You taught me your three-step program: listen, learn, and shut up."

"Tell me what else you learned?" asked Rex.

"That I'm not as tough as I thought, not as smart as I figured, and luckier than I deserve to be."

Rex sized up his son, no longer a boy, for a full minute and said, "Then you got full value from wearing the uniform."

This was to be the last discussion that father and son had of their military years. Both viewed it as an important responsibility to be discharged properly, but not one worthy of rehashing.

When Shawn's medals came through the mail a month after his

discharge, Rex tossed them on his bed and Shawn tucked them away in his dresser, unopened. Understating his father was tough, but he vowed to give it a try. Shawn also promised himself that he would not become one of those veterans who could not let the experience go.

He spent several hours each week listening to Nick explain what he had learned about computers in the Air Force and encouraged him to apply for a job in Chicago at a firm which applied these skills. Several far-sighted companies were interested in hiring Nick, and he chose Metro Dynamics, a company with only thirty employees and one which would give him both the freedom to explore uncharted territory and to engage in decision-making, including equipment selection.

The clincher during the application process was when the CEO, Mr. Belknap, told him, "You're smarter than I am and I promise you I will never forget that. I'm the boss and don't you ever forget that."

Metro agreed to pay for Nick's MBA studies at De Paul. Nick loved his job and through efficient time management fit a graduate course each semester into his schedule.

Shawn began his law studies at Clement, and the two young men reserved Saturday mornings to walk the beach and plan their future in business. Joan was fine with this arrangement, because she trusted Shawn and also because she valued her privacy.

Shawn prodded Nick to devise ways that big money could be made from computers. Their Saturday morning talks were summarized and recorded by Shawn for two years, lest they miss a good idea. He would routinely replay the tapes in search of a theme or the kernel of an idea.

Studying tapes from this lengthy process, Shawn felt he was on to something: Nick was able to see things in different scales and sizes than most people. Since much of the costs of computer manufacturing was related to the size and weight of these devices, miniaturization promised huge cost savings. Shawn encouraged Nick to think visually, but Nick's art and technical drawing skills were limited.

Both men knew they would not be able to apply for patents without accurate drawings, and they spent one Saturday on their walks discussing this challenge. To this point, they had kept all their business to themselves, but it was apparent that this had to change.

"How about if I check with Dr. Wilson to see if she knows someone who can help us?" asked Shawn.

"Sounds good to me," replied Nick.

"Suppose it's about time to let our parents in on our scheme?" Nick nodded in agreement, adding "My folks are beyond curious."

Shawn called Dr. Wilson the following Monday and explained that they wanted to have a meeting at the Butler residence on Friday night and asked whether she could join them for supper.

He explained that he and Nick were starting a business venture and needed her advice. His lofty estimation of her climbed still further as she agreed without asking any prying questions, seemingly trusting his judgment.

As planned, the meeting was held after a fish dinner which Rex engineered. Rex and Rita gravitated quickly to each other and the six sat at a balanced table. For forty-five minutes, Shawn led the discussion and paused intermittently to permit Nick to explain technical information, which he supported with crude drawings.

"Obviously, we need help with our art work," laughed Shawn. "Do you know of anyone who can help us, Dr. Wilson?"

She looked at him mischievously and responded, "Who do you think is the art major around here? I will, however, need help with the technical aspects beyond what Nick has explained."

Tim Brown cleared his throat theatrically and said, "And who do you think is the engineer around here?"

"When we have our work patent-ready, what next?" asked Rex. "I thought perhaps you and I could work on this one, dad." "And I thought you'd never ask," replied Rex.

With the responsibilities now assigned, the Butler-Brown-Wilson (BBW) alliance was formed. Shawn wisely had decided that if they had gotten that far in one evening, that they could schedule another meeting, this time at the Browns, three months from now. Since everyone agreed, Shawn said he would like to explain their ideas at that time for selling the patents and his suggestions for a project budget. He politely requested that if major problems emerged that he be contacted.

"Count on that!" interjected Mr. Brown, and everyone laughed.

After the meeting, Rita and Rex began quietly what everyone else regarded as a private conversation. The Browns went home, and Nick and Shawn walked the neighborhood as they replayed the evening's meeting.

Shawn began, "I think we should cut Dr. Wilson in for 10%."

Nick nodded in agreement, adding "We could make her the chairman of our board and spokesperson, rather than have companies take advantage of us because we look too young."

Three months later, the group met again after a steak dinner at the Browns. Shawn explained that he and Nick had combined their eleven miniaturization ideas into four proposals. He also said that he would not be attending law school the following summer because he would be going out to Silicon Valley to get a feel for how business was being done there.

"If I find the kind of interest I expect to, would you and Nick be able to join me in California for a few days?"

"I'll make myself available," Wilson answered. "How will you know whom to ask and how much to ask for?"

"One way or another, I'll find out," Shawn pledged.

Rita Wilson studied Shawn for a moment and then looked around the room and said, "I believe he will, don't you?"

With affirmation all around, the BBW patent arrangers took another step forward and shared the excitement. Tim and Jane Brown became even happier than they already were and Nick was pleased to be part of a cohesive team. Shawn was gaining confidence by the day, Rex was deeply interested in BBW and Dr. Wilson, not necessarily in that order, and Dr. Wilson was intrigued by the boldness of their venture. All agreed that if they made money, fine, and if not, that they would never forgive themselves for not having tried!

CHAPTER 45

Buddies No More

After a few days of stowing his gear and checking in at Clement, he called Molly Jean Donovan. Telephoning her house was interesting because you were often given a runaround. Over the years, he had been transferred to her father, Matt, who wanted to know why he was calling him. On another occasion, he had been put on hold so long, he hung up. This time, with Agnes Donovan answering, he was on safe ground.

"Hello Mrs. Donovan. It's Shawn. How are you?"

"We all missed you, Shawn," she said eagerly. "When are you coming over?"

"That's what I'm calling about?"

"You could have just dropped in. You know that," Agnes said in a disappointed tone.

"Well I didn't know if Molly Jean…"

"Talk to her yourself. She's just coming downstairs," Agnes instructed him.

"Hello, Butler. I didn't know the Marines had landed," teased Molly Jean.

"Hello, Molly. I want to come over. We could go hang out," suggested Shawn.

In a firm tone that he had not heard before, she stated, "Our hanging out days are over, Butler. If you want to see me, it will be on a formal date. I don't want you lounging around here in the middle of the day. Pick me up at seven o'clock tonight and we'll go to a restaurant, my treat as a courtesy to a returning serviceman, and then there's a movie I want to see. Wear a shirt with a collar and shave. We have some things to talk about. Any questions?"

More off-balance than at any time in combat, Shawn hung up and sat dazed, trying to determine what had just happened. Molly Jean had always been his buddy, but clearly they were buddies no more. Had he done something wrong? Was there someone else? Who was this new Molly? Was she going to send me packing?

As he approached the door of the Donovan home, he sensed that something was wrong. Before he could determine what it was, two of her brothers jumped him from behind and the two others came at him through the front door. He could not have whipped all four but he could have hurt them; however, this was something he did not want to do.

Wrestling happily, all five collapsed in a heap in the home's entryway. Mrs. Donovan had seen this foolishness before and stood with her arms crossed in the doorway of the kitchen.

Molly Jean descended the stairs and barked loudly, "Turn him loose and take a hike, you clowns."

Her brothers had come to think of her more as a fifth brother than a sister, and her current tone had put them off balance. They each made their way out the front door, looking back at her. To add to their confusion, she sported full make-up, instead of her usual token attempt, and had had her blonde hair cut and shaped. Instead of jeans and T-shirt, she wore tiny golden earrings, a soft beige blouse, and a snug peach skirt.

Shawn stood with his shirt askew and his mouth open, as he took in the new MJ. He reached for her, but she pointed him towards the bathroom, so that he could straighten up. After washing up and tucking in his shirt, he exited the bathroom and again reached for her in an attempt to give her the half-wrestle, half-hug, which had become their trademark. She brushed his hands aside, stepped close and gave him their first real kiss. As he started to respond, she withdrew quickly and took his arm, while moving him towards the front door, leaving a chuckling Mrs. Donovan in their wake.

After dinner at Rubio's, an upscale restaurant with Italian-Cuban cuisine, Molly toyed with her wine glass before speaking. She had remained in-charge throughout the dinner and now was about to make her case.

"Shawn Butler, I've known you for nine years and have loved you since the time I saw you speaking with my mother for the first time. She thinks you are what my father should be. You listen to her and obviously value her opinion. She respects you and so do I.

"You are the most considerate man I know. You never badmouth others and don't con anybody, although you're clever enough, if you wanted to.

"Choosing Nick as your best friend is admirable. Your loyalty to him is wonderful since you could easily have chosen someone splashier and more visible. You complete him.

"You're not a drunk and will never be. You're the best man our age that I know. I'd like to marry you and have your children.

"if you're not interested, tell me now. In any event, I don't want to be your friend any longer. I can't bear it."

Shawn responded, "I don't know what to say…"

Molly Jean responded, "Don't say anything now. I know you've been away a long time. On the other hand, you know yourself well and make decisions quickly. I'll give you a week.

"I think I'll pass on the show. You have some thinking to do," she added. "Take me home, please."

Upon entering the Butler residence, Shawn found Rex sleeping on the couch. Rousing his father, he told him that he was thinking of getting married.

Rex shook himself awake and explained to him that "women get married when they find the right guy and men marry when they feel they are ready. Are you ready?"

"The way she explains it, I guess I am," answered Shawn. "Who is the lucky woman?" Rex asked.

"It's Molly Jean, dad."

Shawn witnessed his dad's fist pump for the first time and then they shook hands. Wearing a faint smile, Rex excused himself and went to bed, leaving Shawn to ponder this new development.

At 8 AM the next morning, he was sitting on the Donovan's front steps. When Agnes came out to retrieve the newspaper, Shawn was reading it.

"Come in and have some breakfast," she insisted.

He started to object but was reluctant to cross the Donovan

women the way things were going. How long had he been gone?

"Matt's on duty and my sons are at work. Molly is still sleeping. By the time you've finished eating, she'll probably join us."

"Thanks, Mrs. Donovan," Shawn said softly.

Molly Jean appeared later, not looking terribly surprised to see him.

"I'm sorry to just drop in like this, but I have some questions. Will you substitute a walk with me for your morning run?" he asked.

"Sure. Give me ten minutes," she replied.

"I'll step outside to arrange my thoughts," he said.

He thanked Mrs. Donovan and sat on the porch once again, rising when Molly joined him. She wore little make-up this morning.

"I've given your idea serious thought. As a matter of fact, I didn't sleep much last night," he confessed.

As they strolled down the block, he said, "I have five questions and you may well have a batch of your own. I'd like to go first.

"Go ahead," Molly urged.

"How many children do you want," Shawn asked. "One for sure, but I would prefer at least two." "Where do you want to live?" he asked.

"I'd much prefer to live here. I love Chicago as much as you do." "Apartment or a house?" he asked.

"I'd like a roomy apartment near a park."

"Do you want to work or to stay home with the kids?" he asked.

"I worked hard for my bachelor's degree in business. I want to use my training and would need your cooperation with the children."

"Who will manage our money?" he asked. "We would have to do that together."

"You've answered my questions, and we are on the same page. I'm ready for yours," he pronounced.

"I only have one. Are you ready for a lifetime commitment? I don't look upon this as an experiment. I have seen the wreckage caused by divorces and want no part of something like that."

"Yes, I am. I love you Molly Jean. I'm sorry you had to point that out to me, but I will make it up to you. I'd be proud to have you for my wife, if you'll have me," he announced.

"I'll take you, warts and all, Butler." "Let's shop for a ring," he suggested.

"OK," but the hug she gave him indicated it was more than OK. He hesitated, suggesting, "Let's ask your mother to come along."

Molly looked at him with tears in her eyes. "Keep making suggestions like that and we're going to do just fine. There's hope for you yet," she observed.

Shawn reached out and kissed her. The clinch lasted long enough that a small crowd of neighbors gathered and started clapping. As they separated, Shawn noticed that Molly Jean was blushing, something he had never seen before. Shawn observed that MJ sported a blush nicely. *Why didn't I ever notice how pretty she is?*

When asked to go ring-shopping, Agnes all but jumped up and down. Shawn's plan was to have Molly and her mother reduce the ring choices down to three and then join them. Later, when Shawn peered into the jewelry store window, Agnes waved him over and Shawn approached. Mrs. Donovan had decided to let them make the final selection by themselves but did give Shawn a high five before retreating to another corner of the store. Her enthusiasm indicated how pleased she was at being included in the process.

Shawn read Molly's eyes and then picked the ring she wanted most. Buying the ring was worth it just to see the glitter and depth it lent to those blue eyes. Leaving the store, they held hands, which they had done many times before, but this time it was different. On the ride home, Molly and her mom sat in the back seat, admiring the ring from all angles and hugging each other. Their happiness filled the car, and Shawn could think of nothing to do but drive carefully and smile.

CHAPTER 46

Silicon Valley, The Preliminaries

The next three months passed quickly for all involved. With help from Mr. Brown, Dr. Wilson grasped a basic knowledge of patents and drew accurately. The meeting at the Browns resembled a pep rally with all parties energized and positive.

Shawn explained that he had lined up a patent attorney through Clement and that he and Rex would be meeting with him, now that the drawings and patent language were ready. He reviewed the expenses that everyone was incurring and indicated his willingness to let everyone turn in their receipts. Mr. Brown observed that since everyone was contributing, that a full accounting could wait. All nodded or murmured affirmatively, and that matter was closed.

Shawn spoke to the group about his intent to give Dr. Wilson 10% of any profits because she would be traveling to California and also would be busy as the BBW Board Chair. Again, consensus was reached.

Rita countered "I will accept 5%, nothing more. If I hear dissent, I will reduce the 5%. I know I drive a hard bargain, but it's the way I was raised."

Everyone laughed appreciatively and Shawn went on to the next topic, pay for the patent attorney. Shawn began, "I've been working with Chris Hanophy, who likes what we're doing and loves how we're doing it. He works for a big firm and has to charge us a fair price to satisfy his employer. He wants 2% of the profits or $2,000 to process our four patents. I asked him what he would do, if he was in our shoes. Looking nervously behind him, he wrote $2,000 on a pad and circled it."

"What do you recommend, Shawn," asked Tim Brown.

"I believe he has our best interests at heart. Can we raise $2,000?" "I'll give $1,000," said Mr. Brown.

"I'll donate $500," countered Dr. Wilson. "I'll give the last $500," added Rex.

"That takes care of that. If you give me your checks tonight, I'll pay Mr. Hanophy tomorrow afternoon so that he can begin work."

Hanophy filed for the four patents within ten days, and three were given tentative approval five months later. The fourth patent request was found to be duplicative of a request which had recently been approved. After calling all BBW participants, Shawn was given approval to make travel plans to visit the Silicon Valley ASAP.

Shawn made several calls and discovered that two former classmates were working in San Jose. The Browns and Dr. Wilson provided three more names in this region.

After the flight to California, he decided to spend a few days in San Jose before calling any of the five contacts. Shawn read local newspapers and walked through the lobbies of IT companies, trying to get a feel for the culture. He attended two lectures and read company documents as part of his education. Eavesdropping shamelessly in restaurants and bars, he realized that the language spoken here was sprinkled with computer-insider terminology foreign to him.

To road-test his approach, Shawn chose one of his two contacts, Charles Cheznicki, with whom he had played high school football. Shawn remembered him as a tough lineman with good math skills, polished manners and no-nonsense parents. Having both his work and home numbers, Shawn chose to try him at home, where he might be more relaxed and have time to talk freely. He placed a call at 6 PM.

"Hello, Chuck, this is Shawn Butler, a voice from out of the past. Do you remember me?"

"Yes, of course. How are you Shawn?" Chuck asked warmly.

They spoke for five minutes, discovering that each had served in the military and were engaged to be married. His responses confirmed that Chuck remained the same stand-up guy he knew as a teen.

"What brings you to San Jose, Shawn?"

"I have some ideas I'm shopping around. Can I buy you a meal and pick your brain?" Shawn asked.

Chuck thought a moment, "Why don't you come over now? Pick up a sandwich for me, nothing heavy, because I've packed on some weight, and I'll provide the beer."

After receiving driving directions, Shawn freshened up and jumped in his rental car. He reviewed his pitch during the car trip and soon was ringing the bell. Chuck stepped through the door with a chest bump which sent Shawn two steps backward.

Laughing, Shawn placed the food upon the dining room table, looking around for Chuck's fiancee.

"I've asked her to come over at 9 PM, Shawn. I want you to meet

Tammy."

"And I would like to meet her," Shawn replied.

By the time they reminisced, finished the food and drank a beer, it was 8 PM, which gave him an hour, all the time he would need, before the evening turned social. He projected that it would take him twenty minutes to explain BBW, twenty minutes to answer questions, and a final twenty for Chuck to point him in various directions.

Cheznicki explained that he worked for a small firm, LiteRite, that had ten employees and two promising projects, which they were trying to sell off because they were approaching their level of sophistication and they needed the money. Shawn had learned that the Valley was made up of projects in varying stages of completion. Employees and the companies themselves needed to be nimble to survive and lucky to thrive.

LiteRite was looking for additional work. Chuck was responsible for keeping his company within bounds on their projects, explaining that he was just one of many Midwestern transplants in the Valley with similar job descriptions which required discipline and common sense. He gave Shawn encouragement on his miniaturization theme, telling him that there was much more talk about making things smaller than there were actual projects designed to do so.

He spoke of the MIT and Cal Tech students, graduates or not, vaulting off their campuses and wanting to invent new things, rather than shrink existing devices and processes. Chuck loved his job but spoke of the high potential for burn-out because of SV's fast pace, changing market conditions, and fickle venture capital support.

Just as Shawn was about to ask the key question, Tammy drifted in. She was a charming, unaffected, mid-twenties woman with a brown pony tail. Sensing that she had interrupted something, Tammy excused herself and went into the den to watch television.

Shawn asked, "What would you do, if you were BBW?"

"I would meet with LiteRite and at least two other companies and see how they react." Chuck said. "I can set up an appointment for you next week but promise me you'll try to meet with some other companies. Can you call me at work tomorrow afternoon?"

"Sure. Now, let's meet Tammy."

The rest of the evening passed pleasantly and BBW took another step towards maturity. He phoned his father and asked him to spread the word.

The meeting at Chuck's company was informal and encouraging. Shawn met with Chris Behrens, LiteRite's CEO, who was not much older than he was. Behrens indicated that the current winds might be blowing favorably for BBW, because the bulk and weight of IT devices were presenting increasing challenges. In his opinion, funding was increasingly likely to gravitate to patents resembling those of BBW. The CEO made a strong pitch for the flexibility and ease of communication in doing business with a small company. Shawn promised that this would not be his last contact with LiteRite.

He called the four remaining contacts. In one, Shawn spoke with the daughter of a friend of Dr. Wilson, who was unable to help since she was struggling in a company fighting to stay afloat. She made a half-hearted offer to meet with him, but Shawn declined.

In another, Shawn discerned little interest and picked up a lunch tab with not much to show for it. In yet another, Shawn was told that there was little money in miniaturization and essentially that he was wasting his time and theirs.

The remaining contact, Leslie Donaldson, a niece of the Browns, worked for a 100-member firm, Compulink, which was a high flyer. She and two other women were searching for a project and sat with Shawn around a beautiful conference table.

After listening to him speak for ten minutes, Leslie stood up and said, "Let's take five."

Shawn went in search of a rest room, figuring that he was about to be shown the door. Instead, when he returned, he was introduced to William Hadley, Compulink's CEO, who politely asked Shawn to start his presentation from the beginning. Without missing a beat, Shawn described the three patents pending. Mr. Hadley was obviously interested.

"With whom have you spoken?" Hadley asked.

"I've been working closely with a smaller company, whom I have promised to leave unnamed."

"We would want exclusive rights," Hadley demanded.

"I'm not sure that's possible. Would you meet with the CEO from this company and representatives from the company I represent, BBW, perhaps at the end of next week?"

Used to getting his own way, he wrestled with himself for a moment. Finally he said to Leslie, "Set this up. Plan a lunch meeting. I want to sit next to this unnamed company's CEO. Work with Shawn on the seating arrangement and all other details. I want to meet with our lawyer at least a day before this meeting. Any questions?"

Leslie and Shawn both shook their heads, and BBW moved forward once again, this time taking a big step.

CHAPTER 47

BBW's Super Bowl Week

After a volley of telephone calls, a meeting was set for noon on the following Thursday. Representing BBW would be Rex, Tim, Shawn, Nick, Chris Hanophy, the patent attorney, and Rita Wilson; all would arrive on Tuesday and be brought up to speed. Shawn and Leslie spent four hours on Monday preparing an agenda and making sure all the documents were prepared and distributed. The final agenda item was when Compulink would either make an offer to buy the patents or pass.

On Tuesday afternoon, the BBW contingent took a shuttle bus from LAX in Los Angeles to San Jose's High Sign, a fine hotel. With flowers for Rita and a fine bottle of wine for each of the six, Leslie and her two colleagues joined Shawn in greeting the group. Mr. Brown gave his niece, Leslie, a big hug and they chatted briefly.

Shawn had scheduled a team meeting for 4:30 PM in the hotel and had made dinner reservations, also in the hotel, for 7 PM. Shawn had asked that Leslie join them for the first thirty minutes of the meeting to answer questions about Compulink. She outdid herself with a fine Powerpoint presentation and gave polite, incisive answers to several of BBW's questions.

After Leslie excused herself, Shawn handed a list of concerns to Dr. Wilson and turned the conduct of the meeting over to her. Rita handled the transition smoothly and ticked off a series of items. Much of the time was spent on the work product, the three pending patents.

Wilson praised Nick and reminded everyone that if he wasn't more perceptive and smarter than most everyone else, there would not be a BBW. She asked Nick if the patents did, in fact, reflect his ideas or if BBW had drifted off the Nick Brown track.

He teased, "I vaguely recognize my work."

Then getting quite sober, he lectured, "Initially, my ideas were fanciful abstracts floating free, not tethered to any meaningful framework. Before Shawn forced me to come down to earth, I did not have anything that could have been patented or taken seriously for any reason. Even then, Mr. Hanophy had to shape our ideas that had rough edges into a manageable, negotiable form.

"Thank you all for believing in me. I envy you because I live in a world in which I often am out of rhythm. On the other hand, you are each focused and centered. You have me believing that being out of step is not necessarily bad. But for Shawn, I would have never been welcome on anybody's team. He and the rest of you have given validity and substance to my visions. For that, I will be forever grateful!"

Everybody was stunned because no one had ever heard Nick talk that much at one time. Mr. Brown smiled proudly, knowing full well that Shawn and BBW had done things for Nick that he and his wife could not have accomplished.

Mr. Hanophy was asked about the going rate for the three patents pending. He hedged, stating that it was "tough to say and could range anywhere from five to fifty."

He paused and then realized that the group's obvious disappointment stemmed from their thinking that he meant thousands. Hanophy clarified, "That's five million to fifty million dollars."

The group was struck silent because at the time Rex and Tim were working hard to earn $30,000 per year, while Rita was making $60,000 annually as the distinguished president of a highly respected college. Hanophy cautioned that "the three patents were not worth a nickel unless someone had a nickel and wanted to buy them. I have made several phone calls, though, and if speculators think it's a good idea, money is no object."

When the meeting ended, Shawn asked that everyone remain in the room and address any last minute concerns. He also asked for a show of hands for those interested in a three-hour Silicon Valley tour leaving at 9 AM the following morning. Not surprisingly, all raised their hands, confirming Shawn's conclusion that BBW was comprised of avid adult learners.

The evening's dinner at the hotel was relaxing and enjoyable for all. Rex and Rita talked non-stop with one another, until Rita excused herself. Though resplendent in turquoise and one of the few who could use a splash of gray in red hair to make her even more beautiful, Shawn noticed a grimace as she lifted herself out of her chair.

Shawn trailed her outside and asked, "Are you feeling all right, Dr. Wilson?"

She turned to him and responded, "No, as a matter of fact, I'm not, Shawn. I've had some tests run recently and will receive the results when I get back to Chicago. Don't tell anyone, particularly your father. I've grown fond of your dad and don't want to worry him."

"Whatever you say. I know how much he thinks of you. We would have worked around your absence somehow. You didn't have to come."

Rita looked at him carefully and insisted, "Yes, I did. It's this way, Shawn. I have hundreds of friends and colleagues but have never built my own family. In searching for a man while in my late twenties, I found drunks, hustlers, and retreads. I quit looking and concentrated on being a good aunt. In addition, I have been a godmother so many times, I would have lost count if I hadn't made a list.

"My brothers, in-laws, nephews, and nieces are great but I inherited them. You and your dad are the closest thing to a family of my own choosing that this old maid has. I wouldn't have missed this business trip for the world. Besides, I have always liked drama and long shots," she winked, ending the conversation.

The tour went fine with Mr. Brown doing most of the talking. BBW had spent an interesting, restful day and was ready for the main event on Thursday, the BBW Super Bowl, as Shawn called it.

As they trooped into Compulink's main conference room a few minutes before noon on Super Thursday, each appeared a tad nervous but very positive. What did they have to lose? They smiled at each other and waited impatiently as the Compulink team settled in their chairs.

CHAPTER 48

BBW Goes For Broke

As the meeting began, Dr. Wilson turned to Mr. Hadley and had him introduce his team, which now included a lawyer and a consultant, besides Leslie and her two associates. Appearing ill at ease, Mr. Behrens of LiteRite introduced Chuck Cheznicki.

Rita's smile had the combined effect of turning Hadley into a smitten school boy and relaxing everyone else in the room. As she presented the BBW team members, Rita gave each an opportunity to talk briefly so that they would be warmed up, if and when they were asked to speak later. Mr. Hadley noted this technique and was likely to use it at Compulink in the future.

Hadley showed little interest in Nick because he had several of his type working for him. He did, however, demonstrate keen interest in the exchanges between attorneys, both of whom were razor sharp and on their best behavior. As Hadley and Wilson worked through the agenda, it was obvious that Shawn and Leslie had done a fine job in developing the sequence of the agenda items.

The Hadley-Behrens-Wilson CEO interplay, so important in negotiations of this type, had gone well. Shawn speculated that Hadley would have gone so far as to spread his suit coat over a puddle for Dr. Wilson.

"Mr. Behrens, LiteRite is in good company with BBW. You will be part of our discussion in the next hour," advised Mr. Hadley.

Mr. Hadley then turned to Dr. Wilson and said, "'Your company is tiny but mighty. You have kept your eye on the ball in a way that most IT teams do not. Shawn has choreographed things well and BBW's presentation was smooth and unpretentious. I am also proud of Compulink. If we do not come to a meeting of the minds, it will not be your fault or ours, but simply a matter of timing and choreography."

"It's now time for my team to discuss our decision. Leslie will take you to our lounge. Our deliberations may take two hours or more, not because we are trying to heighten the suspense, but because we will have our board chair and our banker on speaker phone in this important matter. I hope you understand, Mr. Behrens and Dr. Wilson?"

"Certainly. Thank you for your concern," said Mr. Behrens. Dr. Wilson nodded in agreement.

Leslie brought in juice and coffee before leaving an in-house number at which she could be reached. Mr. Hanophy spent most of the next ninety minutes on the phone, Dr. Wilson dozed, Chris Behrens and Chuck huddled on another company matter, and the remaining BBW participants played rummy.

When the phone rang, everyone looked at Rita and froze. Smiling, she picked up the phone and confirmed that BBW was ready to return to the conference room. Magically, Leslie appeared and led the way.

After all the participants settled in, Mr. Hadley turned to Mr. Behrens and Dr. Wilson, asking if they had any final questions. Both shook their heads.

"Our offer is $22 M to BBW for unconditional rights to all three patents. Unfortunately, we could not find a role for LiteRite," apologized Mr. Hadley.

Mr. Behrens was crushed and unable to speak. In a measured tone, Dr. Wilson responded, "Now it's our turn to caucus, Mr. Hadley.

Fifteen minutes will suffice."

Hadley and his team left the room. Meanwhile, Mr. Behrens and Chuck picked up their materials and were about to leave, before Dr. Wilson asked, "Where do you think you're going? You're still part of this, unless you have something better to do. You're not going to leave us now, are you?"

Both Chris and Chuck knew a rhetorical question when they heard one, dummied up, and returned to their seats. BBW and LiteRite turned to Dr. Wilson and wondered what she had in mind.

"Mr. Hanophy, is $22M a fair price?"

"On the basis of what I've learned in the past few weeks, I think it is, Dr. Wilson," responded Hanophy.

"Do you think LiteRite can work for Mr. Hadley, Chris?"

"Yes, I believe we can, unless we forget he is the boss," said a smiling Behrens.

"Then if my colleagues agree, here is my suggested counteroffer: $20M for us and $3M for Compulink to hire LiteRite on a sub- contract."

The fairness and decency of the terms struck everyone as being appropriate. Rex and Tim were particularly glad to see a mature adult at work as a model for their sons.

"Do you want to take a vote, or will nods suffice," teased Tim.

Rita laughed, "Let's see how Mr. Hadley responds. For now, hold your applause."

Upon receiving BBW's terms, Hadley laughed. "It's a deal. Mr. Behrens, can you and Chuck stay and meet with our in-house attorney? Dr. Wilson, you are going to have to catch a plane, so will you trust us to treat LiteRite fairly."

"I would expect nothing less from you, Mr. Hadley," as she shook his hand, which he studied proudly.

Because they had not decided upon how to divide the spoils if they received an offer, the group assembled in an isolated corner of the airport before their trip home. Asking if anyone would object, Shawn stated that he would like to put Mr. Hanophy and his company into the mix for one million, explaining that "I didn't realize how important that Hanophy would be and how good he is. While much of the money will go to his company, I have a hunch we are helping accelerate his career. I would also like to obligate BBW to pay $1M for our legal expenses. In our haste and ignorance, we undoubtedly have left a messy legal tangle and we are all going to need someone to help us with our taxes."

No one objected, so he tore a full sheet of paper into small squares, giving each of the BBW members a square, instructing them to write their initials and a number between one and eighteen to reflect their requested share in millions. The first request went Rex (2), Tim (2), Rita (1), Shawn (3),and Nick (4), a total of $12M.

Shawn chuckled and said, "We are undersubscribed to the tune of $6M. Dr. Wilson, your humility is catching."

He looked at her and she gave him a look which said, Don't you dare ask me to take more. She suggested "Why don't the four of you take an additional million and then put the rest in a Butler-Brown Foundation for disadvantaged children?"

Again, her logic was so compelling that all the participants could do was nod. The final tally was Rex (3), Tim (3), Rita (1), Shawn (4), Nick (5), Hanophy's Patent Law Firm (1), Legal Expenses (1), and the Butler Brown Foundation (2), a total of $20M.

Never one to miss a reason to celebrate, Tim Brown somehow produced a bottle of champagne, popped the cork, and poured the liquid into plastic cups, which Nick distributed. BBW was loopy and exhausted when they boarded the plane. Dr. Wilson nodded off on Rex's shoulder before take-off, and Shawn looked at his father, who signaled palms up, indicating he didn't know why she was so tired.

CHAPTER 49

Wedding Plans

A week after the California trip, Shawn, Molly Jean, Nick, and Joan took a walk on the beach to sort out their marriage plans. They each decided to marry in St. Angela's Catholic Church and after a lengthy discussion, agreed to have separate ceremonies on the same Saturday in October.

Nick and Joan decided to marry first, and Shawn and Nick agreed to be each other's Best Man. As bridesmaids, Joan chose an unmarried aunt only slightly older then she, while Molly Jean asked a married cousin with whom she was close.

Joan and Molly Jean had reached these arrangements amicably. Molly Jean envied Joan's class and reserve and Joan admired MJ's swagger and edgy sense of humor. Further, Joan held Shawn in high regard; anything or anybody that was OK with Shawn was fine with her.

Because they had so many friends in common, the four decided to share their reception later on the wedding day at Diminico's restaurant. They agreed, however, that their honeymoons would be separate, the Browns in Italy and the Butlers in Lake Geneva, WI.

Unspoken in the negotiations was the importance of pushing up the date of Shawn's wedding because of Rita Wilson's declining health. Wilson had taken a sick leave from her presidency at CCC and was now working two half days per week as she transferred the job to her successor.

On the second Sunday in September, the night of the Bears' home opener, she asked Rex to come to her house for the mysterious purpose of "sharing something with him." Without argument, he appeared at her home and found the door ajar. Calling her name, he entered her home.

"I'm in here, Rex."

She was propped up in her bed and had an enchanting aura about her. Smiling sadly, she beckoned him to sit by her bedside. Rex did as he was told and waited for her to speak.

"As you may have guessed, I'm dying. The doctors have given me until Christmas. I plan to hold myself together until the weddings next month, then will enter a hospice.

"I want to tell Shawn myself. Could you ask him to come over here tomorrow night?"

"Of course," Rex agreed. "Is there anything else I can do?" Rita looked directly at him and softly said, "Yes."

Under her penetrating gaze, it took him a full minute to realize what she was asking, but he had to ask her to be sure. "You want to get married?" he wondered.

Rita responded, "Since you insist, the answer is Yes. I've always wanted to marry, but it never happened or maybe I just never let it happen. In any event, I want to die married to you. Can we do it this Saturday?

"I understand that I'll be second-in-line, waiting to see you on the Other Side, but that's good enough for me. I have a big living room and if you and Shawn could move some furniture, we could put a dozen or so of my family on one side, five or six from the college in the middle, and BBW on the other.

"In the hope that you would agree, I've drafted a pre-nuptial agreement which we could turn over to our attorney from the BBW award. Most of my money goes to my nephews and nieces and I want none of yours. I just want you for myself for a few months. Please say yes, you big lug," she pleaded for the first time that he could remember.

"Yes, of course I will. I'm flattered and humbled. Anything else?" he asked.

"That's quite enough, don't you think?" she teased. "Now I've made a list of things to do, so we need to get busy," while reaching up for a starter hug.

The following evening, Shawn knocked softly at Dr. Wilson's door and let himself in. She was seated at her dining room table and motioned for Shawn to join her. For Shawn, who had been briefed by Rex, the words simply would not flow.

She smiled at him radiantly and said, "You and your dad have made me very happy. I'm not asking you to call me Mom and I'm not taking anyone's place. I just want a wonderful man and his fine son at my side when I pass. Do you understand?"

"I think so, but even if I didn't, I'm all for it. You've made my dad very happy. Since you came into his life, his posture has improved and his speech is more animated. When he retired last year, I thought that he would withdraw even further, but just the opposite has happened," he responded. "How can I help?"

"Can you manage the invitation list?" she inquired.

"Of course. Can I use your phone? I'll start after I make a suggestion." he pledged. "My dad asked me to be his best man. Have you chosen your bridesmaid?" asked Shawn.

"Not yet. I've been stalling. If I choose one of my nieces or God daughters, I will offend the rest of a nice group of young women. Why do you ask?"

Shawn hesitated, "This is not a request, just a thought. Have you considered selecting an educator? After all, you've had a marriage of sorts with education all your adult life."

"I work on a male-dominated administration and faculty. Gender-wise, I'm pretty much the Lone Ranger at CCC. I can't think of anyone I would ask."

"How about Andrea from Right? She has as much invested in education emotionally as you do and has not married for some of the same reasons. She thinks the world of you," he added.

Rita laughed, "Others have been listening to me tell them what to do for such a long time, that I've forgotten how to accept a truly fine idea. I think it's a great suggestion. If she is willing, could you bring her over tomorrow evening, so that we can check signals?"

"I'll call her now."

Shawn looked up Andrea's number in the phone directory, and she picked up on the second ring. After Shawn explained the request, he turned to Rita and said, "She wants to know if you're sure."

After Shawn gave her the phone, Rita explained, "Shawn and I agree that you would be the best person to represent me at my wedding. Could you help me out, Andrea?" asked Dr. Wilson.

After listening for a moment, Rita replied, "That's fine. Thank you. Can you come over tomorrow evening to help me get organized? 7 PM would work for me."

Turning to Shawn, she said, "Your mother must have been a wonderful person to have passed along so many endearing qualities. You also have inherited the best traits of your father. You not only do the right things, but in the right way, for people who need them the most.

"What were you doing when I was thirty and looking?" Hesitating, she warned him with a mock-threatening gesture, "Answer that one and this delightful moment could take an ugly turn."

CHAPTER 50

Butler-Wilson Nuptials

The Butler-Wilson wedding occurred on one of those beautiful fall days which makes living in the Midwest worthwhile. The leaves were starting to fall and the morning was chilly but warmed up quickly.

Shawn, Nick, three Diminico brothers, and the entire Donovan five arrived at 9 AM, one hour before the service. With Shawn and MJ directing, this crew moved excess furniture to the basement and the garage. Shawn had arranged to put all the Diminicos and Donovans in adjoining rooms after removing two doors, thereby permitting the members of both families to see and hear the service.

Guests began arriving at 9:45 and by 9:55 everyone was in place. This group of Catholics had become somewhat jaded, being raised in a seemingly endless string of baptisms, first communions, confirmations, weddings, and funerals. Yet they sensed that they were about to be part of something special; consequently, a hush settled over the room.

Rex had given Rita an engagement ring earlier in the week, and she joked that "everything was moving so fast and I'm so slow." Shawn had the wedding ring safely in his pocket. Rita was determined to stand during the service, but she had rented a wheel chair as a "fall back option," as she put it.

On Wednesday, Rita phoned a retired priest, Father Russel,

eighty-five and fragile, who had baptized Rita. She explained the situation, including her serious illness, and asked if he would officiate.

"I may not have more than 15-20 minutes in me for the service, dear," explained Father Russel.

"I may not have more than that myself, Father."

He laughed, "It's just the sort of thing your mother would say, Rita. You, your mom, and your dad were everything a family is supposed to be. At the time your mother passed, your father simply couldn't bear it. He was determined to live until you were on your own, but the heart had gone out of him. It left me wondering if a person can love a spouse too much.

"When I baptized you and looked into your eyes, it was one of the few times I ever regretted being a priest instead of fathering children. There was a nobility in those little peepers that you've never lost.

"Changing the topic, why did you choose me to officiate, Rita?"

"I want to send a message to all the younger people here that twilight can be beautiful, too. I'm telling them that if you find and cherish good people, lovely things happen. I'm telling them it's never too late. Finally, if you're good at something, don't quit doing it because, if you do, part of you will start dying at the same time."

"You don't mind if I use some of that, do you, dear?" "I'd be disappointed if you didn't, father," she replied.

Reflecting on the discussion with Father Russel as she stood in front of him, Rita wobbled somewhat, but Rex had a firm grip on her. An ecstatic Andrea faced a proud Shawn as Father Russel began the service, which he had promised to abbreviate.

"We are gathered here to bind Rita Wilson and Rex Butler in matrimony. I have married hundreds of couples but have never met two people better suited for one another.

"They both have chosen the high road in managing their lives. Since this avenue isn't heavily traveled and there is little signage, it's not surprising that it's taken them some time to find each other.

"Rex has proven himself worthy to marry Rita, because he has already been a good husband and father. When his wife passed years ago, he did not wallow in self-pity; instead, he put his energies into being a good father and model citizen. Another sterling quality is that Rex looks down the road, rather than over his shoulder.

"By contrast, Rita remained steadfast to a college which she helped elevate in each passing year. Her brothers, nephews, nieces, Godchildren, and fellow employees will testify to her worthiness.

"These two mature adults have chosen to share their lives in the remaining time God has allotted them." At these words, there was an audible intake of breath.

"Will anyone dare challenge the worthiness of Rita Wilson and Rex Butler to marry each other on this, the seventeenth of September, 1980." The response was perfect silence.

"Shawn, will you produce the ring?"

Shawn stepped forward and gave Rex the ring, receiving a sparkling smile from Rita for his efforts.

"Rita Wilson, do you accept Rex Butler as your husband, to love and respect, until death separates you?"

"I do."

"Rex Butler, do you accept Rita Wilson as your wife, to love and respect, until death separates you?"

"I do."

"I now pronounce you man and wife. You may kiss the bride," intoned Father Russel.

With that, Rex turned Rita to him and they shared a kiss, so gentle and sincere, that it would be talked about for years. The hush that followed was dictated by a reluctance to break the spell.

Finally, someone began clapping and the rest joined in, before a rash of kisses and hugs erupted. Shawn kissed Dr. Wilson in her wheel chair and she let go of him only after thanking him with her eyes. Sensing a shy male, the Diminico girls surrounded Nick and were taking turns kissing him, before a laughing Joan rescued him. Andrea received the same treatment from the Donovan brothers, before Shawn stepped in. Molly Jean kissed Rex and cuddled with him briefly, while her brothers headed for the beer keg in the backyard.

There were no presents to be opened because Rita had requested that any gifts be made in the form of donations to Second City Hospice. No one dared cross her under these circumstances.

Matt Donovan and Mr. Diminico, neither unfamiliar to the dangers of drunk driving, were collecting car keys and designating drivers. Agnes Donovan and Mrs. Diminico linked arms before making a party sweep and talking with everyone; they were in their glory and had a great time. When the beer was gone, everyone headed to Jerry's restaurant for the reception.

Rita's brothers, Mike and Jeff, had flown in from the West Coast with their families. The siblings were delighted to see their sister so happy, despite the circumstances, and agreed that Rex was every bit the man that Rita said he was.

Hugged out, Rita was exhausted and retired early, after insisting that Rex stay until the guests were gone. Shawn assembled the same crew that started the day and the furniture was carefully put back in place. Rex made it a point to shake every crew member's hand. All realized that a handshake or thank you from Rex was high praise, indeed.

Rita was awakened when Rex joined her in bed and grasped her right hand gently as he drifted off to sleep. He had managed a perfect ending to a perfect day, as she smiled and cried softly.

CHAPTER 51

Rita's Farewell Tour

Rex had moved into Rita's home temporarily. Despite his capable care-giving skills and comforting presence, she concluded after the wedding that it would soon be time for her to enter a hospice.

At Rex's request and because of Dr. Wilson's outstanding reputation, Dr. Liam Kelly, CEO of Second City Hospice, paid her a courtesy visit two days after the wedding. Rex detained him as he was parking the car and filled him in on the details of their recent marriage. Later, after he answered several of her questions, she nodded off and Dr. Kelly suggested a nap.

Rex walked him outside and had little trouble in talking him into sharing lunch at a nearby restaurant. Upon stepping inside, Rex pointed politely at a back booth and the cheerful waitress walked them to the location he requested and left menus.

"Your wife enjoys an excellent reputation on the West Side, Rex, but if you'll pardon the observation, she's even better than advertised. She doesn't feel cheated by her illness and obviously loves you deeply. Most people don't even know anybody that formidable, and here you are, married to her. As you know, she's more concerned about you and Shawn than herself."

Before baring his soul, Rex wanted to know more about Dr. Kelly. He learned that Kelly had grown up in a big South Side family and had married a young woman from the West Side. He had four children, eleven grandchildren, and was expecting his first great grandchild. Kelly's wife had died a slow, painful death five years ago, at which time he quit practicing medicine and opened Second City Hospice.

Rex asked about his wife and Kelly said that she was the rock upon which their family was built. He said convincingly that he had found a truly good woman, whom "I could never match and didn't try. Pure and simple, this woman was just better than I was, no matter how hard I tried. Perhaps your experience was different," Dr. Kelly inquired.

"Not at all. I thought I was doing something wrong, because she always operated at a higher level," responded Rex.

"My wife had an extra gear that I didn't have and so does Rita," Kelly interjected.

"My first wife did, too, but it was a different gear from Rita's due to the kind of lives they led. Anyway, each had a capacity or a reservoir which I do not," Rex said.

"I think we're talking about the same thing," agreed Dr. Kelly. "I just hadn't thought about it in your terms. This difference we're discussing becomes painfully apparent when the woman nears the end. My wife had a perspective which I could never fully share. She made a case for everyone and saw value in people that I could not appreciate. She was particularly kind to people with whom we were not close. When asked once why we did not see a couple very often with whom we had had great fun, she told me that anybody can have a good time with them and that we should socialize with others who need us more."

The food came and they ate their sandwiches. After exchanging hospice details in the parking lot, they stood momentarily, enjoying the beautiful day. Two kids in a rusty Ford slammed on the brakes a mere two feet away, with one yelling at them "to go back to the old folks home." The distinguished military veteran with a terminally ill wife and the retired physician who had done little else but help people since he was a boy simply folded their arms and stared at the noisy pair. Sensing that they were in over their heads, the boys looked at each other blankly, before the driver pulled away slowly.

With Rita's guidance and Second City instructions, Rex had packed her bags for the trip to the hospice. Her lack of balance, bathroom issues, and a dramatic increase in the pain from the cancer which had radiated from her lower stomach to several major organs made the decision to leave her home a no-brainer. She made a strong effort to stay awake during the trip to Second City, which was near downtown.

Rita had asked Rex to drive past Wrigley Field and then on to Lake Shore Drive south into downtown. She called it her farewell tour.

She gazed out the window, saying, "What a city! It's like a human checkerboard. We have clusters of Irish, Italians, Poles, Greeks, Jews, Blacks, Orientals, and dozens of other groups, who are starting to mix and match.

"There's a vibrancy and strength here that would be tough to duplicate. Though proud to be who we are, we are painfully aware of our limitations, using them as street gestures against an outside world that often holds us in contempt."

As they approached Wrigley Field, she noted a Latin group

walking slowly and talking rapidly. "Look at them, sharing their dreams, hopes, and fears. Aren't they wonderful?" she asked.

Rex responded, "Yes, they are. Many people worry about our future, but when I see groups like this, I don't worry. They'll figure a way. Won't they?"

Rita smiled in agreement and turned her attention to Wrigley Field, home of the Cubs. "I'm glad I'll never see the Cubs win the World Series. I feel that one of the reasons that Chicagoans have such wonderful families and strong neighborhoods is that we and the Cubs have never considered ourselves quite good enough. There's something noble about our struggle, and I feel privileged to have been a part of it. I'm not sure it would be healthy for the city to have the Cubs win.

"I know it's a little out of the way, but will you drive back to Western Avenue and then south past the Biograph Theater, the scene of the 1934 John Dillinger shooting. That scoundrel always captured my imagination!" Rita pronounced.

"He robbed and killed, but he had soul, and he gave people hope. Millions rooted for him.

"I had dozens of boys and girls like him in my art classes. When I dealt with rascals, they knew I liked them and that somehow I understood. I admired the way they held their chins up in a world that treated them badly. When they picked themselves up and came back for more, I used to wink at them, indicating we knew something that most of the rest of the world didn't understand.

"Stop as close to the Biograph as you can, please. I want to recreate the shooting in my mind. There are some of us who feel that the only way Dillinger could have been caught was through betrayal. He was too tough and smart to be beaten straight up. Had he not trusted that Romanian woman, some of us feel he would still be on the run, like a pinball on a perpetual roll."

Rex marveled at the rogue side of this wonderful woman, who seemed to have a soft spot for bad boys. How many other dimensions did she have, which he was unlikely to discover?

"I'm getting tired. Take me to my new home, Jeeves, by way of the Outer Drive," she laughed.

By the time he turned on to Lake Shore Drive, she was sleeping contentedly. Rex was proud to be her chauffeur.

Rita settled in quickly at the Second City Hospice. She had declined chemotherapy and decided to let nature take its course. Since she still had her hair, which draped attractively on her pillow, Rita was easily the most attractive of the fifteen women in residence, because many were ravaged by their medical treatments.

All but a few of the nineteen men acquired the habit of walking by her room slowly and looking in on her. Rex, a frequent visitor, initially was annoyed by the intrusion but then realized that for these men, Rita would be the last beautiful woman they would ever see.

Shawn visited her twice, not staying long, since she could fall asleep at any time. He laughed when she reminded him to take out the trash and brush his teeth.

Rita apologized, "I'm new at this mothering thing, but I certainly like it. I have so much to say and so little pep. Thanks for sharing your dad. You and Molly Jean will make wonderful parents, if that's what you want.

"I'll visit with your mom on the Other Side. We'll have lots to talk about," she promised Shawn.

"I'm sure she'll love you. Everyone does," he observed.

"That may be so, but they all belong to others. Your dad is mine and you are part mine, if only for a brief time," she stated. "I know it's selfish and that it shouldn't mean so much to me, but it does."

Shawn responded, "There are hundreds of people who would do anything to repay you for your service and kindness. What I will remember most about you is that when your name comes up at public gatherings, everyone speaks more softly out of respect for you.

"What a wonderful legacy you will leave."

Rex stayed at the hospice on a cot which Dr. Kelly provided. On the ninth night of her stay, he turned to leave and she would not let go of his hand.

"Please stay," she requested. "The pain is worse now. I may need both your hands, and I want to die holding on to you."

She soon closed her eyes and was gone. With great effort, in part because he did not want to let go, Rex disengaged Rita's death grip and went to find Dr. Kelly. The next evening, the kindly doctor remarked that he did not see it as a coincidence that two of the hospice's male residents passed within twenty-four hours of Rita's death. Dr. Kelly suggested that these men may have expired because their intrusiveness had been keeping them alive.

CHAPTER 52

Weddings A Pair

The Browns were the driving force behind the Nick-Joan wedding, while Agnes Donovan, after a meeting with Rex, propelled the Shawn-Molly Jean ceremony. The older adults were mildly tense but the four principals took things in stride, because they had known their partners for many years and were well familiar with their new in- laws. Wedding day surprises, then, were unlikely and none occurred. The Brown-Conley nuptials were scheduled for 8 AM. Being told that Joan was not given to smiles, Jerry Diminico, with the help of a friend from Western Union, had the following telegram delivered to her at the church at 7:45 AM. "My Wonderful Joanie-

Nick is not nearly good enough for you. Fly to Nashville tonight, and I will take you to Paris and make you mine.

Your teddy bear, Elvis Presley"

The telegram apparently had the desired effect. To everyone's surprise, Joan was radiant, even a little giddy. Courtesy of Rex and the Diminico brothers, Joan's parents, each in varying stages of dementia and now living in an assisted living facility, were escorted to and from the church with great care and without incident. Both Conleys did recognize Nick and chatted with him briefly. Seeing Joan so happy, Nick loosened up and even teased Shawn about his tux, telling him that it was made of Silicon.

By any measure, it was a wonderful ceremony. The priest and the altar boys were tipped handsomely, and the event may have broken the matrimonial record for smiles per person. The altar was beautifully decorated with flowers and candles. Nick and Joan kissed like they meant it, all four parents were teary-eyed, and the beautifully adorned church altar sparkled.

The church had cooperated nicely by allowing those connected with either wedding to use the church hall at any time during the morning. Dozens of participants and guests took advantage of this courtesy and sampled the coffee and punch provided.

The Butler-Donovan ceremony also went well, though the Donovan brothers were badly hung over. The respect that Shawn and Molly demonstrated towards each other permeated the throng assembled in the tidy, old church.

Shawn and Matt Donovan had met two nights before at Jerry's restaurant for dinner. Shawn anticipated the standard warnings from the father of the bride, after being asked by Matt to "hear him out."

"As you know, Agnes and I love MJ deeply. I'd be lying to you if I told you that we are ready for her to leave our home. She's been a steadying influence for her brothers, who need all the help they can get. I don't have to tell you what a comfort she has been to her mother.

"For me, Molly has been a reminder of my shortcomings as a husband. Times are changing, and cushioned by the police department, I have not changed with them. When I steamroller my way through a family crisis, I look at her and her body language tells me I'm not doing things the right way, even when I'm doing the right thing.

"This is where you come in. My wife loves you because you give her full credit as a responsible adult. My daughter loves you because you do the right things in a low-key, sensitive manner. She knows that you always take people's feelings into account and hold up your end.

"You have set the bar high for yourself, higher than I would have for any son-in-law. Here is what I expect from you. Stop by whenever you can. Continue to help me with my sons; they need you. Let's go out for a beer once in a while and compare notes. Check in with Agnes as often as you can; she's your biggest fan. Most importantly, continue to love my daughter as you change and grow. She's as good as she appears and will do anything for you if you treat her squarely.

"Your patience in listening to me has been admirable. What can I do for you?" Matt asked.

"I'll gladly do everything you've asked. I only ask one thing of you. When you have a chance, please visit my dad. He likes you and values your friendship."

"Done."

As they exchanged vows, Shawn peered directly into Molly Jean's eyes. If there was any question that she was making a lifetime commitment and that she expected one in return, her posture and firm voice dispelled any doubts. Besides assuming the role of wife, she also seemed to realize that it was up to her to fill in for Shawn's mother, a woman with great qualities, and for a stepmother who was an academic legend in Chicago. While some may have concluded that these were tough acts to follow, she welcomed the challenges.

Compared to her father and brothers, she figured Shawn and his dad would be a day at the beach.

After warming up at his own wedding, Nick performed admirably. He looked relaxed and moved smoothly, both recent additions to Nick's repertoire. Nick had always been there for Shawn and that was unlikely to change.

Agnes smiled non-stop, and Rex and Matt cut imposing figures as fathers of the groom and bride. Their leadership was needed for the reception at Jerry's, which was closed to the public until 4 PM. When the spoons were clattered as a demand for the brides to be kissed, the four newly weds kissed in unison, eliciting an endless barrage of "two-for-one" jokes, some in questionable taste.

When the Donovan brothers tried to sit this one out with their hangovers, Andrea, no longer the shy librarian, got the biggest laugh when she went to Steve, the huskiest of the brothers, dropped onto his lap, and gave him a noisy kiss. This display of affection stirred all the Donovan brothers, and a hysterical Shawn felt compelled to defend Andrea. When his attempts proved futile, Molly Jean discharged her brothers with strong shoves, while sarcastically thanking Shawn for his help, which she derisively termed "pitiful."

Thirty minutes later, Shawn and MJ slipped out and walked casually to their car, holding hands as they had done many times before. Neither was in any hurry to get back to their apartment. By their reckoning, they had nothing but time and wanted to savor the moment.

Nick and Joan also picked a good time to leave. Heading for their car, Nick, who had done so well up to this point, made the mistake of looking around.

"Your parents aren't here, Nick. It's just you and me now," she reminded him as she took his arm after poking him in the ribs.

He now realized that his life had become more complicated. Nick had become accustomed to checking with Shawn and then his parents. Joan had now moved to the front of the line, and if he forgot that, then troubles would arise. Nick was going to have to help Joan dissemble the many barriers that he had erected between himself and the world around him since he was a little boy.

Both couples had money, education, health, and good family support, making their marriages likely successes but not sure things. There were traps everywhere into which careless young married couples with similar advantages had fallen. On this day, though, optimism ruled. Observers assumed the marriages would be successful and instead devoted their time to speculating what forms these successes would take.

CHAPTER 53

Newly Weds

For their honeymoon, Shawn and Molly Jean stayed in a beautiful cottage on Lake Geneva for a week and remained in contact with Chicago by reading the *Chicago Tribune* and listening to WGN radio. They ate lunches and dinners at McDougal's Tap on the water, owned by the portly Jim McDougal, a retired Chicago policeman, and his wife. Jim served drinks and Kitty prepared pot roast, corned beef, or whatever she was in the mood to cook.

Learning that they were newly weds, the McDougals fussed over them. Bringing a bottle of brandy to their table after dinner each night, Jim told truly funny cop jokes. Shawn and Molly gathered that, after the second or third drink, that the stories were being embellished, but they did not mind a bit. One evening when a party from an adjoining table called for a drink as McDougal was in mid-story, he replied, "Not until I deliver the punch line." Stories well told without interruption trumped food and drink at McDougal's.

In the cottage on their last honeymoon evening, Shawn received a phone call from Danny Boyle in Chicago. Shawn and Danny had worked together frequently, since Shawn attended all the Democratic meetings that his schedule permitted. Danny attended both weddings, gave tasteful presents, and impressed everyone favorably.

"Shawn, this is Danny. I'm sorry to bother you on your honeymoon. Do you have five minutes for me?"

"Of course, Danny. I'm sorry that I didn't make more time for you at the wedding," he apologized.

"No apology necessary. I had a great time. Your friends and family are world class."

"Here's why I called. I have a proposition for you. As you know, I work for the County Democratic Committee. Tom Leahy, State Senator from our district, died last night and we need to replace him in Springfield for twelve months. They are having a special election in six weeks. Will you help us?"

"Sure, I can work around my law studies. Which candidate will I be working for?" Shawn asked.

"For the first time in our dealings, you're missing the point. The Dems are going into young and smart mode. We want you as our candidate. You'd be cinch to win," Boyle predicted.

Thrown off balance, Shawn explained, "I will need time to sort this out, time which you don't have. I've just signed a lifetime contract with a tough customer who's sitting right next to me," he joked.

Privy to the entire conversation, Molly Jean responded with a playful kick to his shins but appeared interested. From extensive exposure to the police force and community agencies, she grasped how important it was to grab opportunities when they presented themselves. Shawn and MJ understood that the carousel was not obliged to stop for them again.

"Molly and I need a conversation. Can I call you in the morning?" asked Shawn.

"It would be more convenient if I called you. Can I reach you at this number at 9 AM?" inquired Danny.

"Fine. Talk with you then," promised Shawn.

Shawn was prepared to make a lengthy plea to spend six months in Springfield and to offer Molly Jean a chance to come with him. He also had to think of how he would finish his law degree at Clement. MJ got to her feet and began pacing.

"Do you want to do this?" she asked. "Yes, I do."

"For a number of reasons, I don't want to go to Springfield, but I do want part of the action. I won't hurt your chances and think I can be of some help. Won't you have an office here, also?" Molly asked.

"Yes, of course."

"Couldn't I work part time in the Chicago office?" MJ inquired. "Certainly."

"How about you finishing law school?" she wondered.

"Clement and the Democratic Party work together on numerous ventures. Clement is nothing if not flexible. I have almost completed my coursework. I may have to delay taking the bar exam, but I can live with that," Shawn stated.

"Two questions. Are you prepared to wait a year to have a baby, because even without a bouncing Butler, we will still be busy?"

"I'm willing to wait two years, but no longer," Molly responded. "That's more than fair. My second question concerns your schedule during my short campaign. Even though as a Democrat I should win convincingly, important people are going to be gauging my future prospects in part on the basis of our performance during the next six weeks. I need you with me for that time. You engage people easily and win their respect quickly."

"I'm suppose to start work for the Metropolitan Sanitary District on Monday, but they have a political dimension and I'm betting that I can delay my start date without being penalized," she assumed.

"Then it's a deal?" Shawn asked.

"Yes. Let's certify this arrangement," she challenged him. "What did you have in mind?"

"A nightcap back at McDougal's," she suggested. "You're on."

Before the Butlers left the room, Nick called and explained that Mrs. Conley had passed. Shawn offered to drive back to the city immediately but Nick indicated that this would not be necessary.

While the Butlers had enjoyed a fine week, the newly married Browns had called off their honeymoon trip, due to Mrs. Conley's stroke. It took both Joan and Nick to manage this situation, because Mr. Conley was frantic and angry concerning his wife's death which he could not accept. Nick was able to sit with him and calm him down but when Mr. Conley saw his daughter, he quickly became agitated.

After his wife's passing, Mr. Conley refused to eat and started throwing things. His doctor insisted upon restraints, against which he struggled mightily. The situation deteriorated quickly from that point. He went in and out of comas for four days before passing. Losing both parents in a hurry, Joan became slightly withdrawn.

Nick, however, was more shaken than Joan. She had seen this coming for years, but Nick had underestimated the severity of the Conley's problems. During the crisis, Nick's parents stepped in and were a great comfort to Joan. At the same time, Nick, who had learned the therapeutic value of a hug as a small child, and Joan hugged each other for several minutes at a time. In an already solid relationship, Nick and Joan were drawn even closer by the passing of her parents.

CHAPTER 54

State Senator Butler

With Nick handling the details, Molly Jean impressing everyone, and Shawn shaking so many hands he cramped, everything fell into place. Senator Butler won the special election convincingly with 65% of the vote. They then turned to the chore of building the Butler office team.

Shawn was able to hire a retired former state senator, Cecil Andford, to work with Nick in setting up the Springfield office. Mr. Andford, as he liked to be called, was starchy but seemed to know everything about Springfield and had a line on anybody who had ever worked there in public office.

Andford could abide anything but bad manners. Since Shawn and Nick had been properly raised by courteous adults, Andford treated them with the respect he was being given and they got along fine. On the occasions when a visitor to the Butler office was rude or demanding, Mr. Andford would materialize and lead the offender on a one-way trip into the hall. Team Butler members wondered how he managed to disperse problem visitors but were too smart to ask.

In an effort to balance the generation gap, Nick found a sixty-year old staff assistant, Mary Burke, who immediately became everybody's favorite aunt. She had been overheard to say, "Shawn and Nick are such nice young boys. I would never let anything bad happen to them."

No one left the Butler office or spoke to its staff on the phone without having their problem addressed. In addition, Mary handed out licorice sticks, patting the recipient's arm while doing so. She gave a second stick to hard cases, asking, "I'm sure you have someone nice to share this with, don't you? Make sure to tell your friend where you got it, dear."

On the rare instances when Mary was unable to manage a situation, Mr. Andford could. The Butler office team was firmly in place, permitting Shawn the opportunity to prowl the Capitol.

He made it a point to meet each of the predominantly veteran crew of Democrats, one way or another. The grouchy Democrat House Speaker had called him to his office and told him that until further notice, he should be "seen but not heard." Shawn did not intend to heed this warning but realized that he would have to tread carefully.

Now at least slightly familiar with all the Democrats, he felt it was time to step across the aisle, tricky business for a freshman. Since he knew few Republicans personally, Shawn asked Mr. Andford to fill him in on the thirty-seven names listed on the Republican Senate roster. Explaining his intent to co-sponsor bills and otherwise cooperate with Republicans, Shawn worked with Mr. Andford in identifying eleven likely prospects and six question marks, with twenty being a definite no-can-do.

From the no-can-do list he spotted his arch-enemy and St. Orem's former linebacker, Marty Steinbrenner. There were two ways to deal with the Steinbrenners of the world: try to hide from them or walk through their front door. Shawn was a front-door guy and figured the sooner the better. He did not want to have Steinbrenner catch him unawares in a hallway so that he could put on a show for his colleagues; instead, he preferred to surprise him.

Knowing that staffers invariably arrived before the representatives, he decided to wait in his outer office and catch Steinbrenner on his way in the following morning. Because he refused to identify himself before Steinbrenner arrived, he was engaged in a mild dispute with a staff member, when he heard the burly senator talking in the hallway as he lumbered towards his office.

Shawn stood off to one side so that he could jump in front of Steinbrenner as he entered, shake his hand quickly, hand him his business card, and begin talking. Steinbrenner was looking over his shoulder, finishing a conversation, when Shawn presented himself.

"Hello, Marty. I'm Shawn Butler, Illinois' newest legislator. You will remember me from St. Ignio's. As I recall, St. Orem's hung on to beat us in a close game in the city playoffs several years ago."

Turning to leave, Shawn said "I'm headed for a meeting now but perhaps we can get together for a beer. It was good to see you again!"

Steinbrenner stammered, "Butler…"

"Yes, that's right, Senator Butler," he said, turning at the door. "Don't be a stranger."

In his wake, he left a puzzled staff member and a steaming Steinbrenner. Shawn knew the battle was just beginning.

Feeling good about himself, Shawn walked quickly in search of Senator Gary Sloan. From the eleven likely Republicans, he had identified one of particular interest, Rep. Gary Sloan from downstate Carbondale.

He had done some research on Sloan, discovering that he was a Mensa member, centrist in a Republican Party moving right, heart patient, bachelor, skeptical Catholic, and son of a world-famous medical researcher. Shawn went directly to Sloan's office and introduced himself to his aide. As they finished their discussion, Sloan stepped into the doorway and gave Shawn a stern look.

"What's a Democrat doing over on this side of the building?" Sloan asked.

"Wanting to see you this morning before your dance card fills up. I imagine things are pretty hectic here," Shawn ventured as he approached Sloan and shook his hand.

"Your intuition has let you down. Since you're here, why don't you come in. You are my first visitor and will probably be my last before my 10 AM committee meeting," Sloan conceded.

"Would that be the Health Committee" inquired Shawn.

Sloan studied Shawn, stating, "I'm impressed. You probably know more about me than my colleagues on this side of the aisle."

Shawn responded, "I wouldn't have stopped by until I did." "What do you want, Butler?"

Realizing he could not con Sloan if he wanted to, Shawn decided to reply directly. "I would like to work on a bi-partisan project. Since you're smarter and more available than most of your fellow Republicans, I thought I would start with you."

Catching himself from laughing, Sloan inquired, "Are you staying in Springfield this weekend?"

"Yes, I have too much legislative material to learn to go back to

Chicago, but I'm newly married and Molly Jean's coming here on Saturday." Seeing Sloan's disappointment, he quickly added, "However, I am available for a few hours early Saturday if you have time for me. Do you usually stay here on the weekends?"

"Most of the time. Travel presents problems for me," Sloan acknowledged, while tapping the left side of his chest. "There is a lot of real estate between Springfield and Carbondale."

"Is it your heart?" asked Shawn.

"Yes. If I live like a monk, I'll live as long as you will. If I get frisky, I could go in an instant. My damaged heart keeps me on my toes," he joked sadly. "I take a two-hour walk and flop on Saturday morning. I sit when I get tired. Would you care to join me and talk about ways of doing the state's business together?" asked Gary.

Shawn realized that this question was more plea than suggestion. This loner was reaching out to him and Shawn would have accepted, even if it was inconvenient, which it was not. They agreed to meet at 8 AM on Saturday in a local park and exchanged phone numbers if weather presented problems.

CHAPTER 55

A Bipartisan Idea

On the day of their meeting, the sky was overcast, but rain was not expected until mid-afternoon. Senator Sloan was sitting on a park bench when Shawn arrived.

Before Shawn sat down, Gary decreed, "Taping our conversation is out. I've been burned once already. I will, however, take notes and would be offended if you didn't."

Shawn fished out a folded sheet of paper and ball point from his jacket pocket, and Gary began to walk slowly. Shawn let Sloan set the tone for the conversation, since he could not currently do anything bipartisan without him.

For the first hour, Butler and Sloan sparred back and forth, reviewing the prime issues of this year's coming session: health, transportation, higher education funding, and the environment. Each understood that a bipartisan effort was doomed if both Shawn and Gary were not enthusiastic about the problem and in total agreement with their proposed solution. Both agreed that their bill could not be too costly and must make each party look good. There could be no downside to whatever venture was sponsored.

Butler-Sloan eliminated health care because the federal government was the elephant in the room, which left no space for the union of a loner Republican centrist and a young freshman Democrat. Mr. Andford had told Shawn that there was already a large transportation bill coming from the Republican side; Sloan confirmed the existence of this bill in draft form and said that the sponsors were heavy hitters. The higher education funding issue was triangulated with unions, university chancellors, and the state community college office, leaving no action for bit players.

Shawn was glad that the walk was over because Gary looked spent. They returned to the bench where they started and decided that their most likely possibility, by default, was somewhere within the sprawling, complex, environmental issues of Illinois. Shawn suggested getting Nick involved because he was creative and smart. Gary said that he had a person with similar qualities on his staff, Jennifer Osborne.

Reflecting the original Butler-Sloan discussion, Shawn had encouraged Nick to think in terms of low cost, low risk, and high visibility. During the following week, Nick and Jennifer met from Monday through Thursday for two hours each day in Sloan's conference room.

On Wednesday, Shawn and Nick sat down for a status report. Nick was vague when asked how Jennifer measured up as a working partner, and Shawn decided to let it pass.

Again focusing upon the benefits of playing small ball, Nick explained that their idea was to retrofit two trucks and to form two teams to conduct mobile water analyses. Illinois had recently faced a series of polluted water situations, and lengthy response times had aggravated the problems and drawn stinging public criticism. By deploying two fully supported five-member teams, it was anticipated that responses could be reduced to twelve hours or less.

There were other advantages to the mobile trucks. Rather than having samples shipped back to Chicago or St. Louis, the analysis could be done on-site. Another consideration was the PR value of having a clearly marked state truck nearby within hours of a disaster. Citizens like to see their tax dollars at work, particularly when lives and property are threatened. A conspicuously parked Illinois Water Emergency Analysis truck could alleviate panic in a crisis. Finally, these teams, composed of a driver, chemist, engineer, geologist, and diver could train local emergency teams when not responding to emergencies.

Shawn was impressed and told Nick so. With Nick's blessing, Shawn planned a meeting of all concerned for Friday afternoon. The meeting, which promised to last at least two hours, was delayed for a variety of reasons until four o'clock. There were four participants: Shawn, Nick, Sloan, and Jennifer Osborne.

Senator Sloan, who had spoken with Jennifer only briefly before the meeting, convened the gathering in his conference room and politely asked Shawn whether he had anything to say. Shawn laughed when he said that he only knew enough about the idea to know that it was cheap, safe, and highly visible, adding, "What's not to like?"

Senator Sloan joined in the light mood and asked Jennifer to begin the explanation. She spoke at length and would have kept going if Senator Sloan had not interrupted her, asking for Nick to weigh in. Very smoothly, he picked up where Jennifer had left off, but only managed three sentences before Jennifer jumped in and insisted on continuing the presentation. Shawn and Nick took her rudeness in stride but Sloan squirmed and squinted. Nick retreated mentally into that distant place of his.

Sloan finally cut her off, while indicating that he liked the idea. Shawn agreed, and the senators specified the visuals they would need to support the presentation Shawn would make to the Democratic Senate President, Eric Flynn, and Sloan, to the Republican Senate Minority Leader.

When the meeting ended, Sloan asked Shawn if he could stay for a moment. Shawn nodded to Nick, telling him he would stop by Jennifer's office and collect him. Senator Sloan needed a moment to collect himself because he was having difficulty putting himself in an apologetic posture.

Sloan began, "I'm sorry about that. Jennifer evidently has trouble sharing her toys. Nick's fingerprints are all over this project and he has done fine work. I'm really excited. In case you missed it, this is my excited look," he joked.

"I don't doubt that Jennifer was of some help, but she has Springfield fever and has trouble thinking small, or at least less than spectacular. On the other hand, your guy gets it."

Shawn explained, "Nick doesn't need the applause and is the most forgiving person I know. He is my friend and if he is the only one I ever had, I would get by.

Looking at Shawn, Sloan quipped, "I really ought to try this friend thing. I've heard a lot about it."

Pausing, he observed, "Thank you, Shawn. It's nice doing business with adults. We could use more of them in the Legislature.

"By now, Jennifer will have concluded that this session did not go well for her and will probably receive my criticism more constructively than if this had not happened. I believe she has the capacity to be a fine staffer."

They agreed to meet the following week and shared a handshake and a smile. The Butler-Sloan bipartisan effort was taking shape!

CHAPTER 56

Bipartisan Expansion

Shawn spent the next week going about his business as Nick and Jennifer drafted a bill, Mobile Water Emergency Analysis (MWEA). Shawn had made a fifteen minute appointment with Democratic Senate President Flynn for Friday at 2 PM, citing MWEA as the purpose and having a copy of the draft delivered to the Senate President's Office on Friday at 10 PM, purposefully leaving little time for review. This would be the last time he would underestimate Flynn.

When shown into the Senate President's office, Flynn was holding the MWEA copy between his thumb and forefinger as if the document was diseased. His expression suggested that he had eaten something that did not agree with him.

"What's the meaning of this, Butler?" he roared.

Without hesitation or fear, Shawn proclaimed, "I wanted to see if a small bipartisan project is possible. It is. I wanted to see if I could find a Republican I could work with. I did. Finally, I wanted to see if my chief of staff has what it takes to work with the other side of the aisle by preparing a worthy project. He does."

Giving Shawn a hard look, Flynn stated "I showed this draft to two other Dems at lunch. They seem to think that there is a place for it," the President grudgingly admitted. "So I accept your unsolicited bill draft and will take it from here. That will be all."

Having Rex for a father and football as a sport prepared him for moments like this, so he gathered his materials quickly without making eye contact and headed for the door. The Senate President studied him carefully and spoke again before Shawn could leave the room.

"Butler, do you think you can prepare another one of your small bipartisan projects, this time on higher education funding for private schools, or is the Butler team just a one-trick pony?"

"We can do it, sir," as he turned and faced the Senate President.

"Call tomorrow at noon for the name of your Republican partner and the topic I choose," instructed Senator Flynn. "Any questions?"

"No. sir," Shawn replied.

"Well, you only have seven days to complete this education draft. Why are you wasting your time blocking my doorway?"

Shawn turned and smiled his way back to his office, feeling as though he was back in the Corps. As he briefed his staff, Team Butler heard opportunity knocking and was eager to answer.

Later that day, Shawn received a call from Senator Sloan, telling him he was sorry that Shawn had been brushed aside. Sloan said he was angry that Shawn had been treated poorly and would be willing to make a public statement to that effect. Senator Sloan thought it unfair that he was going to have his own star polished as the result of a project for which Butler was the driving force.

"Please don't say or do anything rash, Gary. MWEA may turn out to be one of the best things that ever happened to me, no matter how indirectly. I enjoyed working with you and hope to do so again.

"Don't worry about me. I'll be fine. For now, we both have things to do.

"I know where to find you on Saturday mornings. Thank you for your support," offered Shawn in closing.

Nick was pleased that he was able to contribute through MWEA and was busy preparing a second bill, one which would likely be stronger and tighter than the first because of what he had learned about bill-drafting. Shawn again marveled at how Nick could create a major impact and make it look easy.

They exchanged information on long, slow runs each weekday morning, while lifting weights and swimming on the weekends. Butler and Brown were finely tuned and ready for bigger things.

Nick continued to work effectively, despite getting a call from Joan's doctor that confirmed that Joan was expecting. He confided to Shawn at dinner that this news far eclipsed BBW's Silicon Valley triumph. Nick said that Rex had already gotten the call from Mr. Brown and had responded with a hearty, "All right!"

Shawn was delighted because Nick and Joan were so pleased and because the baby coming along would be so loved. He chuckled to himself when envisioning the excitement in the home of Tim and Jane Brown, while congratulating Nick.

Shawn later received a terse call from Senate President Flynn, asking him what committee assignment he wanted. Without hesitation, Shawn answered, "Environmental Affairs." With his nerve and Nick's brains, he had long felt that they could be of the most help to the citizens of Illinois by promoting environmental causes. He knew Nick would be proud to bring a baby into the crowded Chicago area, for which he had worked to make the air and water cleaner and chemical use safer.

Flynn responded, "Done. Contact Senator Banks later today but not before 2 PM. I must speak with him first."

Before Shawn could answer, Flynn hung up. Things were starting to fall into place. Team Butler was on a roll!

CHAPTER 57

Shawn's Campaign Plan

Shawn was now faced with the eternal dilemma of politicians, how to apportion time between doing the people's work and campaigning for another term. His special election had given him only thirteen months to put his Springfield team together and to campaign in Chicago, whereas other legislators enjoyed a full forty-eight months to plan and balance these responsibilities.

While his Springfield office was running smoothly, the voters he needed to receive a full four-year term lived in Chicago. Shawn invited Danny Boyle to visit him in Springfield for three days, an invitation for which he apologized to Danny as being overdue. Shawn met with Mr. Andford and Mary to emphasize that Boyle was to be treated as very important. He had barely begun his explanation before both nodded that they well understood Boyle's critical role in Shawn's re-election.

While Shawn sat in committee meetings and on the Senate floor, Danny visited with Mr. Andford and Mary, and the three became fast friends. Appreciating their roles, Boyle took each to lunch separately, while the remaining staff member covered the office.

Danny impressed Andford with his knowledge of Illinois politics and picked the former senator's brain for details. In return, Mr. Andford was intrigued by Boyle's political insights of Chicago. After lunch with Mary, Danny felt warm and fuzzy. Though a seasoned political operative, Boyle still was able to learn from Mary's people skills. His visit helped everyone, and, as usual, he truly enjoyed himself.

On Danny's last night in Springfield, Shawn hosted a working dinner with Boyle, Nick, Andford, and Mary. To stress that Andford was not just window dressing, Shawn deferred to him on several occasions during the meal.

Over brandy, Shawn smiled at Nick and said, "We have to make some adjustments in Team Butler. Nick is going to be a papa and will be needed in Chicago for most of the next few months."

Turning to Mr. Andford, Shawn asked him if he had any interest in playing a more central role in the Springfield office. "I'm not asking can you, because your ability has been established beyond a doubt but do you care to spend your time this way, with heavy responsibilities from Tuesdays through Fridays?

Shawn paused, "While Nick and I are fussing over a solitary baby not yet born, we know you have many people in your life, including three grown children, eleven grandchildren, and..."

"And a new great-grandchild," Mr. Andford chimed in, amidst laughter. "Of course, I'll step up, particularly since you asked so politely. Thanks for your courtesy. You know, many senators lose their civility immediately upon their arrival here. I don't see that happening to you. If I do, I'll let you know."

"Then it's settled. If he is available, Nick will work weekends with me in Chicago and often Nick will not return with me to Springfield. If I am unavailable for vital campaign business by phone, try Danny Boyle. Mr. Andford and Mary will run the Springfield office when we are campaigning in Chicago," Shawn summarized.

By the time he got back to Danny's office in Chicago late on Friday afternoon, they were able to meet for thirty minutes. Boyle then asked if Shawn would take a ride with him to see the Butler campaign headquarters, which Molly Jean had approved. As they parked near the small building draped with Butler banners, Shawn sensed that something was in the wind.

Danny jumped in front of Shawn and opened the door widely for him as they entered the headquarters, just in time to be met with a huge roar. Every campaign worker was there. Shawn kissed MJ, and shook hands and hugged his way through the group. He was especially careful to treat the three dozen volunteers well, knowing their importance.

Boyle asked Shawn to say a few words. "Some of them haven't heard you speak. They want to know what you stand for and what the campaign structure looks like. Explaining your bipartisan approach would also answer some of the questions I've received."

After telling Boyle he needed five minutes to collect his thoughts, Shawn drew Nick into a hallway and tested his preliminary thinking. Consistent with his style, Nick said little in response to Shawn's trial statements but instead made faces which spoke volumes. Thanking Nick, Shawn headed for a makeshift podium.

Banging on the microphone and smiling, Boyle got everyone's attention and introduced himself as the Butler Campaign Coordinator. He thanked everyone for attending this "hastily arranged event" and gave Shawn several well supported compliments. With a rush of enthusiasm, Danny then introduced Nick Brown, "the best chief of staff in Springfield and owner of one of its finest minds."

Nick took the podium and looked carefully around the room. He did not need notes and made eye contact with many attendees.

"I have known Shawn Butler since we were in pre-school," he began softly. "He's always included me in things. Shawn could have chosen a more dynamic chief of staff; instead he picked me because we work well together.

"He was the Best Man at our wedding and will be Godfather to our child," as he swept his arm towards Joan who was six months along and smiling happily. The crowd cheered.

"I have never seen him treat anyone cruelly. Shawn is honest and his word is golden. When he shakes your hand on a deal, no paperwork is necessary.

"He and I can not campaign effectively without you. In the unlikely event that Danny Boyle can't answer your questions, ask me or Shawn," urged Nick in a louder voice.

"But now, it is my privilege to introduce to you the senator from this district, who wants four more years to do the people's business. Will you help us make that happen?"

The crowd responded with a strong, "Yes." An emotionally charged Nick, however, was not satisfied.

"I can't hear you," Nick teased.

The crowd erupted and Shawn bounded to the podium, shaking Nick's hand on the way. Before speaking, Shawn looked at Molly

Jean, who nodded her approval.

"A few years ago, this election would be a walkover for a Democrat. This is no longer the case, since large numbers of Republicans have moved into this district after graduating from college and professional schools. They are strongly allied with corporate interests, so their candidates have money and connections.

"If any of you have joined my ranks, expecting an easy victory, let me tell you otherwise. Yes, I'm a nice guy, but so is my opponent, Ned Strickland. I played football against him and also know he's tough and not afraid of hard work.

"I have a terrific wife and a great staff, but that is not going to be enough to insure my re-election. I feel that we are going to have to be contrarians to be successful.

"Here is what I propose. We are going to win on the strength of what we are *not* going to do. We will promise not to make any intrusive campaign phone calls on my behalf. We will promise not to send out any mailers. We will promise not to hang any signs in the district, other than on our headquarters, truck and bus.

"Too often, the candidate is on the defensive. We will put the burden on the voters, asking them one question, and one question only: What have you done for Chicago lately? Our message, then, is that we are not going to bother the voters with typical campaign tactics but that we want to know how they are helping our city improve. If they don't have an answer on the spot, ask them to call our office when they have one.

"For my part, I am going to be everywhere. I'll be outside when the churches and movie theaters let out, at the major intersections during rush hour, and as close to public libraries as the law allows. I will be a walking, talking hand-shaking machine. I want everyone in our district to know what their representative looks like.

"I plan to knock on at least one door of every block in our district. I will ride shotgun on a long, flat-bed truck with two signs: (1) Butler for State Senate and (2) What Have You Done for Chicago lately? On the truck, we will place a full-size poster of me which we will use when I am not there, explaining that I'm indisposed. Staff and volunteers will ride on a sixty-four seat bus. There will be no preferred seating. If I see my staff members clustering, I will break them up.

"We are going to be noisy. If we awaken an infant, we will apologize and offer the parent a diaper. If the noise irritates someone, hand them a piece of hard candy. I want the dentist vote, too.

"If complainers are terribly persistent, remind them that we will never call their home, clog their mail box, or leave signage in our wake. When we are around, everyone will know it, and when we are gone, the surroundings will be left as we found them."

"We will have blue T-shirts for volunteers and ask that you choose comfortable shoes. If you play a stringed instrument, bring it. Invite singing groups to join us. We will be a party on wheels.

"If my plan is too over-the-top for anyone, I ask that you leave now. If you choose to stay, I guarantee you that we will have more fun than any campaigners have ever had."

No one moved, and most were smiling, realizing that they were about to become part a grand experiment and liking the feeling. Someone yelled, "This is going to be a retro campaign."

Shawn smiled and pointed at the woman who had yelled, shouting "Retro. I love it. I will use that in my speeches. Please talk with me before you leave. You've helped me already."

The group chanted "Retro" several times with Shawn urging them on with fist pumps. The electric buzz in the air bonded everyone in the room. The Butler campaign had switched into high gear.

CHAPTER 58

The Campaign

The Butler Campaign was a blur, mixing improvisation, music, short speeches, and corny jokes on and around the truck. Team Butler on wheels became so popular that two volunteers at campaign headquarters handled nothing but calls regarding the four-per-week parties. The events were scheduled strategically throughout the voting district. The city police insisted on receiving an advance campaign schedule, but Shawn chuckled when he realized that the police, on duty and off, attended these events because they and their families enjoyed themselves, not because they expected trouble.

Inevitably, the newspapers picked up the story and assigned reporters to follow Team Butler. Danny and Shawn had set a few rules regarding alcohol use, but everyone behaved themselves, because they did not want to be relieved of their duties. Shawn, Danny, and Nick spent hours training these volunteers.

A jealous Marty Steinbrenner assembled a dozen gang members to break up a campaign party. Meanwhile, Shawn had prepared a contingency plan with Matt Donovan to stop any rough stuff.

While the police were on their way, Shawn and Marty wound up nose to nose and a crowd formed. Steinbrenner had put on at least thirty pounds but was still strong. He rushed Shawn, who dodged and tripped him. Badly embarrassed, Marty threw several wild punches before grabbing Shawn in a vise-like grip, as the police arrived.

Between the Butler name on the campaign truck and support from the police working the event, they were prepared to arrest Steinbrenner. Shawn said, "No, leave him go. Senator Steinbrenner won't be back, will you, Marty?" Steinbrenner looked like he wanted to go home.

Republicans tried copying the Butler mobile campaign concept with little success, largely because they were too controlling. Team Butler knew how to wing it. Many older Democrats were somewhat jealous, but Shawn kept them happy by sparing them a few hours to speak at their campaign events. Mindful of his tender years, he made it a point to listen and learn when in the presence of his senate and house colleagues, several twice his age.

Shawn was considered a rock star and quickly achieved iconic status. When she was not helping Joan, MJ spent time preventing him from getting a big head by good-naturedly teasing him about his shortcomings, such as his animated but clumsy attempts at dancing. Privately, his staff members referred to him as a dancing retro robot.

Shawn liked the way the campaign was going and saw that November 2, election day, would almost coincide with Joan's due date. Election day came first and Team Butler won in a rout, capturing 61% of the vote.

His Republican opponent, Ned Strickland, conceded early on election night, congratulating Shawn sincerely. "Once again, I played on a bigger, stronger squad against you and again, you outfoxed us. Your closely knit teams in high school had fun and beat us when that should never have happened. In this election, we Republicans were so impressed with our size and money, that we didn't notice how starchy and muscle-bound we are.

"When I heard what the Butler Campaign was doing, I went out one night to watch your campaign from across a street. Even at that distance, it was obvious that you were on to something. I learned a lot from this experience, and I plan to live my life a little differently as a result. I will push our two daughters to work hard in learning things but I'm going to see that they have fun while doing it," he stated.

"I won an election but you're ahead in an important category, 2-0," Shawn countered generously, in reference to Ned's daughters.

"It's time for you to build a family, Butler. People love Molly Jean and she helped you, perhaps more than you know.

"You're a natural politician. You can go as far as you want."

Shawn replied, "Thanks, Ned. You have class.

"I want to learn what I missed during the campaign. Will you have lunch with me next week?" asked Shawn.

"OK, but don't put it on your public schedule. I would be honored to sit down with you, but I can't tell anybody. I hope you understand?" asked Ned.

"Sure thing. Shall I wear a big nose and glasses?" joked Shawn.

There was money left in the campaign treasury and Shawn asked Nick and Danny to spend it by preparing a personalized, framed thank you note for each volunteer. The text was designed to display at least two unique contributions made by each volunteer and a statement of how much Team Butler appreciated their efforts. Shawn, Nick, and Danny would later sign all of the documents personally; there would be no Xeroxed signatures on a Team Butler thank you card.

Nick and Danny jumped on this task eagerly and the volunteers received their thank you packages from Shawn in person within ten days. There were many emotional moments when Shawn knocked on their doors, and he was met with happy tears and enthusiastic hugs.

Shawn doubled over laughing when Jerry Manion, perhaps their hardest worker, assured Shawn that, "if necessary, he (Jerry) would take care of anybody who caused the Butlers any problems." Shawn sobered quickly when he realized that Manion was serious.

The three principals met in a debriefing meeting three days after the election. Nick and Danny, always willing to listen to Shawn, waited to see which way he was going to take the team.

"Danny, why did we win so convincingly?" began Shawn.

"You were a good candidate and ran a novel campaign," replied Danny. "You surprised your opponent and everyone else."

"How do you see it, Nick?" Shawn persisted.

"You only had thirteen months to make mistakes, and you didn't make any promises, that you would gag on later," answered Nick.

"So I caught everyone by surprise and didn't do much wrong. That's not exactly a ringing endorsement, is it?" he asked rhetorically. "Those certainly are not sufficient reasons to vote for me four years from now, are they?" he continued.

"I say we start our next campaign tomorrow. Here is an idea which Nick provided but that we did not have time to implement this year: Team Butler goes transparent. We prepare and distribute a monthly flyer on how I'm spending my time and energy in doing the people's business. We will put the leaflets in bars, Laundromats, and stores. I don't want them stuffed in screen doors and rained on. I don't want litter. I want residents to clamor for these flyers. I want voters passing them on to their neighbors.

"If necessary, I'm willing to spend some of my Silicon money to fund this leaflet. I'll ask MJ to interview residents for a half-page each month. Nick, can you be the editor of this document and ride point on it from the Legislative side? Danny, will you submit a short article each month on local Democratic doings?"

Both men nodded and the next reelection campaign had begun. Shawn showed them the Team Butler mantra to appear on each flyer.

A Senator's Plea for Help If I stand pat, give me a shove.

If I betray you, show me the door. If I miss the point, enlighten me.

If I don't smile, make me laugh.

If I don't have your vote, tell me why.

Shawn Butler

CHAPTER 59

Butler-Brown Babies

In the afterglow of the election victory, Team Butler added a small but most welcome member, seven pound, ten ounce Maggie Brown. Maggie displayed a shock of black curls and an impish smile, while her father was stunned and wore a silly grin for days.

An inveterate multi-tasker, Joan puzzled Nick by packing things after her water broke but before the trip to the hospital and then giving telephone instructions the following day to her substitute teacher. Nick thought that the baby would need her full attention.

"She's just a baby, Nick, not the center of the universe," she assured him. "The sooner she realizes that the world does not revolve around her, the better it will be for all of us. She is pretty cute though, isn't she?" asked Joan, while hugging Nick and the baby at the same time.

Joan was quite composed and the baby settled in nicely with her. Shawn and Molly Jean visited often, bringing meals and Team Butler news. Life in the Brown home fell into a tolerable rhythm.

Nick did the right things on cue for Maggie and, consistent with his nature, played an effective supporting role. He spent hours studying his daughter, changing her diapers, and giving her bottles. Though Nick was initially stiff and awkward around this little visitor, Maggie seemed to sense his good intentions and gave him the benefit of the doubt. Her smile made him light-headed.

Matt and Jane were so entranced with their granddaughter that they found themselves, on one occasion, tugging on each side of Maggie, with each wanting to hold her. Catching themselves, they laughed and helped Jane get a good grip on the baby, while Matt waited his turn.

"She'll be better company, if we don't stretch her out of shape," laughed Jane.

When Maggie had just begun to sit up, Shawn and Molly Jean came into the house one evening, carrying food and a few new toys. The four adults watched the baby as she sat in the middle of the living room floor, tearing the packaging and playing with her toys. With little patience, Maggie flipped, bounced, tore, and damaged her presents.

Shawn could not help but notice the differences between Joan's methodical nature and Maggie's impulsive approach. While sure that this gap would shrink in time, Shawn wondered if their differences would create a problem in the future for mother and daughter.

Molly Jean and Shawn agreed that it was time for them to start a family. Maggie needed someone to play with, and so did they.

Molly Jean became pregnant easily but had a difficult eight months and then was restricted to bed rest at home until her delivery. Her physician, Doctor Ryan, came to the Butler home one evening when Shawn had just returned from the store.

"Good. I wanted to visit with both of you," announced Ryan. "There is no easy way to put this. Our tests have confirmed that this will be your last pregnancy, Molly. I'm going to have to do a few procedures when you deliver, in order to keep you safe."

MJ looked at Shawn sadly and said, "It appears as though we will have an only child."

Shawn had never seen MJ ruffled before. Her upbringing had prepared her for most anything, but not this. He had never seen anything or anybody rattle her.

Joan stopped in later and Shawn had the good sense to get out of the way. He walked to Nick and Joan's home, a mere two blocks away. If the two women had things to talk about, so did their husbands. Maggie was sleeping when Shawn and Nick dropped onto the couch.

"Office business?" inquired Nick.

"More important than that. It concerns our families."

"Is your home too small?" Nick guessed as the reason for the conversation. Both men were now paying more attention to the size and comfort of their homes. Despite their new wealth, Shawn and Nick lived in modest homes.

Chicago's north and west sides at the time were laced with tens of thousands of brick single family residences, termed bungalows. They had basements that flooded with the slightest provocation, three bedrooms, kitchen, living room and a dining room on approximately 1,300 square feet on the main floor, and a triangular attic, usually unfinished. The homes were constructed on narrow lots. Courtesy of the regulations implemented after the Chicago Fire, these houses were 18 inches apart on one side with a sidewalk on the other.

Identical on the outside, these homes varied widely on the inside. With Silicon Valley money, Shawn and Nick had improved their bungalows and were prepared to spend more money if their wives so desired. Built in the early part of the twentieth century, these homes had a great appetite for electrical and plumbing upgrades. Most of the roofs had been replaced at least twice.

"No, we have room for the three of us and we will be comfortable physically," replied Shawn. "Instead, I'm wondering if I can adjust to changes in my district. I served in Vietnam but can only speak and understand a few hundred words of Vietnamese. My pigeon Spanish isn't fooling anybody either. I connect reasonably well with the Poles in my district, but the Russian language and customs baffle me.

"I told you in the beginning that if there came a time that I couldn't relate well with my constituents, I would quit. Just being a placeholder and getting my ego stroked is not fair to the people who vote for me.

"As you know, the Catholic churches have Spanish and Vietnamese masses. Why couldn't we do something politically along those lines for the sub-cultures in our district?"

Nick replied, "I think we can. I will meet with Andrea Russo next week, because Right JC has already fought this battle," Nick advised. "I'm sure you will not be surprised to learn that CCC was ahead of everybody in addressing this challenge initially. Perhaps these institutions will let us board their sub-culture train before it begins rolling too fast for Team Butler to jump on."

"Pursue this, please. Keep me posted, Nick, but you have bigger questions, don't you?"

Nick paused, then pointed out, "The White Flight has begun.

People like us have begun moving to the suburbs. Do you want to stay here?"

"Yes, I do. Chicago is in my blood. I would feel like a traitor if we bailed, but you could move out west of the city. We could work something out," Shawn pledged.

"As corny as it sounds, I do not want to leave you. I have a great wife, a super baby, and wonderful parents close by. "Only if Joan said she did not feel safe or if I couldn't find suitable schools for Maggie, would we leave," Nick explained.

"Fair enough, but you have more money than you can spend. You could build a great life elsewhere," Shawn noted.

"That Silicon Valley windfall we shared was almost too easy, wasn't it? Joan and I have discussed the money. We don't think of it as really ours. We feel once we provide for the baby and a modest retirement, that we want to give much of it back to Chicago's poor," Nick confided.

Shawn was rarely caught off guard by Nick and blinked twice before saying he recently had much the same conversation with Molly Jean. He explained to Nick that the Butler situation was more complicated, however, because Matt and Agnes Donovan lived almost paycheck to paycheck.

He told him that one of her brothers was going to dry out in an expensive rehab clinic again. Shawn and Molly Jean had agreed that, without anyone else knowing, each brother would be given a modest annuity from the Butlers that they could begin collecting every year when they turned fifty. Hopefully, this allowance and social security later on would be enough for each to live on.

Both men agreed that the Butler-Brown Foundation would be a fine vehicle for their philanthropy. Shawn asked Nick if their subculture project could be folded into the activities of their foundation.

"I need to take a walk and digest all this," Nick said distractedly. "I'll get back to you."

CHAPTER 60

Shane

Assuming that Nick would somehow make the pieces fit, Shawn went home. He wanted to brief MJ on his talk with Nick and get her impressions. Before he had a chance to say anything though, she gave him "the look," and off they went to the hospital.

Shawn had called the hospital days before and the paperwork was ready for him. Though checked in promptly, he need not have hurried. Molly Jean delivered Shane (named after the lead in the classic western movie) quickly but remained in surgery. Dr. Ryan surfaced and said the baby was fine and would soon be ready for inspection, but that MJ was resting for the second phase of a two- step procedure, which so far was going well.

Since it would be at least an hour before he could see Molly, Shawn went to the observation room of the maternity ward. Two giddy males about his age were standing and pointing at their newborns. They congratulated Shawn and asked him if he had a girl or a boy.

"A boy," Shawn replied and pointed to his offspring. The three of them laughed, backslapped, and even danced a little.

Feeling as if he could fly, Shawn noted Shane's little hat and button nose. He couldn't help but conjure up a collage of Molly Jean, his biological parents, and stepmother as he admired his son. Nick joined Shawn in front of the glass and inspected Shane, while explaining that Joan would leave to visit MJ as soon as he returned home to watch Maggie. The new fathers discussed the changes they were going to have to make and were eager to do their part.

As the babies dozed, Nick summarized his suggestion to the sub-culture problem: a two hour meeting at the Chicago district headquarters one night every month hosting each major sub-culture, six meetings per month in all. Staffers would be compensated in the form of a half-day off on Friday afternoons.

Perhaps the most attractive aspect of this idea was that it would provide an opportunity for leaders within each sub-culture to emerge and for Team Butler to monitor this process. There would be a Vietnamese night, a Latino night, etc. Shawn immediately saw the wisdom in this idea, because they would not be staging a clumsy attempt to mingle sub-cultures. When Shawn needed to be in Springfield, he would be connected to the meetings by telephone, and Danny Boyle and Jerry Diminico would manage the meetings.

Later that evening, Danny was enthusiastic when Shawn shared this idea with him. Boyle indicated that the Democratic Party had experienced numerous social problems, when it had attempted to mix and match ethnicity. The Party concluded that the identity of these groups needed to be maintained for at least another generation before the sub-cultures could be assimilated politically.

Boyle observed, "Team Butler always seems to be at least one step ahead of the Party in making needed changes. It's a good thing the other districts are not too proud to copy your ideas."

Shawn was quick to credit Nick and staff when their new projects were successful. Team Butler was gaining a reputation for political innovation in and around Cook County. Requests began pouring in for

Shawn to share his processes with other Democratic districts and organizations; all requests to date had been filled.

For those leaders whose egos were reasonably in check, Shawn, Nick, and Jerry were asked to visit their districts and convene with leaders and staffs in large conference rooms. Regarding legislators whose desire to provide better services was tinged with envy and insecurity, these male leaders (and they were all men at the time) usually asked to meet with Shawn, Nick, and Jerry behind closed office doors at Team Butler headquarters, without any staff members from either district present.

In any event, Shawn always found ways to complement the other Democratic leaders and never talked down to their staff. Because Nick was often baby-tending and occasionally was intimidated by hyper-aggressive leaders in these meetings, Shawn grew to rely more heavily upon Jerry, who feared no one but always showed respect for individual Democrats and the Party itself. Jerry understood that Nick was "the brains of this outfit," in Shawn's words.

Shawn stressed the importance of team play, both in Springfield and Chicago. He shuffled staff quickly if things were not running smoothly but always showed compassion when making staff changes. He fired only one person, a woman who refused to attend alcohol rehab. Shawn demonstrated loyalty so well, that he rarely had to use the word.

Neither he nor his staff made enemies. By always giving and not asking for anything in return, Shawn's popularity continued to grow. His star was rising and he was not bullying anyone in its ascent.

CHAPTER 61

Rex Fades

Rex only visited Shane in the hospital once and did not stay long, alternating smiles and winces. He was losing mobility rapidly and had taken two falls in the past six months. The nerve damage Rex had suffered in combat now caused constant pain. He refused medication because he felt it diminished him as a human being.

Shawn had arranged for an extra phone in Rex's home so that his father could call him in case of an emergency. Nick and Joan were a fallback option in case Shawn was unavailable. Shawn had suggested to Rex the possibility of moving to a medical facility but received only a cold stare for his idea.

When Shane was six weeks old, Courtney brought him to visit Rex one evening. She asked to use his phone to call Shawn in Springfield. When she reached him, Molly gave the phone to Rex.

"Shawn, I have two wonderful visitors. The baby is generous with his smiles, even sharing them with this old fossil.

"Life around me keeps getting better, while my own life is slipping away. What a comfort it is to me knowing that, thanks to you and Molly, things are going well."

He turned serious for a moment by asking "When are you coming home, Shawn?"

Because his father had rarely asked when he was coming or going, Shawn hesitated before answering, "I'll be home on Saturday, dad."

Molly Jean knew that Shawn had planned to stay in Springfield over the weekend, but that his father's question had prompted a change in plans. She was determined to make this visit with Rex special and held Shane for a moment in case Rex's arm had fallen asleep. She then switched the baby to his other arm as she returned him to Rex.

A minute later he observed, "You know, you're in the same league with my wives. I've never said that to anyone else."

MJ laughed and cried, waiting for Rex to fall asleep as he held his grandson. While drifting off, he looked at her with what she imagined as the kind of love he had shown to Courtney and Rita.

In the midst of his pain and the immense satisfaction he gained from holding Shane, Rex fought sleep as he tried to focus on Molly Jean. He saw images of his wives behind her. This moment was exceptional for both of them, and neither wanted it to end. Molly retrieved the baby long after Rex began sleeping, and she then walked the short distance to her home.

Twelve hours later, MJ got a call from Rex, indicating that he had already requested an ambulance. She assured him that she would call Shawn and see Rex at the hospital. Shawn was unavailable, so Molly left a message. He returned the call quickly, explaining that he would begin the three-hour drive from Springfield immediately. MJ then called Nick and he came to the Butler home to watch Shane. All bases were covered.

Molly Jean drove very carefully, as did all the Butlers and Browns now that there were babies in the picture. Molly Jean double-timed to

Rex's room but stopped short as two doctors exited Room 324, the number they had given her at the desk.

The bigger, older doctor exclaimed, "How could he possibly refuse medication in his condition? His tolerance for pain is extraordinary."

His younger colleague responded, "I'll go you two better. First, he refused to crawl into bed before he used the toilet and insisted on closing the door. Second, he wanted to know all our names and whether we would be working the same shift tomorrow evening. When we assured him that we were all scheduled to be here tomorrow, he explained that he wanted as many reasons as possible to live for at least another twenty-four hours. He then thanked all five of us by name and insisted that we thank Benny, the ambulance driver.

"This man knows how to get off stage."

Molly smiled as the two doctors went down the hall shaking their heads. She entered 324, found a chair, and held Rex's hand. She marveled at how he managed to sit proudly erect in bed, while in such pain. Knowing Rex as she now did, Molly supposed she would have agreed to marry his son, sight unseen, had she been single.

MJ fell asleep holding his hand and that is how Shawn found them. Rex managed a smile as Shawn entered, and Molly, newly awakened, kissed Shawn and Rex before leaving.

"Sorry to take you away from Springfield, Senator," he teased.

"What can I do, dad?"

"Sit down and listen. I don't have much time or breath left. I would have passed sooner, but I was hoping that MJ would have a baby, and she outdid herself with Shane. He's wonderful.

"I've also seen you grow into a splendid husband and father. You are everything your mother deserved in me, if I was more sensitive and smarter. In addition, I would not have met Rita if not for you. I think she and your mother would have liked each other, don't you?" he asked rhetorically.

"You've been a great son. I never had to threaten or warn you. Just telling or showing was enough.

"Do you have anything you want to say to me?" Rex asked.

"No, dad. I yield my time to you. You're promoting me better than I've ever been able to market myself," Shawn laughed. "I'm lucky to have had you for a father. Sure you don't want to stick around?" Shawn asked.

"Can't a guy die around here without someone trying to talk me out of it. Remember, it's not too late for me to send you to your room. Now let me sleep, because I have some things I need to do tomorrow."

Shawn walked over to his father and kissed his forehead, something he had never done before. Because he did not see his father conscious again, he was glad he had done so.

Rex died in his sleep that night. The funeral service in his home was lightly attended, but those who were there realized that this is the type of memorial he would have wanted: relatives and a few good friends, without a fuss. Tim Brown, ably assisted by his wife Jane, managed the event in his effective, light management style.

Shawn spoke movingly about Rex's military service and two marriages. He then told of how it was being the son of a great man.

"When he looked at me, I stood up straight. When he and I were in public, he insisted I respect everyone around me. Because of the way he treated me, I try to put others before myself.

"He drank and ate in moderation, and so do I. When he was around, nothing bad was going to happen. He wouldn't allow it.

"Partly because of the high regard he had for women, I have come to believe that females are inherently better than males. It's not our fault, men. It's just the way things are.

"He never asked me to do anything he wouldn't do himself. Since he used words sparingly, I try to finish my remarks before people are tired of listening.

"In conclusion, he would not want any long faces here today and asked me to thank everyone for coming. As you may remember, my father thanked everybody for everything, with a sparse phrase or a stern nod. He told me last week that he tried to give as good as he got. When your time comes, my father, Rex Butler, said he hopes you all will be able to say the same."

CHAPTER 62

Tragedy Strikes

The Butlers and Browns had lived charmed lives for generations. Collectively, they had enjoyed good health and been accident-free. Shawn constantly reminded members of both families that Butler-Brown was "on a roll." Births, education, jobs, and deaths had come in an orderly fashion; hence, their lives were predictable and, on balance, satisfying. Even the Silicon Valley windfall was accomplished methodically and under the radar.

Like most prolonged winning streaks, it halted suddenly. Butler-Brown had been riding a crest for so long that the families had no conditioned reflexes to handle tragedy.

Since he was in high school, Jimmy Donovan, the youngest of the four brothers, had been drinking heavily. He drank earlier in the day than his brothers and switched to hard liquor sooner. His Irish good looks had faded, his teeth had become mottled, and his once impressive physique had deteriorated.

Because of Jimmy's drinking problems, Detective Matt Donovan had twice helped him retain his driver's license and leaned on the warehouse supervisor at Harrison Wholesale Company occasionally to help him keep his job. Jimmy's battered old Ford was a rolling metaphor for the messy life he led. Matt and Agnes had spent almost all of their modest savings in an unsuccessful attempt to treat his problem with rehabilitation efforts.

At 5 PM on a rainy September Friday, Molly Jean was pushing Shane's tarp-covered buggy on the sidewalk towards the Donovan home to visit her mother. Jimmy, her brother, well fortified with the half pint of bourbon he drank during his work day and the three boilermakers he chugged after work, turned sharply into the Donovan driveway just as MJ was crossing. She reacted quickly by shoving the buggy out of harm's way, but the shove propelled her directly in the path of Jimmy's car. The crunch was heard at least a block away and she died instantly.

The terrible sound drew Agnes Donovan from her kitchen, while Jimmy made a clumsy attempt to breathe life into his sister. Failing in his efforts, he staggered past his mother, who went to Molly Jean's lifeless body.

Before kneeling at MJ's side, she motioned to the widow next door to retrieve Shane, who had rolled from his overturned buggy onto the lawn. The neighbor, Mrs. Landry, stood behind Agnes briefly before telling her that the baby appeared fine and was no longer crying. Agnes asked her to take Shane into Landry's home, away from the confusion. Mrs. Landry complied after scooping up the diaper bag, bottles, and cereal boxes.

Tim and Jane Brown materialized and looked for directions from Agnes, who had a horrible premonition and ran towards the house. Tim Brown decided to stay with MJ's body, while Jane left to call Shawn, who was working downtown. Before Agnes could reach her porch, a single gunshot from one of Matt Donovan's snub-nosed .38 caliber pistols rang out. Jimmy had stepped into the tub of the bathroom on the main floor and shot himself in the head. Agnes wobbled out of the bathroom and slumped on the couch, thoroughly defeated. Within ten minutes, she had lost two of her five children.

Shawn and Matt Donovan converged on the accident site at the same time from different directions. Both had been given accounts of the accident-suicide by telephone. Their eyes locked in misery.

"Go ahead and hit me. I deserve it," Matt demanded.

"I want what Courtney would have wanted, peace. Besides, you didn't do anything," Shawn stated.

"That's part of the problem. I didn't do anything for years while the four of them acted like fools, and I kept my head in the sand," Matt admitted.

"Beat yourself up later. Right now, Agnes needs you. I don't even have to see her to realize how badly she feels."

"You Butlers and the Browns are better people than we are. We will never catch up," Matt conceded.

"Start now," suggested Shawn. "If you can't put Agnes back together, your whole family will come apart. Besides, you two raised Molly Jean. Failures could not have done that."

"You're right again," mumbled Matt as he hurried into the house.

Shawn checked in with Mrs. Landry, who hugged him and indicated she would keep Shane as long as necessary. A widow in her sixties, Mrs. Landry was one of the strong women who had helped the United States win WW II. She relished the challenge of caring for Shane. The baby was in good hands.

Not surprisingly, Nick surfaced. Saying nothing while waiting to be directed, Nick continued to be a great comfort to Shawn, who asked him to think of how to handle the funerals, an awkward matter at best. When Nick made a circle with his index finger, Shawn nodded his understanding that Nick was going to walk around the block and think this matter through.

On his third lap, Nick stopped and stood near Shawn who had just overseen the loading of MJ into a hearse. Nick told him that his suggestion would involve Mr. Donovan, and the two friends walked into the house.

"Could we talk, Matt?" asked Shawn.

Matt pointed to the backyard and for privacy's sake, the three men walked to a corner of Donovan's property . Both Nick and Matt turned to Shawn for leadership in this matter.

Shawn said, "We have two funerals to arrange and need to plan them in a way that is best for all concerned. Matt, before Nick makes his suggestion, do you have something you would like to say?"

In a tortured, small voice, Matt said, "I only want whatever Molly would have wanted."

"So do I," Shawn chimed in.

"Then I think I have something that may work. Hear me out," Nick requested. "I propose that we have two funerals in one. Lay the bodies side by side. They were close, if I understand correctly. I heard MJ say once that she changed a few of Jimmy's diapers.

"The press is going to have a field day with this story. You have brother-sister, an alcohol-related accident, two deaths, the wife of a sitting state senator, and the children of a police detective for openers.

"I suggest we hold a press conference the day before the funeral. You each make a public statement and then answer all questions. On the day of the funeral, we admit press photographers into the church two hours before the service for thirty minutes. Let the press click away, then clear them out of the church and lock the door.

"I recommend that we make no statements the day of the funeral; it's too easy to say something we will gag on in the future. I also suggest closing the caskets. Only family and friends will be admitted to the church from a list we will generate. We probably should release the list to the press," Nick concluded.

Nick stopped talking, because his part was complete. Shawn and Matt looked at each other, nodded, and shook hands.

Shawn gave Matt the last words which were, "Molly would have approved."

CHAPTER 63

Twin Funerals

St. Stephens was a beautiful church built on a corner lot at the turn of the century. The building had been given two major upgrades since. Its signature was a tall gold steeple which caught sunlight from numerous angles, often creating a spectacular effect; the reflection never shimmered quite the same way twice.

After WW I, the church bought an abandoned brewery, a structure which had fallen into disrepair. St. Stephens razed the adjacent plant and constructed an asphalt parking lot, an expanse which had been recovered four times. Parishioners loved the ample parking spaces and easy access to the adjoining street which the lot provided, primarily because it was difficult to be boxed in if you left church before mass ended, as many did.

Father Dorney was standing in front of the church, waiting for Shawn and Matt Donovan. All three had agreed to meet one hour before the press conference to be held in the church hall.

As they settled in the back of this multi-purpose facility, Matt asked Shawn if Molly could be buried on the Donovan family plot. Shawn said that MJ wanted to be cremated, because each felt that the sprawling cemeteries made no sense when surrounded by cramped urban living conditions. Father Dorney flinched at the topic of cremation which had long been the subject of controversy in the Catholic Church.

"You would, however, be welcome to put a headstone on your plot," offered Shawn.

"And, with your permission, I would like to inscribe it "Molly Jean Donovan-Butler," responded Matt.

"Agreed," said Shawn.

Turning to the priest, he asked, "Do the closed caskets bother you, father."

"Not at all," he replied. "Leaving them open would simply encourage viewers to replay the tragedies."

With the big issues out of the way, they discussed seating and a speaker list. Nick had drawn a seating chart, being careful to blend the two families to avoid a Hatfield and McCoy effect, and Matt had made a few notes of his seating preferences. The two men disposed of the seating matter quickly, without dispute.

Shawn insisted on speaking first at the funeral because he wanted to set the tone, explaining that he was going to say, "that he had married into a good family that hit a rough patch." He would close with "If there is anyone here today who came to promote trouble between the Butlers and the Donovans, go away now and let us honor our dead without added grief. No one is blaming anyone here." During the press conference, reporters were disappointed that there was not going to be more of a story. Harmony was the theme of the twin funerals, and accord does not sell newspapers. In case anyone missed the solidarity, Shawn and Matt locked arms midway through the conference.

On the next day, dreary and blustery, the mourners filled the huge parking lot and filed into the church. After Father Dorney gave a brief introduction, Shawn made his remarks. Then it was Matt Donovan's turn as he looked around the church.

"Fueled by alcohol and caused by our youngest son's folly, a terrible accident took Molly Jean from us. Our son could not deal with what he had done and killed himself with one of my pistols.

"In police work, suicide is often viewed as a sign of cowardice. In this case, I don't think so. I see his act as a mixture of love for his sister and deep disappointment in himself. He had hit bottom and didn't see any way to climb out.

"Wherever you are, Jimmy, we still love you. I know that MJ does, too. We miss you both deeply.

"If I had been a better father, we would not be here today. My wife did her job, but I failed to do mine.

"In my occupation, the combined effects of alcohol abuse and immaturity are predictable. Why I chose to ignore this bad chemistry in my youngest son is a puzzle which will haunt me to my dying day.

"Molly was gutsy, witty, pretty, and smart. She commanded respect. When she married Shawn Butler, a fine man, Agnes and I hoped some of the Butler class would rub off on us.

"Shawn, we hope you will bring Shane (not present) around to see us often. We will be looking for traits of Molly in him."

"The Donovans have some holes to fill. Please help us, Shawn. We need you now more than ever."

Shawn nodded firmly and Matt slumped on the podium. It was just as well that Matt had already made his point, because he could not have gone on. All three of his sons came up and helped him to his seat, and Matt and Agnes hugged.

Father Dorney splashed holy water on the caskets, as Jimmy headed for the family plot in his hearse and Molly Jean to the crematory in hers.

CHAPTER 64

Russo, the Nanny

Andrea Russo had become a fixture in Team Butler. She was an extremely capable volunteer, fiercely loyal, and smart enough to make big problems small and little problems disappear. The stock response when a team member needed to find something or have a statement clarified was "See Andrea!"

In return for her service and simply because they liked her, Rita, Molly Jean, and Joan had taken Andrea to clothing stores and beauty parlors, making sure that she dressed fashionably and applied makeup properly. Andrea looked forward to her outings with the Team Butler women, who accorded her special treatment. She also had dramatically improved her social skills by functioning in a fast-paced political environment. Men who had ignored her completely before were starting to notice. In her early fifties, she had morphed into an interesting, pretty woman.

Shortly after her retirement from the junior college, Andrea took her mother to Italy and joked that her mom had brought half of the country back with her. You knew you had arrived if Mrs. Russo asked you into her house for espresso. For those who would never travel to Italy, a visit to her home was a stimulating second best.

Andrea lived with her mother in a bungalow near Right JC. Like other nearby homes, it was the same on the outside, but a ringing tribute to Italy and Catholicism on the inside. The rosaries, paintings, and rugs were the real deal.

Mrs. Russo grew roses and handed one to many of her neighbors without comment once each year in August. If you didn't get one, it meant that you had been a poor neighbor that year, perhaps by not keeping your walk shoveled or by making too much noise. A Russo rose meant more to most neighbors than they were willing to admit.

Neighbors tried to check on her safety without her noticing; this was tough because she had a sixth sense and eyes like a hawk. In the words of a teacher living next door, "I don't know who is looking after whom, she with the Russo radar or we with our random checks."

She and Andrea were regulars at St. Anthony's and arrived fifteen minutes early each week for Sunday mass so that they could sit in the same place. On one occasion when an elderly man and his wife were already occupying the pew, Mrs. Russo stood and glared at them until they moved.

Andrea's domineering father had died suddenly when she was in grammar school, and Mrs. Russo had never auditioned for a replacement. The widow relished her independence.

With her newly found allure, Andrea easily got escorts, when needed, for weddings or funerals, but she discouraged any serious love interests. In fact, she had never gotten over her infatuation for Shawn. Since his visit to her at Right's library when he was newly enrolled, she had never thought seriously of another man.

Andrea had long concluded that she and Shawn were not meant to be. She was fine with that as long as he stayed in touch. Simply being around him was good enough for her. Being a small part of his distinguished legislative career gave added meaning to her existence.

When little Shane was born, she could not have been happier. She had gone on two shopping tours with Molly Jean and Shane and babysat Shane once when MJ went for groceries. When with the baby, she gave him her undivided attention and looked at him directly. She loved to hug him but quickly returned him to a position facing her so that they could look into each other's eyes. Andrea had changed diapers for her nephews and nieces, so doing the same for Shane presented no great inconvenience.

Shawn knew that he must do something about the Mrs. Landry situation because asking her to care for a newborn by herself indefinitely was unfair, despite her protestations to the contrary. Shawn and Nick discussed the situation in his Chicago office, and Andrea was close enough to overhear.

Nick hesitated, "Joan said we could take Shane for a while."

"And I love you both for volunteering, but I need a long-term solution. Shane thinks that Mrs. Landry is his mom, and she has grown quite attached to him. What am I going to do, Nick?" asked Shawn.

At this time, Shawn had to leave for a meeting outside the office and asked Nick to give the matter some thought. Shawn indicated he would be back in the office by 5 PM. Nick sat at his desk and began drawing arrows to represent the problem, with Shane at the center. He was struggling mightily when Andrea pulled up a chair.

"I couldn't help but eavesdrop, and I have a suggestion. I love Shane and want to be his nanny. I respect Shawn and would never let him or his son down. I'd be more than willing to share Shane with Mrs. Landry, whom I've never met," pleaded Andrea. "If Shawn or I see that my care isn't right for Shane, I will step aside," said Andrea.

Nick looked at her for a full minute without speaking, which she found unnerving. "Would you give me an hour to think about how I will present this to Shawn," Nick finally asked.

"Certainly," responded Andrea.

When Shawn walked in, he shuffled his phone messages and handled several small matters with staffers and volunteers. Getting around to Nick, he waved him to a conference room and was surprised when Andrea followed and closed the door. Confused, he looked to Nick for an explanation.

Nick began, "I think I have a workable Shane solution for you. Andrea and Shane already have sized each other up and appear to be a good fit. She says she would like to be his nanny and feels she has earned your trust.

"On the basis of what you have told me, we should also keep Mrs. Landry on board, for say, two days per week. It would seem foolish and ungrateful to do otherwise. We would pay each woman at the same hourly rate. Besides, Andrea is going to need a break. If Shane is anything like Maggie, he will soon be everywhere and into everything. Andrea has assured me if this is not working out, that she will quit," Nick summarized.

Shawn walked over to the window and stared vacantly outside. "Let me speak with Andrea privately, please," Shawn requested.

After Nick closed the door, Shawn looked carefully at Andrea, saying "There are many sides to this proposal that we need to consider. Not everyone has my best interests at heart. People will say we are sleeping together, though we won't be. Being a nanny will interfere with your love life and perhaps hinder the care you provide to your mother." He paused, "Your thoughts?"

Andrea responded confidently, "I balanced my mother and my job at Right. I can manage my mother and Shane. I'm never going to have a husband or children, Shawn. You and Shane are as close as I will get. I've helped you for years, without ever asking you for a single thing. Now, I'm calling in all the good will I've built up.

"If it hadn't been for you, I'd still be sitting home with my mom. You have opened up the world for me, and for that I am very grateful.

"I want to be close enough to help you when you need it and to help your son grow, learn, and prosper. As much as I love you, I will not push Shane to become a version of you.

"If I'm not the answer, tell me now and I'll move on, but if you give me this chance, I'll make you proud," Andrea assured him.

"Sorry to put you through this but I had to see how serious you were. You're hired. Take Nick and visit Mrs. Landry," Shawn said, while hugging her like an uncle would, remembering how careful he was going to have to be from now on, not to send the wrong message.

CHAPTER 65

Life With Shane

Shawn had become a Democratic Party leader in Chicago by helping anyone from either party, and a leader in Springfield, largely on the basis of Nick's political innovations. He missed Molly Jean, especially on holidays. Molly had been a lover, confidant, and friend, in no particular order. He had not found anyone who was able to fill all three roles or even willing to try.

In Shawn's estimation, MJ was one of a few, man or woman, who had lived her entire life with both feet on the ground. Despite Shawn's growing importance, he felt uncertain on occasion and realized that he had become partially dependent on MJ for balance and perspective.

Shawn was working so many hours, he did not see Shane's first steps or hear his first sentence. The Russo-Landry combo worked well; they sometimes paired up and took Shane to a movie or the library. Where Shawn stood in the pecking order was brought home to him when three-year old Shane refused to take his hand as the four of them were leaving the house one day. Instead he reached for the hands of Andrea and Mrs. Landry and then nodded for Shawn to follow. Miss A and Mrs. L, as Shane called them, were always there for him.

When Shawn was available, he often took Shane to visit the Browns or the Donovans. About six months older, Maggie liked to wrestle with Shane and occasionally swatted him. Shawn let him fight his own battles and cry himself out when necessary. Though initially insensitive, Maggie always consoled Shane towards the end of a visit and was a big hugger. When Joan started to correct her daughter for playing too rough, Shawn would discourage her, saying Shane was going to have to learn to take care of himself.

"Easy for a Marine to say," quipped Joan.

"Not as easy as you think, but it's in his best interests," countered Shawn.

Shawn and Joan remained on good terms because they never allowed a difference of opinion to fester. He enjoyed her company because she had many characteristics in common with his father, including great posture and a quiet dignity. As she got older, Joan became even prettier, taking good care of herself and her family.

The Butler visits to the Donovan home were a different matter. Agnes had not fully recovered from that fateful day and only came to life when the Butlers stopped by. Her sons realized that she was suffering and started acting more like responsible adults, drinking less and doing small chores for Agnes. They also started doing uncle things with Shane, including piggy back rides and squirt gun fights. Some positives had emanated from the tragedy.

Once inside the door, Shane would go to Agnes immediately because he thought all mature women liked him, and he was generally right. Agnes frequently had a treat for Shane but made him search for it. She would only tell him which room it was in. When he found the toy or candy, she congratulated him enthusiastically and he would giggle happily. On Chicago's northwest side, where hugging was always in season, Shane may have set a hug record.

He was impressed by the Donovan pictures of policemen, which adorned the walls and also displayed in picture frames. On one occasion, Shane shattered a picture frame by accident, and Agnes gave him a broom and supervised the clean-up.

When Shawn came to retrieve him, he ran to his father, saying excitedly, "Grandma showed me how to use a broom!"

"Why do I get the idea that there is an unfortunate story behind this bit of news?" surmised Shawn.

Matt used to enjoy "borrowing" Shane so that they could visit the police station. It took the little boy a few minutes each time to get used to the size of the policemen and the bustle of the station, but once he adjusted and put on a police hat, blew one of their whistles, and handcuffed his grandfather, he was hooked. It was not unusual for Matt to go off by himself and cry when Shane had gone home, partly because of the reminder of the children he had lost and partly because of his growing love for Shane.

Andrea made sure that Shane had other children to play with, since she had spent much of her childhood at home near her mother and realized the importance of socializing with other children the same age. From years three through eight, Shane and his circle of friends did not think it strange that Shane's nanny played with them on jungle gyms and swings. After almost fifty years, Andrea finally found a big chunk of childhood she had missed.

Andrea also umpired baseball games and did not play favorites; no one disputed her calls. Shane often remarked, not bitterly, that Miss

A treated his friends better than she treated him. Andrea merely took his comment as a sign that she was doing her job. Andrea had come to love him deeply, but it was a tough, fair love.

Shane knew that his father worked often but that when Shawn was home, he devoted most of his time to him. His life was different than that of most kids his age but was full and stimulating.

CHAPTER 66

Shawn's Career Decision

Now in his fourth full term as state senator in February, 1983, Shawn was drawing wide attention as a potential Democratic party candidate for the US House of Representatives. He had avoided comment religiously but had reached a point where he could no longer do so, without embarrassing some very loyal people who were backing him. When in doubt, he turned to Nick and suggested a long beach walk to plot his intentions.

On one such occasion, both men were dressed in parkas and stocking caps, leaning into the biting winds. They started near North Avenue and headed toward Lakewestern University, a distance of four miles. Shawn had stashed two energy bars in his jacket and Nick was carrying two bottles of water, despite the cold.

Shawn began, "I'm the right age, forty-three, have a solid military background, and hold two degrees, the second in law. I've bitten my tongue when I would like to have unloaded on some of my colleagues and have worked with some key centrist Republicans to help our citizens.

"I've lived in the city all my life and know thousands of Chicagoans. I am not seen as a grandstander or a hot dog. I'm single, not divorced, with a good son. Thanks to you, people in Springfield think I'm smart. Thanks to my parents, I'm not carrying any baggage and am thought of as a decent human being," Shawn stated.

"On the other side, I know little about DC and what I do know, I don't like," Shawn added. "Shane and Maggie are high school juniors and will soon be in college locally. By the way, did you know Maggie and Shane won't date anyone unless the other gives the OK?"

"Yes, and when they ride the CTA together to St. Ignio as we did, that Shane insists Maggie study on part of the commute?" Nick asked.

"Talk about a role reversal," Shawn observed with a hearty laugh and Nick joined in.

"Joan and I can't get her to do anything we want her to do but she will listen to Shane. He's really a fine young man," Nick said.

"Maggie's a peach, too, but she just had one mother, a practicing teacher at that, while Shane had four: Courtney, Andrea, Joan, and Mrs. Landry," Shawn explained.

"What are your thoughts," Shawn asked? "I will not go to DC without you."

Nick responded, "My parents are in their twilight years and struggling to live independently. My dad's becoming forgetful and mom has lost mobility. My father has become nasty when he can't sort things out. Joan, Maggie, and I have been troubleshooting their problems for the past few years."

"It's difficult to see your dad as nasty. He's one of the reasons you're such a nice guy," Shawn contributed

"Thanks, Shawn. The reason this is tough to accept is that he has been mean to Joan. She was always a big favorite of his. She understands thoroughly but it has still been tough for both of us.

"If you want to go to DC, I will go," Nick pledged. "I'll simply have to make some adjustments. I've been coasting for a long time and our life has been very good. How about you?"

Shawn stated, "I have mixed feelings. If I am going to make a move, now is the time. I love this city, though, and as a state senator, I can be here anytime the Legislature is not in session.

"As a US Representative, I would have to learn the growing suburbs, many of them staunchly right wing Republican, not the centrists with whom I have done business successfully. Those suburban residents deserve better representation than I would be willing to provide. Politically, our nation is moving towards the extremes, while I am entrenched center left.

Shawn hesitated a moment, "Let's stay where we are in the state senate, Nick. Can you put together a meeting at the Democratic Party headquarters next week and draft a statement from me declining regretfully? I want you, Danny, Andrea, and a few others to attend to demonstrate that I am not there simply to have my arm twisted or my ego stroked."

"Yes, I'll do it," said a secretly relieved Nick.

CHAPTER 67

Pivotal Meeting

The requested meeting took place in the main symposium center of the beautifully appointed Democratic headquarters south of downtown Chicago. It turned out to be much more than what Team Butler expected. Sitting four-term US Senator Ike Gibbons (D-Bloomington, IL) and Lieutenant Governor Connie Rigney (D-Joliet, IL) sat quietly with their associates when Shawn and his entourage entered. Team Butler was seated front and center. Francis T. Delaney, the no-nonsense chair of the Cook County Democratic Party, was the moderator and began the summit promptly at the top of the hour.

Mr. Delaney began, "Originally, this meeting was designed to draft Shawn Butler as the Democratic nominee for US House-17. Despite his tender years, Mr. Butler has served his district and this state admirably for fourteen years. During his tenure, he has walked a delicate bipartisan line, treated everyone with respect, and passed crucial bills with little fanfare. How do you see it, Madame Lieutenant Governor?"

Without missing a beat, the vivacious Mrs. Rigney took the baton, "Never seduced by the sound of his own name or the doors which it opened in Springfield, Shawn has contented himself to do the people's work without showboating. Navigating treacherous waters, he has trained Democrats, made peace with Republicans, passed needed bipartisan legislation, and treated everyone with respect, even those who didn't deserve it.

"His love for Chicago and our state bleeds through every thing he does. This sort of loyalty and good behavior should be rewarded, don't you agree, Senator Gibbons?"

"I thought you'd never ask, Mrs. Rigney," replied the first African-American from Illinois to serve in the US Senate. A polished orator with Civil Rights chops, he wondered "if Mr. Butler would be interested in being the Democratic nominee for junior US senator from Illinois?

"Since we are catching you cold, I insist that you accept my campaign team as yours." Spreading his arms to include the others in the room, he stated, "We had a private meeting and do not believe you can compete without campaigners experienced at the national level. This provision is a deal breaker. Well, Mr. Butler, what do you say?"

Sensing Shawn's indecision, Danny Boyle held up a sign requesting a pit stop. Shawn was grateful for this excuse to buy time. "Mr. Delaney, Danny tells me that his kidneys are floating and that he needs a fifteen minute break," quipped Shawn.

"Mr. Boyle's interest in saloons is well documented. I doubt whether there is enough left of his kidneys to do anything but float. You have *ten* minutes to deliberate, Mr. Butler, so that we can allow our distinguished guests to move along," ruled Mr. Delaney.

Shawn replied firmly, "Thank you, sir."

Team Butler was directed into a pleasant conference room adjacent to the symposium center. Shawn took the seat at the head of the table but was too stunned to speak as were most of the others.

Never tongue-tied, Danny Boyle surmised, "You've hit the

mother lode, Shawn. Veteran Democrats know we can't win any longer the old-fashioned way, by nominating candidates who have worked the most years for the party. The career Democrats respect you because you've never given them reason not to, and the younger members like you because you have helped them. You have not stepped on anyone's neck to get where you are or jockeyed to move up the ladder. As a result, the Party is solidly behind you. Congratulations!"

"What do you think I should do, Jerry?" asked Shawn.

"Take the nomination and run with distinction. I think you will win, but even if you don't, you will automatically become a Party leader and decision-maker," advised Jerry Diminico.

"Andrea?" asked Jerry.

Not tipping her hand, she responded without enthusiasm, "You're the only one who knows if this is the right thing for you."

Shawn looked at Nick, who was sitting at the end of the table reserved for Team Butler but remaining miles apart from its members. Nick had always told Shawn what he should be doing and never concerned himself with what Shawn wanted to hear.

Guessing what Nick would say, Shawn was afraid to ask. Instead, he stood and said, "I'm going to accept the nomination."

Without making a sound or glancing Shawn's way, Nick glided out the door and was gone. Everyone noticed but turned away and entered the symposium center, minus Nick.

Waiting for his team to group around him, Shawn said slowly, "I accept your gracious offer. I will make you proud."

After a flurry of handshakes, Mr. Delaney told Shawn that he would arrange a meeting with his new campaign team one week from today in the room they now occupied. "Nobody goes public until then," Delaney emphasized, shaking his fist at Team Butler menacingly.

As they headed for their cars, Andrea, who had not missed a thing, asked for a private moment. Stepping off to the side, Andrea grasped Shawn's arm and said softly, "I've never been more disappointed in anybody in my entire life. You and Nick have always been best friends. In addition, he is the reason you are financially secure and that everybody thinks you're so smart. You didn't even ask his opinion; that was cowardly on your part. You couldn't face him, could you?" she sneered.

"Since we met, you have never failed to do the right thing until now. I've been told that everybody has their price, but I thought Shawn Butler was the exception. So did everyone else. We all know now that you would throw any of us under a bus to feed your ego. You've cheapened yourself beyond repair.

"I've not married, partly because I never had the courage to trust someone but mainly because I couldn't find someone who measured up to you." Turning to leave, a badly hurt Andrea hissed in a scathing tone, "How could I have been so wrong?"

She left Shawn standing alone, flushed with embarrassment. No one, not even his parents, had ever humiliated him to this degree. Perhaps, he thought, this was because he had never done anything to deserve it more.

CHAPTER 68

Living With Betrayal

Shawn roamed the beach for hours before returning home. When he walked through the door, Shane smiled from the kitchen table, while displaying a mouthful of Mrs. Landry's superb casserole. Now a gawky 5' 10," he had started teasing his father because Shane's recent growth spurt made him slightly taller. He was such a good, trusting young man that his father became teary-eyed from time to time when he looked at him. This was one of those moments.

Because of his betrayal of Nick, Shawn had trouble returning Shane's smile and maintaining eye contact. To make this conversation more difficult, Shane had adopted Andrea's stance of being loyal and honest in every matter, which challenged a politician who was engaged in a constant ethical balancing act.

Emotionally and socially, Nick and Shane were much alike, and news that his father had been cruel to Nick would have devastated Shane. Maggie would be more likely to understand but Shane, not so much. Nick and Shane lived by absolutes, while Shawn and Maggie were comfortable with compromises made in gray areas.

Had Nick known that Andrea found it necessary to scold Shawn, he would have been upset. Their lives were deeply intertwined. Miss A served as his caregiver, big sister, aunt, teacher, and mother.

Since Molly Jean passed, Shawn, Nick, Miss A, Mrs. L, Joan and Agnes had combined to insure that Shane got what he needed, including reasonable discipline and plentiful encouragement. All adults close to him had his best interests at heart.

Seeing Shawn's discomfort, he asked, "What's wrong, dad?" "We have an office problem," declared Shawn, turning away. "I'll bet Uncle Nick can help you solve it," responded Shane.

Shawn was stricken by these words and would have had difficulty replying at all if he had not been saved by the ringing of the telephone. Shawn took the call and said that he was needed at his district office. Thoroughly uncomfortable, Shawn hurried to his car.

Betrayal did not suit Shawn well. Molly Jean would not have let him get away with this foolishness. Among other things, she had been his moral compass. While driving, he groaned since he could almost hear MJ condemning his mistreatment of Nick by telling him in flat tones to "Make things right, Butler!"

Shawn remembered his father telling him that women are simply more honest than men. Painfully, he reviewed how his mother, step-mother, wife, Mrs. Landry, and Agnes Donovan would evaluate his recent behavior. He was certain that they would have adopted Andrea's position. Since the surviving women in his support group did not tolerate any foolishness from Shane, why would they have accepted it from Shane's father?

After soul-searching in his car for a while outside his well lit Chicago office, Shawn went inside to see who was there working for him at 7 PM. He checked the sign-in board and saw that there were four volunteers preparing a mailer under the supervision of whom else but Andrea Russo. With major help from a techie volunteer, he had designed this special board prepared with lights that flashed on when a volunteer pressed a switch. Shawn noticed often that working volunteers would glance fondly at their lighted name and decided that the expense was well worth it. Everyone liked to see his or her name in lights.

Shawn engaged each volunteer in a brief conversation before asking Andrea for a minute of her time. He did not sit behind the desk in his office but rather at a small table with her. She looked at him closely but sat quietly. She had already done her talking.

Speaking softly, Shawn explained, "I lost sight of some things, forgot who my friends were, and was rude to Nick. Thank you for calling this mistake to my attention.

"Be assured that I will not be a candidate for the US House and that I will continue as an Illinois senator for as long as my staff and the voters will have me. The only reason I have gotten this far is because of Team Butler, not Shawn Butler. Getting caught up in myself at this point in my life was incredibly dumb, but I managed to do it somehow.

"Will you forgive me and help me prepare a letter to Mr. Delaney with copies to the key players at the meeting he held?"

Andrea countered, "I will be happy to work on the letter but the forgiving part may take a while. You're on probation, Senator Butler."

"Fair enough, Andrea. That's better than I deserve. Let's get to work. I'll call Nick, Jerry, and Danny."

He reached Nick at home, explained his change of heart, and asked him to come in to headquarters. Sounding happy, Nick agreed.

Shawn then called Jerry at his bustling restaurant with a similar explanation. Jerry listened carefully and did not sound surprised.

Jerry laughed and quipped, "You always do the right thing, even if it takes a while. Do you want me to come to HQ?" Jerry asked.

"No, things were out of control briefly but no longer. We'll put the letter together this evening. Let's talk on Sunday."

Jerry closed by saying, "My driver will bring pizzas your way, double sausage. No charge, but tip him. His wife's sick."

"Gladly. Thanks, pal!"

Reaching Danny at home, Shawn provided the explanation he had given the others. He added, "I know you stuck your neck out for me. I'm sorry for complicating your life. You deserve better."

Danny took a deep breath and summarized, "What you're telling me is that you're turning down this offer because your staff and the people who voted for you are more important than your personal ambitions. As you know, I'll argue about anything with anybody, even if I have to take the weak side, but I can't debate this one. One thing though, I would like to see the letter before you send it."

"We're putting it together this evening, because Mr. Delaney deserves a prompt response. Can you join us?" asked Shawn.

"I'm unshaven and in sweat clothes," explained Danny. "Then we'll have no trouble recognizing you. Come on over."

Encouraged by Shawn to make the letter as brief as possible, this group boiled their thoughts down to three paragraphs. With Team Butler in high gear, the letter took forty-five minutes to complete.

Shawn planned to give Mr. Delaney his copy in person tomorrow and send the others by special delivery. With smiles all around and pizza waiting, Team Butler was again on the same page.

DEAR MR. DELANEY:

PLEASE WITHDRAW MY NAME FROM YOUR NOMINATING PROCESS. I REGRET ANY INCONVENIENCE MY REVERSAL WILL CAUSE.

I WAS SO TAKEN BY YOUR KIND OFFER THAT I UNWISELY SHUFFLED MY PRIORITIES. BE ADVISED THAT FROM NOW ON, THEY WILL REMAIN IN THE FOLLOWING ORDER: (1) OUR DISTRICT RESIDENTS, (2) CHICAGO, (3) MY STAFF, AND (4) THE DEMOCRATIC PARTY.

THE MODEST SUCCESS I HAVE ENJOYED TO DATE IS DUE TO A DEDICATED SUPPORT TEAM. THEY TRUSTED ME WHEN I TOLD THEM THAT MY FINAL POLITICAL GOAL WAS TO BE AN EFFECTIVE STATE SENATOR REPRESENTING A PORTION OF THE WORLD'S GREATEST CITY. I VOW NOT TO DISAPPOINT THEM EVER AGAIN!

SINCERELY YOURS,
ILLINOIS STATE SENATOR, SHAWN BUTLER

CHAPTER 69

Butler and the Environment

While early in his 29 year career as a state legislator in which he was regarded as the ultimate team player by fellow Democrats and a worthy partner in selected issues by Republicans, Shawn decided to carve out a signature topic. As an undergrad, he had taken a science class from Dr. Mitch Bowen, a young, intense professor of environmental science at Triple C. Bowen was a true believer and focused upon regional issues when possible, such as Lake Michigan water distribution, Midwestern toxic waste dumps, and O'Hare Airport hazardous chemical handling and applications.

As a gesture of appreciation to Dr. Bowen for his community service, Shawn had volunteered on two Saturdays to assist him in his many projects. While saying little to him, the professor particularly appreciated Shawn's help, because the Butler stamp of approval as a student leader tended to attract more helpers and to validate the merit of Bowen's projects.

At Clement one fall day, Dr. Bowen conducted a water use seminar at a left-leaning institution, a good fit for both. Shawn cut a class to attend this well-attended lecture and waved to the professor on the way out. Dr. Bowen called him over and finished his discussion with the appreciative students with whom he was talking.

Shawn and Bowen took seats in the now vacant classroom and assessed each other. Bowen had a few streaks of gray, but otherwise remained lean and athletic. Running had kept Shawn's weight down, and Bowen registered his approval.

Bowen began, "I never thanked you properly for the support you gave me at Triple C years ago. You are a good man. I'm not surprised to see you here. Third year law student?"

"Second."

"Can I assume you're a veteran in this vet-friendly haven?" "Yes sir, I am," responded Shawn.

"Something challenging, I'll bet. Perhaps a Marine?"

Shawn nodded. Changing the topic and a little embarrassed, Shawn asked, "What's your specialty now, sir?"

He responded, "I haven't had time to develop one. In my estimation, industrial chemical misuse is our biggest challenge. FYI, I'm taking a graduate chemistry class at the University of Chicago, trying to learn more about this problem.

"In a related issue, new toxic waste sites are being discovered every week. They are becoming more dangerous and trickier to treat all the time."

Switching gears, Dr. Bowen asked. "What kind of law are you going to practice?

"I haven't a clue, but I plan to stay in Chicago and make it a better place to live," replied Shawn. "It sounds corny when I say it that way, doesn't it?"

"Not to me it doesn't," responded Bowen quickly. "Will you do something for me once again, Shawn."

"Name it," countered Shawn eagerly.

"Simply keep me in mind. I have a hunch we're not through working together, and I have trouble selling my ideas. Being the oddball that I am has its advantages, though, because I am able to think independently and see things more clearly than most. For example, I believe you will become an important force," he predicted.

"Don't forget the little people you met on the way up," Bowen closed while slapping his chest and chuckling. "Maybe we can collaborate and do some good."

With that, Dr. Bowen was gone. Shawn reflected on the many Bowen-types he had come across as he learned more about Chicago. Citizens of Bowen's caliber were treasures and served to neutralize greed and corruption, acting as antacid tablets. He vowed to work with these community servants whenever possible.

Shawn became chair of the Illinois Senate Environmental Committee during his fourth term. Upon receiving this appointment, Shawn called Dr. Bowen and offered to buy his supper at Diminico's restaurant on Friday.

Shawn inquired, "Is it OK if I bring somebody?"

"Sure, if you think he or she can help the cause," responded Bowen.

"Do you want to bring someone?" asked Shawn.

"I don't have anyone to bring," conceded Dr. Bowen.

This painfully honest reply confirmed Shawn's conclusion that he was on to somebody special. Of the hundreds of people he knew, few would have been willing to make this admission, perhaps Shane and certainly Nick. Shawn believed that naked honesty of this kind was a sign of self-understanding. He could not wait to get Bowen and Brown at the same table.

On Friday evening, Shawn and Nick entered Jerry's place and waved at Mitch Bowen as they approached his table. He introduced Nick and Mitch and then excused himself. Obviously well known, Shawn made the rounds of the tables, handing out competitors' pizza coupons. After taking his seat, he explained that this was a stock gag he pulled on Jerry. Shawn was not surprised when Nick and Mitch were sitting in silence.

"Well, I'm sure you two had a lot to talk about," quipped Shawn.

Shawn explained his idea of having a legislator (Shawn), an environmental science professor (Bowen), and a business man (Nick) combine forces to solve environmental problems. Shawn asked Bowen to name a topic and the professor indicated he was still working on hazardous chemical use at airports. Turning to Nick, he prompted him to ask questions. When the pizza arrived, Shawn took two slices and joined Jerry Diminico, who had completed the dinner rush.

After an hour, Shawn tried to rejoin his table but both occupants waved him off. He laughed when he noticed that both Nick and Mitch were speaking and writing at the same time.

This informal meeting kicked off years of successful environmental projects in the form of federal, state and private sector grants, public- private partnerships, and public and private sector research. Shawn's name was regularly associated with these projects and he always gave full credit to Bowen and Brown.

Mitch and Nick became fast friends. Joan fixed Bowen up with a serious female physics professor and they dated for two years before marrying, with Nick as best man.

Opening up to Shawn, Nick exclaimed, "Until I met Mitch, I didn't know that there was anybody as eccentric as I am. What a relief to know I'm not one of a kind!"

Nick added, "I only have two male friends and I've been the best man at both of their weddings. What are the odds?"

CHAPTER 70

Shane Grows Up

Shane attended LW and majored in environmental science. From the day he walked in the door, he had future graduate student written all over him. Despite being on a different campus, he gravitated to Dr. Bowen and worked for him as a Triple C intern during the summers.

Meanwhile, Shawn was doing work for the Democratic Party by training new legislators and sponsoring environmental legislation. He did not parent much, because Shane still relied heavily upon his support group. As far as Shawn knew, his son was not dating anyone special. Shane had picked up Nick's habit of taking long walks. He admired Joan deeply and enjoyed simply sitting with her, without talking much. For Joan, Shane acted as a Maggie substitute, who was always out and about.

Shane grew up too fast for Shawn, who due to his work in Springfield, would go weeks without seeing him. When father and son did visit, discussions focused upon regional scientific developments.

Shawn talked with Mitch about graduate studies for Shane, indicating it was time for his son to leave the nest. Dr. Bowen and Shane sorted out the application details. A strong student, Shane was accepted in the doctoral program at Princeton. He loved the research activities there and telephoned Shawn twice a week.

Shawn traveled to New Jersey once to visit Shane, shortly after he started school there and planned another trip at the end of Shane's third year to attend his Ph.D. graduation. Shane said cryptically that he had someone he wanted to meet, and Shawn supposed this person was a professor, probably a Bowen type. Shane insisted upon picking up his father at the airport.

When Shawn went to claim his baggage, he encountered his son holding the hand of a small, pretty red-haired girl. Looking terribly lost, each wore jeans and non-descript tweed jackets. The sight of this couple touched him because they looked vulnerable and yet so close to each other.

"Dad, this is Katy O'Malley. She's the one," he said; blushing while he held up her hand with an engagement ring.

Looking from one to the other, Shawn stopped short and was unable to respond. He offered his hand to Katy and she took it tentatively, while giving him a shy, heart-tugging smile. Realizing a handshake was not nearly enough, he gave her a big hug.

"My father wants to talk with you, sir," she noted quietly.

"I'll bet he does," said Shawn, starting to recover.

"You and my dad, Bernie, are staying at the same hotel, where we will be having dinner. Could you meet him in the bar at five before we eat at six?" she asked.

"Fine."

Shane explained, "We will go back and change and you will have an hour or so to get settled. OK?"

"Sure. Have you called Andrea and the others regarding this matter?" asked Shawn.

"Yes I have," he replied sheepishly, hinting that they had been in the loop for some time.

With that, they were gone and Shawn was left shaking his head, realizing that since he had delegated many of his parenting responsibilities, it was reasonable that he would be the last to know about his son's love life. He was getting what he deserved. Now it was up to him to make an apparently good situation even better.

I wish MJ was here, he thought, not because Shane's mother surrogates had not served him well, but because she would so thoroughly have loved Katy. However, she is not here and Shane and Katy are, and it is time for me to be a father-in-law. As he dressed for the evening, he liked the idea more all the time.

Bernie O'Malley was half way through a bourbon and water when Shawn joined him at the bar. He was beefy and balding, cradling his high ball as if there was nothing in the world more important.

They measured each other and shook hands. Shawn pointed to a vacant table in the corner and Bernie nodded. When they settled in and Shawn had been served a beer, Bernie began speaking painfully.

"I didn't see this engagement coming. I guess I thought she would live with me forever. Katy raised herself and spent most waking hours in a classroom or the library.

"By way of explanation, I'll give you the short form. I'm a salesman and travel most of the time. When I was home, my wife tried matching me drink for drink and couldn't keep up. She was institutionalized and died several years ago of a stroke.

"Not a happy story, is it?" Bernie conceded. "Your wife passed also, didn't she," he asked.

"You want unhappy, I'll give you unhappy. Molly Jean was run down and killed by a drunken brother. Top that!"

"I didn't know. I'm truly sorry," Bernie said as he put his drink down and studied Shawn. "How did you handle it?"

"I did not lay down guilt trips or pout publicly. Her parents are fine people and I took the high road, which they deserved. It would have been easier if I could have blamed them. I have had some miserable nights but, other than the holidays, I am doing OK.

"Shane was raised by four wonderful women on a tag-team basis. A man my age, who is my best friend, helped me," Shawn stated, while changing the topic. "Is your daughter as good as she seems?"

"Better. While my wife and I were making a mess, she plunged into her books and waited for things to improve," Bernie confided. "They never did." He paused, "Will your son treat my daughter well?"

"Yes. He wouldn't know how to treat Katy badly because he's had six adults treating him well all his life," Shawn replied. "My concern is that he seems terribly naïve. I don't know how he'll react if things turn sour," he admitted.

Bernie interjected, "Katy also is quite naïve. Look, I'm starting to make some money and I can help them a little."

"I have an idea," Shawn countered, "Though I could help them too, let's not. How about if we let them wrestle with their problems and see how they do? They might surprise us. We can keep in touch and step in any time you deem it necessary."

Bernie toyed with his drink for at least a minute and then pronounced, "I like it. Your idea makes sense. Let's go play Twenty

Questions and see what kind of future they are planning!"

What they discovered is that they planned to marry in six weeks in Chicago; the choice of city was a courtesy to Shane's "multiple mothers," particularly Mrs. Landry, for whom the travel might have been a burden. Both young people felt that a Hartford, CN trip for this aging group was too strenuous and complicated. Andrea had arranged the details for a wedding Mass. Dr. Bowen will be the best man, and a childhood friend of Katy's will be the bridesmaid.

"Sorry, dad. This seemed like the best option," explained Katy.

"I'm on board and impressed with both of you," observed Bernie.

All three looked at Shawn, who said, "I'm trying to keep up but I haven't heard anything I don't like or that presents a problem."

Further discussion disclosed that Shane had found a job as a professor in a downstate IL university and Katy had accepted a job as a biology teacher in a neighboring town. While Shane resolved a few graduate school details, Katy was going to make a trip to find housing.

"What do you want us to do?" asked Bernie.

Katy looked at both fathers and suggested, "We want each of you to show up in a reasonably clean tie for the wedding."

CHAPTER 71

Shane's Wedding

A week before the big day, Shane took a walk with Nick and talked of his selection of Mitch as best man. Shane said "You're so lucky to have Joan and Maggie. Dr. Bowen came from a dysfunctional family. If being my best man helps to make him a better family man, then it will have been worth taking the risk of offending you by not asking you to stand up for me," reasoned Shane.

"I doubt there is anything you could do that would offend me," Nick assured him. "I have always thought of you as what a son of mine would be, if I was lucky. In fact, your dad and I have joked that you and Maggie may have been switched at birth."

The wedding Mass was intimate and low-key. Shawn walked down the aisle with Agnes and Andrea on his left and Mrs. Landry and Joan on his right. He was going to make a comment about a logjam but wisely refrained. Jokes about women and their weight, however indirect or well-intended, do not often play well.

Katy was such a pretty bride that even Father Dorney did a double take. There were enough tears to elevate the humidity in the church.

The reception was also classy, with all on their best behavior. Bernie had cut down on his drinking and charmed everyone. He, Tim Brown and Matt Donovan exchanged one-liners. Matt's three sons each had one beer and switched to cokes, to everyone's relief.

Shawn danced with every woman and did not once sit down.

When he and Andrea danced, she said, "Shane looks so happy and his bride is radiant. What a pleasure to be on Team Butler!"

When Shawn approached Mrs. Landry, he sat next to her wheel chair, assuming she would want to sit out a dance.

"Don't get too comfortable, Senator Butler. The last item on my bucket list is to dance at Shane's wedding and if you'll get someone to help me on my feet, I will do it or die trying."

Motioning to Tim, they brought Mrs. L to a standing position. Shawn took a firm grip on her and after a few halting steps, she found her footing and got through the song successfully.

On the slow trip back to the wheel chair, Shawn declared, "I have a question. One thing I've always wondered…"

Mrs. Landry jumped in, "My first name is Mrs. and it will always be Mrs. to any living soul. Any other questions?"

After depositing her back in the wheel chair, Shawn said, "Thank you for everything. Shane is a better man because of you."

"You're not so bad yourself, Shawn. Now go on and dance with the other women. My list is complete and I'm tired."

After kissing Mrs. Landry on the cheek, he moved on to Joan, who smiled at him broadly. "Working the room, are you, Butler?"

"I'm dancing with all voting age women. Are you old enough to vote?" he teased.

"I'm old enough to cost you an election, if you don't straighten up," Joan assured him.

As they moved onto the dance floor, Shawn said, "Once again, you're the classiest person in the room. Thus has it always been. How are you able to look so queenly?"

Joan explained, "As a small child, I walked through our alley and didn't like what I saw on the pavement. Ever since, I stand straight and see faces, mountains, and stars, not discarded items and waste. I'm not above my surroundings. I simply ignore ground level.

"Tell Shane if he doesn't ask me to dance, I'll never forgive him," she reminded Shawn as he excused himself.

To get a dance with Agnes, he had to cut in on Matt. She said, "This is a wonderful day, Shawn. Molly would be so proud."

"Let me get weird on you for a moment. I feel that somehow MJ is still tuned into our lives," Shawn suggested. "I can anticipate what her responses would be, even to the exact phrasing."

Agnes looked at Shawn and replied, "I feel it too, but being married to a detective, I've never felt comfortable talking to him about that sort of thing. If you and I are right, we have given her a pretty good show, haven't we?"

"You and the others have crafted such a good person in Shane, that I hope the world can tolerate him," said Shawn. "Katy is also very special. How in the world did they find each other?"

When the music stopped, they hugged. Making full eye contact, Agnes said "Thank you," quietly and sincerely.

Shawn replied, "I was about to say the same thing," winked and was gone.

Shawn found Tim and Jane sitting and laughing by themselves. "Can I steal Jane for a dance," Shawn asked.

"Of course," responded Tim, who made a bee line for Donovan

and O'Malley at the bar.

Jane, an accomplished dancer as a young adult, arched her back and studied Shawn as they moved around the floor. "I'm trying to picture you as the little boy who came along and found Nick in the shadows.

We'll never be able to repay you for including him."

Later she added, "I miss your mom and Rita was wonderful, too. You're a lucky guy."

"Luckier than anybody deserves," he agreed, spinning her free towards Mrs. Landry, who was sitting alone and waving Jane over.

"Thanks for everything, Jane," he said earnestly.

He found Maggie being teased good-naturedly by the Donovan boys. She gratefully noticed Shawn's presence and quipped, "Saved by the father of the groom."

As they reached the dance floor, he noticed how attractive she was. "You look like a million bucks. Are you having a good time?"

"I'll bet you've already used that million bucks line on Shane's mother-subs," Maggie replied. "Ordinarily I would say yes, I'm enjoying myself, but no, I'm really not. It's a wonderful day for many people, but it's a painful reminder to my parents that I'm not like Shane, Katy, or either my mom or dad. I wonder if I'll always be a disappointment to them. I know I'm loved, but they never seem to approve."

Shawn stated, "I know your dad better than anyone. He has told me that he is glad you're not like him. He admires your swagger and the fact that you don't shrink from challenges. Your father respects your willingness to take an unpopular stance, if circumstances dictate. You are anything but a disappointment to him.

"Your mother, though, is a little harder to read," offered Shawn.

"Tell me about it," seconded Maggie sarcastically.

"Because you asked, I think she envies you. Since I can remember, her parents were homebound and in poor health. She had to be quiet and color within the lines. There weren't many hugs at her house, since all emotions were restrained. As a result, she's stately and you're impulsive because you have had the luxury of being able to make some mistakes. She didn't have the opportunity you did," Shawn concluded.

"You sure about all that?" asked Maggie.

"Not entirely, but it seems to fit, doesn't it?" supposed Shawn.

"Yes, I guess it does," she said thoughtfully.

"Everybody loves hugs. They don't hurt or cost. When's the last time you hugged your mother without a reason?" asked Shawn.

"It's been a while," Maggie admitted.

"Why not give it a try?" coaxed Shawn.

"I might just do that. Thanks."

"My dad used to say you glowed." Before departing, Shawn observed, "I understand what he meant."

Maggie approached Mr. Donovan, "Care to dance with me, sir?"

"Sure. What a wonderful group of people! You have to be exceptional to be considered average around here," Matt remarked.

"I think you're right," Maggie responded, "but I never felt I truly belonged. I always felt I was here on a pass, but Shawn makes me feel good about myself."

Matt observed, "Shawn understands people because he gets close to them without cramping their style and while not looking up or down at them.

"He treated your dad that way and look how tight they are. People want to do things for and with Shawn; consequently, he leads effortlessly," Matt explained.

Maggie reacted, "But there's more to it than that. If Shawn knew he was going to die tomorrow, he would not owe anyone anything. Unlike the rest of us, he wouldn't be scrambling around mending fences and apologizing to people with his last breath.

"Shawn has built in equilibrium," said Matt. "No one or nothing can knock him over.

"You're perceptive, Maggie. Don't apologize because you are different. Make it work for you. Everybody loves you and you *do* belong," Donovan insisted.

"Now go find someone younger who will make you laugh and brighten up this place. It gets murky in here, unless you are smiling," Matt told her.

CHAPTER 72

Challenges

Shawn's legislative duties were going well in the 1980's and he had more friends than time to enjoy them. Katy was on leave from her school district and uncomfortably pregnant with twins. With no mother to confide in and a father clueless in such matters and a thousand miles away, she suffered in silence. Shane was caught up in his research and provided little help.

For the Browns, this decade was a downer. Tim was in failing health and Jane became more caregiver than wife. After completing a degree in social work, Maggie drifted from one social agency to another and one male companion to another. Maggie was neither happy nor unhappy, while free-floating.

By the time Shawn got involved in Katy's predicament and had her flown to Chicago to see a highly regarded specialist, Katy was in her seventh month. The expert, Dr. Sharon Burns, discovered that Katy was carrying fraternal twins, with a male lodged in reasonable comfort and a female doing everything possible to survive. Dr. Burns observed that "Katy scarcely had room for one child, much less two."

The doctor took the children early, rather than have them both perish. The boy, Jack, weighed almost five pounds and the girl, Emily, was just over four pounds with breathing difficulties. Shane and Katy took Jack home in six days but Emily remained in the hospital. It was touch and go for a week, before Emily became stable. Ten days later, Emily was released to two very insecure parents.

Jack took most of Katy's attention, and Shane handled Emily as though she were a grenade. Emily cried most of the time, ate poorly, and rarely smiled. One evening Maggie visited out of curiosity.

As soon as Maggie and Emily discovered one another, matters began to improve. Maggie asked if she could hold Emily and a desperate Katy nodded. Maggie slow-walked the baby and asked for a bottle, which was quickly provided.

This tender moment was the genesis of a relationship which was to last for thirty important months. At first when Maggie was unavailable, Emily would pitch a fit, but soon the infant realized that if she waited a short time, Maggie would materialize and tend to her.

It was clear that Shane and Katy, left to their own devices, were overmatched. Maggie's help had become indispensable, since Katy was terrified of Emily's breathing problems. Shawn decided that Maggie could be a full-time nanny, if she was willing, and that Shane and Katy would be invited to move back to Chicago full-time. Shane agreed to the move and was all but certain that he could conduct his research through Dr. Bowen.

Consequently, an expanded family was formed. Andrea provided information regarding Emily's condition and took a supporting interest, which Maggie welcomed. At least twice a week, Katy, Maggie, and Andrea would huddle and check signals. Of course, Mrs. L made a cameo appearance on occasion and glowed when she tended to Emily.

With the attention she received, Emily's health was improving. Against doctor's orders, Maggie took her into a swimming pool and the baby took to the water immediately. Maggie bought gym clothes for the two of them and Emily delighted in pointing out the matching reds and blues, as they went through their workouts. Maggie used every opportunity to fill Emily's lungs with air, and the toddler seemed to understand the routine.

Bernie O'Malley got involved in Emily's most challenging health problem, puny lungs. She tired easily because her lungs would not inflate properly. O'Malley had dozens of men friends, in part, because in his own words, he was a "man's man." When Shawn pressed him to explain, Bernie laughed and said that this term meant that he was a cross between a misogynist and a horse's backside.

O'Malley had two friends at a Boston medical institute. He was able to get Emily, when almost two, into four clinical trials to enhance lung development. Maggie and Emily got on and off planes and in and out of cabs with ease. On the first three trials, Emily's chart disclosed the dreaded "no significant difference." The fourth procedure, though, which forced air directly into her lungs at high speed, while causing some pain and significant discomfort, yielded encouraging results. As long as Maggie was nearby, Emily could handle most anything.

The Boston medical group contacted a Chicago area clinic and arranged for Emily to receive the successful experimental procedure twice per week for three months. Soon after therapy began, Emily was scrambling up stairs, though she tired sooner than other children her age. When Jack grabbed a toy that Emily wanted, she chased him. While not able to catch her brother, she began to make it interesting. Maggie, Katy, and Shane shed tears of joy.

Jack had been told that Emily was special and he treated her with kid gloves. He took crayons she wanted one day, and she jumped to her feet, grabbed the crayons, and pinched her brother hard. With tears in his eyes, Jack protested, "Emy's not special no more." Indeed, she was not but instead had become much like others her age, with all the good and bad involved in that. Once again, the Butler-Brown team approach was successful.

Though Maggie would gladly have remained the main fixture in Emily's life, she knew that this was unwise for all concerned. Maggie began disengaging from Emily by leaving the Brown's house before bedtime and letting Katy take over, with Nick managing Jack. As the baby's lung function improved, she became more independent. When putting on her shoes at age four, Emily aggressively refused help, scolding Maggie by saying, "Not Maggie, Emy."

Wearing a soft cast from a paddleball accident, Maggie attended the Butler Christmas party when Emily was almost five. Showing her perceptiveness, Emily took a moment away from the action and stopped by Maggie's chair to inspect the cast. Emily cocked her head while staring at Maggie, stating, "Maggie's special." Sadly for Maggie but inevitably, Emily no longer needed a nanny.

Before and during Emily's rehabilitation, Shawn and Shane would traipse all over Chicago with Jack, visiting Wrigley Field, museums, the beaches, and parks. Matt Donovan joined them, schedule permitting. When there was a hole in his schedule, Bernie O'Malley would fly in and visit. Initially checking into hotels, he began bunking with Shawn on his stays. His presence often provided an excuse to get everyone together, with the twins scurrying about rapidly and several conversations going at once.

On one of his visits, Shawn toasted Bernie's leadership in getting Emily's problem solved. Even the twins were given juice cups so they could participate. When Shawn had finished his brief remarks, Bernie lifted his glass and looking at each person, said, "I've had to improve my game to play in this league. How I wish I had discovered Butlers, Browns, Diminicos, Donovans, Russos, and Landrys earlier in my life. I surely would have been a better husband and father. Thanks to you, though, I finally get it. Maybe I still have a chance!"

Everyone clapped and agreed that there was clearly hope for him. O'Malley had played himself onto the team, not by bullying or carousing, but by responsible behavior and calling in favors from friends.

CHAPTER 73

Agent Orange

Shawn had everyone fooled, including himself. He handled his duties so smoothly that he could do them with only half his usual energy. With Nick's brains and the unfailing allegiance of his staff, Shawn was able to put his legislative duties on cruise-control.

A lifelong fitness advocate, he stepped up his workouts by running more miles and doing additional weight-lifting repetitions. Despite his conditioning, he seemed to be getting weaker by the day. Never given to headaches, Shawn's day started with faint head pain and generally ended with what resembled a full blown migraine.

He watched his diet carefully. He ate less red meat, more vegetables, and endless helpings of fruit. Nothing seemed to work.

Surrounded by some of the best medical minds in the world in Chicago, he finally scheduled a complete physical, using two doctors who owed him favors, Dr. Gibson of the University of Illinois Medical School and the VA's Dr. Milford. He chose these two because each had an ego firmly in check and would not compete with one another. Shawn had a sneaking suspicion that his condition, if in fact he had a condition, was related to his military experience.

He asked Nick to sit with him and the two doctors on a Friday afternoon. Shawn looked at the other three and decided he was badly outclassed from an intelligence standpoint; nonetheless, they all turned to him to lead the discussion.

Shawn explained that he was a widower with two grandchildren and that Nick, a lifelong friend, handled all his business, personal and professional. Shawn briefly described his symptoms and told them he had all weekend free from any obligations.

The doctors began peppering him with questions, as Dr. Milford asked Shawn where he was stationed in Vietnam and how much time he had spent in forested areas. Shawn emphasized to the doctors how careful he had been in keeping himself clean while in- country. When Milford nodded to Dr. Gibson, he began asking about Shawn's headaches, sleep habits, workouts, and nutrition.

As the doctors concluded their questioning, Shawn and Nick were asked to leave for a short time. Shawn refused, indicating that he and Nick wanted to hear the whole story. The doctors looked at one another, shrugged, and plunged in.

"I want to test you for dioxin, the operative element in TCDD, Agent Orange," announced Dr. Milford.

"I want imaging tests, particularly a brain scan," chimed in Dr. Gibson. "If we are wrong, we will have wasted a few days.

However, your loss of energy and headaches concerns us both." Shawn said, "Tell me what you want me to do."

"Report to this office at 7 AM tomorrow morning. Fast completely and drink water only," Dr. Gibson directed. "We will shoot for a late afternoon Sunday briefing. For now, I want you two to leave so that we can coordinate the testing schedule and analyses."

In the parking lot, Shawn asked, "What do you think?" Nick replied, "If I was sick, I would want both helping me." Shawn nodded,

"Chicago has so many great people."

Shawn went to Shane's home, despite a growing headache. The twins yelled "Grandpa" and tackled him. He bluffed his way through a wrestling match, despite his discomfort. He then asked Shane to put the children in front of the TV, before explaining the problem to Shane and Katy.

"How can I help?" asked Shane.

"Keep late tomorrow afternoon open. You, Nick, and I will meet with the doctors then. Don't worry. It may be nothing."

He smiled at Katy, sitting next to her and taking her hand. "This is what happens when you hang out with older people," he laughed.

Shawn slept between tests over the weekend. Nick drove Shawn and Shane to a 5 PM meeting at Dr. Gibson's roomy, comfortable office.

The doctors were not good poker players; Shawn and Nick knew the news was bad. Shane was unaccustomed to high stakes emotional encounters and did not grasp what was happening.

"Dr. Milford and I have reviewed the test results several times," explained Dr. Gibson. He then looked at Dr. Milford.

"It is our strong belief that you have terminal brain cancer, probably service-related. Your dioxin level is high. The US sprayed 20M gallons of this defoliant in Viet Nam between 1962 and 1971. You got your share.

"The cancer has spread to your lungs and other organs. An operation is not an option. You may have two months.

"I know you said you washed yourself carefully, but remember you were inhaling a mist while wiping off a liquid. I'm sorry," Dr. Milford concluded. "Of course, you will want a second opinion."

Everyone looked at Shawn, who spoke slowly. "I knew something was terribly wrong. Thank you for spending your weekend in telling me where I stand." He shook the hands of both doctors.

Shane was impressed that even in this grim situation, Shawn did not forget his manners. Courtney and Rex had taught him well.

CHAPTER 74

Meeting His Maker

During his five weeks at Second City Hospice, Shawn had completed his obituary, made cremation arrangements, paid his bills, and held a close-out meeting with Nick at the office. Shawn had met all the hospice's staff members and already outlived four fellow patients. When he visited his dying colleagues, he carried the *Chicago Tribune*, asked them to pick their favorite section, and then launched into a discussion on one of the day's stories. More often than not, his enthusiasm was contagious and able to cut through the medication and pain of people with but a few days to live. Shawn carried extra copies of the newspaper because he frequently stirred latent curiosity and left patients skimming the *Tribune*'s various sections.

During the previous week, his son, Shane, had driven him to suburban All Saints Cemetery, where Courtney and Rex were buried. Etched in marble was "Corporal Rex Butler," a rank his father wore briefly but proudly. Courtney was "Mrs. Courtney Butler," which hinted at only a small portion of her true value. Shawn rested his hand on Shane's right shoulder as he reflected upon the marvelous consistency which his mother displayed. Each in their own way, the Butlers were formidable parents to whom Shawn was deeply indebted. When he matched them with those of his classmates and friends, none, other than the Browns, seemed to compare favorably.

Shawn met with Dr. Liam Kelly, whom he had met through Rita

and who treated patients at the hospice as he wound down a medical career distinguished by compassion and a sense of humor. Liam was a mere 5' 7" and 150 pounds, but his baby blue eyes radiated strength and optimism, which drew others to him. Liam conveyed the belief that each day was worth living and that his patient was more important than anybody or anything else.

Last week, Shawn overheard a terminal patient of Doctor Kelly say, "Even though I'm getting sicker each day, just being around Dr. Kelly makes me *feel* better." Shawn could not have agreed more.

"I want you to ration your energy, Shawn," said Dr. Kelly. "For what? I've already done everything I've wanted to do." "I need your help with the others," said Liam.

"Who is going to help *me*?" quipped Shawn.

"You don't need help. You're a helper, not a helpee."

"Didn't they teach you any grammar in that backwater med school you attended?" wise-cracked Shawn.

"Seriously, Shawn, you have a limited supply of energy left. You can spend it all at once or ration it for seven, maybe ten days."

"Is there any business we have left between us?" Shawn inquired.

Dr. Kelly studied Shawn. "You're not thinking of killing yourself, are you? These people admire you, and if you commit suicide, it will invalidate much of what we represent."

"Relax, Liam. I get what this place stands for, Death With Dignity. I'm simply trying to decide where and when to pass," replied Shawn, acknowledging that the hospice experience was a splendid opportunity to end life in an orderly, dignified manner.

"Then you're simply trying to live life on your terms, and I respect that. People like you Butlers are the engines that have propelled our country forward. Your compassion is edgy but effective. I wish I was more convinced that we have people coming along willing and able to replace you."

"Thanks for those kind words. I was always able to generate momentum for myself and those around me, though often not certain of the consequences. I treated those around me as if they were as tough as I was, while knowing in my heart that many were not."

On that note, Dr. Kelly left, and Nick, who had been waiting, entered. Nick's posture, seemingly indexed to Shawn's deteriorating physical condition, had suffered lately. He still had a full head of hair, though gray now, that never quite responded to even the most expensive care. No matter how politically powerful he became, he always projected a little-boy-lost persona, which most women found appealing. Never quite sitting, Nick draped himself over a chair and, as usual, waited for Shawn to initiate the discussion.

"Loose ends?" inquired Shawn.

Nick shook his head no, looking quite sad. "Hey, come on! It's me who's dying, not you."

Shawn's attempt to lighten the mood fell flat, so he suggested, "Let's get out of here." As they left the building, he surprised Nick by hailing a cab and instructing the driver to take them to Oak Street Beach, an odd request on a brisk October day.

While in his teens and twenties, Shawn used to drag Nick to the beach. After they got there, Nick became the most contented person within miles. While Shawn would swim and do push-ups, Nick would run or simply stand on the water's edge, gazing at the horizon which framed Lake Michigan, while planning and analyzing their next moves.

On this day, Shawn wanted to walk along the "rocks," the term used for the cement pilings which helped brace Chicago's shore from Lake Michigan's waves and which doubled as an expansive walkway.

Shawn set a strong pace, but Nick, with his distance running background, easily kept up. Used to continuous chatter on their walks, Nick glanced over at Shawn several times and watched him start to sweat heavily, despite the fifty degree temperature.

"Are you all right?" Nick asked.

Shawn pushed on without reply, ignoring Nick's repeated offers to sit on one of the thousands of low-maintenance, cement-based park benches that grace Chicago's lakefront. Shawn was determined to go forward as the setting sun reflected beautifully off the waters near the shoreline.

He started to stumble and sway, but pushed on, before dropping in a heap. As Nick came to Shawn's side, he pealed off his jacket and made a pillow of it to prop under Shawn's head.

"Thanks for everything, Nick. Maybe I could have done it without you, but I doubt it. You were my guiding star, making me a better leader and a more complete family man. When I let you down once, I never forgave myself."

Listening carefully, Nick did not speak but continued to make his friend comfortable by arranging his clothing. After calling for an ambulance, Nick sat close to Shawn, shielding him from the wind as he had protected Shawn in so many more subtle ways since they were children.

Shawn grabbed Nick's hand, convulsed, and died instantly. A teary-eyed Nick removed Shawn's expensive watch, leather wallet and key chain with his free hand and did not disentangle himself from Shawn until the emergency crew arrived. The two women on the team exchanged information with Nick before loading Shawn's body.

Nick stood motionless and stared as the emergency vehicle, with lights blinking, rolled slowly in the lingering twilight along the rocks and turned ceremoniously into a passageway under Lake Shore Drive. He smiled wryly, noting that Shawn died as he had lived: with splendid timing, few regrets, and his best friend close by.

OBITUARY

Shawn Michael Butler

Shawn Michael Butler, 60, died on October 13, 2001 on Chicago's lakefront, after a battle with Agent Orange-induced brain cancer.

Shawn graduated from St. Ignio High School in 1958, Right Junior College in 1960, and Chicago City College in 1962. He was awarded a law degree from Clement College of Law in 1972.

He was a decorated U. S. Marine with two Vietnam tours, and an Illinois state senator for twenty-nine years.

Shawn was the beneficiary of a Silicon Valley windfall in 1970, combining with Nick Brown to fund the Butler-Brown Foundation which pays the full college costs of the youngest child in needy Chicago families with five or more children. To date, 213 high school graduates have received Butler-Brown subsidies. Chaired originally by the late Dr. Rita Wilson, retired Chicago City College's President Emeritus, the Foundation guarantees that at least ten children per year will receive a Butler-Brown award in perpetuity.

Shawn was a self-described gypsy Catholic who loved all of the city's Catholic churches, a Democrat known for his bi- partisan political endeavors, a beach lover, a fitness buff, and an environmental activist.

He was branded by his signature greeting, "What have you done for Chicago lately?" Shawn was known to lose interest in those without a ready answer.

Shawn was pre-deceased by his wife, Molly Jean Donovan Butler; mother, Courtney; stepmother, Rita Wilson Butler ; and father, Rex, and survived by his son, Shane; daughter-in-law, Katy O'Malley Butler; and twin grandchildren, Jack and Emily. Mr. Butler has been cremated.

At 3 PM on October 20, 1991 in the Daley Center Plaza, a brief ceremony has been planned by Shawn's lifelong friend and advisor, Nick Brown. Shawn's son, Shane, will conduct the service and requests that donations be made care of Dr. Liam Kelly at the Second City Hospice.

Mr. Brown reminds everyone that the ceremony will be held outside, consistent with the wishes of Shawn, who proclaimed recently, "If they want to pay their respects to me in the world's greatest city, have them dress for it. I hope the weather is crummy, so I can see who really cares!"

www.ingramcontent.com/pod-product-compliance
Lightning Source LLC
LaVergne TN
LVHW021220080526
838199LV00084B/4300